# BLACK WIND PASS

GALE
CENGAGE Learning·

**LIBRARY OF CONGRESS CATALOGING-IN-PUBLICATION DATA**

Names: Davis, Rusty, author.
Title: Black wind pass / Rusty Davis.
Description: First Edition. | Waterville, Maine : Five Star Publishing, a part of Cengage Learning, Inc., 2017.
Identifiers: LCCN 2016037254 (print) | LCCN 2016042134 (ebook) | ISBN 9781432832889 (hardback) | ISBN 1432832883 (hardcover) | ISBN 9781432834593 (ebook) | ISBN 1432834592 (ebook) | ISBN 9781432832841 (ebook) | ISBN 1432832840 (ebook)
Subjects: | BISAC: FICTION / Historical. | FICTION / Westerns. | GSAFD: Western stories.
Classification: LCC PS3604.A9755 B58 2017 (print) | LCC PS3604.A9755 (ebook) | DDC 813/.6—dc23
LC record available at https://lccn.loc.gov/2016037254

First Edition. First Printing: January 2017
Find us on Facebook— https://www.facebook.com/FiveStarCengage
Visit our website— http://www.gale.cengage.com/fivestar/
Contact Five Star™ Publishing at FiveStar@cengage.com

Printed in the United States of America
1 2 3 4 5 6 7 21 20 19 18 17

# BLACK WIND PASS

## RUSTY DAVIS

**FIVE STAR**
*A part of Gale, Cengage Learning*

GALE
CENGAGE Learning·

Farmington Hills, Mich • San Francisco • New York • Waterville, Maine
Meriden, Conn • Mason, Ohio • Chicago

# BLACK WIND PASS

# CHAPTER ONE

Dimness had long since cloaked much of the land behind him to the east as Carrick rode his tired gray stallion through the rocky narrow path of Black Wind Pass. Below stretched a vision that had never left his mind, one that had been scoured into his memory. It had flitted about amid the carnage of Shiloh, the despair of Andersonville, and the rot of that Texas jail where he paid the price of revenge. He had almost wondered, at times, if it was a delusion. Others had them when the mind was teetering on the brink of lunacy or beyond the reach of the world. He had come close. Too close.

Now, it was real. The Buffalo Horn Valley of what was now called Wyoming Territory lay before him. If he had a home range in this world, something he increasingly doubted even as he doggedly approached it with more resignation than joy, this was it. This past day, he'd almost turned away. He wasn't sure if there was anyone he wanted to see; or who would want to see him. People always changed; usually for the worse. Not the land—the hills and the streams. They were eternal. If the trip was a fool's errand in every other respect, at least he could see the land one last time.

He'd been squinting for an hour as the sun lingered on the horizon, crow's-feet of grit and weather radiating out from red-shot eyes. Now the sun slid beneath the distant hills and he could see. Buffalo Horn Creek was a wavy line reflecting the lighter sky against the growing darkness. He looked into the dusky shadows. There! Half a day away, a bit of white peeked out from behind trees planted by a small boy who was bigger than they were. The trees seemed to have all but swallowed the house they surrounded. Everything changes. Crazy Uncle Charlie Wilson's cabin, built here at the pass, was still standing, though, as defiant of its projected and dire fate as Charlie was of every rule in the book, a trait he helped pass along to his nephew.

The old house was too distant a ride for tonight. He wanted to see everything in the full light of day. He rode down the hill to Lincoln Springs, a place he remembered as little more than a crossroads that hadn't sprouted either much of a name or a population. The ramshackle town had grown considerably in his absence, judging by its number of brightly lit saloons. Ten years was a long time. The last letter came in early 1862. It talked of disease. After that, nothing. Even though most soldiers pretty well worked out what that meant, nothing was ever certain. He'd find out who was left tomorrow. When he stayed with Sherman after the rest of the unit went home to fight Indians, he lost any touch with the territory and any news from home, unless it was some Indian raid gory enough to make the Eastern newspapers. He sent one letter after he got out of Andersonville. Nothing ever came back to the hospital. After he got out, there were other things that needed doing. He had done them. He bore the scars to prove it. Now he was back. Maybe some things would be the same. Most likely not. If there was some other place to go, he'd have gone there, but when he imagined leaving the life he had been leading behind, this was the only place in his mind.

Lincoln Springs was unconcerned with his arrival. Another lone, dusty tramp slipping through shadows on an early summer night was hardly anything unusual. The fact that his gun was the only clean part of him was not remarkable. In Wyoming in 1871, no one looked too closely at another man's gun, let alone the man as a whole. As for names, they were flighty things that mattered less and less the farther West a man rode. A man might have as many as he could remember.

Everett Morrisson was the name written on the window as the proprietor of the saloon, which had a crooked, creaking wooden sign reading "Saloon." The name meant nothing. Maybe his would mean the same. Then again, Texas range gossip spread everywhere the longhorn cattle went. Some people might not remember the past the way he did. No reason to find out. The cautious lived longer than the bold, or so the wise old men who cackled by general store cracker barrels in every two-bit town always told him.

He tied the horse. Stretched. Flexed the gun hand by instinct. For a moment he waited outside the open doorway, sensing what was on the other side. No danger on the wind, only noise. He looked around as he entered the place. He'd seen a hundred like it on the trail north from Texas and the one west from Kansas. Same smells—mud, unwashed men and stale tobacco smoke. There was almost enough room for the tables it held and a space to drink at the bar. A row of chandeliers battled the smoke to give the place light. They barely did better than a draw. It was crowded and noisy. Hot, too. There was beer and whiskey. The beer was cheaper. He looked for familiar faces. None. He expected to feel regret, but experienced only relief.

The doors opened wide; pushed hard. Three weathered riders stalked in. Flinty faces caught the light of the oil lamps. Their eyes sent unanswered challenges as they sauntered to the bar, heads high as if they owned every man in the place. Ripples of silent resentment filled the room as raucous talk turned to muted murmurs. "Whiskey," said one man, whose sense of command showed he was the lead wolf of the pack. His scarred face and leathery skin bespoke a rough and tumble past. He slapped

9

his gloves on the bar as he took inventory of the saloon and its denizens. His glance settled on Carrick. It stayed. He frowned. Never a good reaction, even if it was a common one.

"New up here, cowboy?" he called out roughly, as though Carrick owed him an answer.

"What's it to you?" Caution was like gold and good intentions. Never lasted very long.

Red flushed the weathered face, making the rider bracing Carrick look purple. He gave the floorboards a long look as he gripped the wood of the bar. His head turned to focus on the stranger. He spoke with anger and menace. "You know who you're bracin', tramp?"

"Nope." Carrick was past thought. This was instinct. Feral. A Texas judge told him he was a born and natural killer. He'd seen it as plain common sense. Attacking whatever was going to attack sooner or later came natural. At least he didn't spit on floors.

The rider was talking. He touched his chest, gestured at the men with him. "Jeff Crowley. Brothers Gordon and Dan'l. We ride for Double J."

The brand meant nothing. Irritation was rising along with the unreasoning anger when anyone decided his business was theirs. "What of it?"

"Double J owns most of this range, tramp. We keep the peace for Double J. When we ask, you answer. So, now that you know your place, what's your name and what's your business?"

"Private and personal."

Crowley slapped the bar hard with one open palm. Echoes lingered in the now-silent saloon. "Don't know your name, your face, or how you took the wrong trail here, but you better leave, now. Not the place for your kind."

"Nope." He made a small sip last a long time before the glass

10

returned to the wood of the bar. "Rode all day. Not ridin' all night."

Crowley stared at the defiant loudmouth. There was always one. A lesson had to be taught. Stomp one fool hard, ten other fools get the message. He motioned with his head. The two burly men with him moved towards Carrick. Their boots crunched the dirt on the floor, breaking the silence to the counterpoint of jangling spurs. They stopped and stood a few feet away, arms folded. The wordless threat of being dragged out in ignominious disgrace was clear to every man in the place.

Carrick again sipped the watery beer. Its foamy surface rippled from the long exhale of breath. Probably ought to get this done, he told himself. Eyebrows lifted, he affected to notice the two men for the first time. "Why, lookee here." He grinned in their faces. "You boys waitin' for your dancin' partners?"

As the crowd guffawed, delighted to see a fool stand up to the bullies they were afraid to tackle, one Crowley rushed in and swung blindly. The beer glass was solid enough that the sound of it hitting the man's head made the crowd cringe. As he slid to the floor in a shower of thin beer and thicker blood, the second brother stopped his charge. His hand went down to his belt.

"Don't!" called Carrick, whose hand had already been to his. "Been a long day, boys." His hands drummed the gun butt. "Never was much on manners when folks try to push me. Unless you want to make this personal, it ends right here. Got nothin' 'gainst you or your outfit. Don't like bein' pushed. I'm gonna walk away, and this ends. I don't want to hurt anyone." A wasted speech. Their eyes gave it away. It wasn't over. His eyes went from one Crowley to the other. Which one would go first? He needed to know. He took a sideways step away from the bar, watching both men. One step. Two steps. About ten more to the door and he could maybe say he kept his promise to himself of not doing any more stupid things because they felt good at the time.

The leader surprised him by drawing first. His shot went wide. Carrick's didn't. Gunshots mingled with the sound of the saloon's front window shattering. The leader slid to the floor with a bullet at the base of his throat.

The last Crowley was game but slow. Carrick tried to hit an arm but missed. The brother's shot nipped Carrick's hat. So much for mercy. Carrick's next bullet took the man in the chest. He collapsed in a moaning heap.

Carrick kept the gun in his hand as he surveyed the customers. Most dove for the floor when the shooting started. Now they peered from around toppled tables. "Didn't mean that to end that way, folks. They pushed a mite too hard. Somebody know how to tend a man? Don't think they're all dead yet. That second fella what got shot might live."

The bartender sent a kid out running. Nobody else moved. The men must not have had many friends. Carrick sat at a corner table. Nobody talked to him. He didn't have friends, either. Place had to have law. Law always has questions. He'd wait around and answer them rather than have somebody on his trail following him.

Within minutes, a big man walked in, star on his worn jacket. He seemed to pay no attention to the bodies beyond a quick glance. Maybe this had grown into that kind of town. A gray-haired round man bustled in and went to them.

The man with the star loomed over Carrick. Carrick took inventory. The man was as large as a mountain, but it was a mountain with one very large paunch that hung over a belt and a gun belt. Two bloodshot eyes trying to blink themselves awake said he knew his way around the saloons. The gun he wore looked more like an ornament than a weapon. He looked like a man who was worn and weary—called away from a home he

12

would rather be in and forced to hear a tale he had heard far too many times before. The lawman inspected. Didn't look pleased.

"Dan Hill, sheriff here. Tell me."

Hill was old enough that Carrick should have remembered him, but the face was another unknown. Carrick thought about saying howdy first in case the man had been a family friend; decided against it. If an outfit named Double J owned the range, maybe more had changed than he thought. Anyhow, he couldn't remember who exactly was and wasn't friends with his old spread. Not a time to find out. Hill might not have even lived here back then; lots of folks had come West since the war. Hill seemed like he'd been here forever, though, but he didn't seem to react to Carrick's name much, if at all.

In a flat tone, Carrick told the tale in its bald simplicity, not really caring enough to make it anything more than the way it was. Way too familiar a story. He'd seen it a thousand times. Done it a few, too. Sworn off doing it again, but that wasn't his fault. The sheriff nodded when the spare recitation was completed. "Stay here." He walked among the tables, talking to this one and that one. In a few minutes, he was back, looming over Carrick with resignation and irritation.

"They pushed hard. You pushed back harder. Not something I recommend as a habit but the law has no beef with you. Not sayin' others will feel the same. Double J steps wide and fancy here."

"Never heard of it."

"You must be new to Wyoming."

"Didn't say that, but I only rode into Wyoming Territory a few days ago." It was the way Army folks taught a man to lie. It was the truth, even if it was not the way things really were.

Hill seemed to chew on the response a minute before asking, "Passing through?"

13

"Not sure."

Hill's face seemed to sag. "Might want to, son. Double J's not gonna hire you, and that leaves only the little spreads that only hire at roundup—them and Lazy F. Lazy F and Double J don't quite see eye to eye, but I don't see Lazy F having much longer to hold its land unless they get back that railroad contract Jackson Jones took away from them. Not sure Francis Oliver takes to men who brace Double J in the open like that. Not really his style. Think you better ride on, son. Lots of ranches off to the east and the south, there, where the railroad runs."

"I'll think on that advice, sheriff. I will that."

The sheriff sighed with a patience born from years of trying to enforce the law in a place where young men had to have liquor and had to have guns—a combination that never failed to result in death. The man opposite didn't quite fit the mold of the drifters who came through on a wild high spree that ended in the growing cemetery, but hard cases looking for easy touches came in all shapes and sizes.

"Sheriff?"

The sheriff waited, feet turned to go. The stranger was not going to take the advice. That meant for Dan Hill that the longer they talked, the more chance there was someone would tell Jackson Jones that the sheriff he put in office to make the town what Jackson Jones wanted it to be was friends with a man who had wiped the floor with the Crowley boys. That would not be good for his next election in a few months. He had already classified this man as trouble and wanted nothing more than to be as far from him as possible. Instead, he had to put his hands on the table and lean down to catch the lazy voice of the stranger.

"Sorry 'bout that fella on the floor there," Carrick said, gesturing and craning his neck up at Hill. "Man wanted to be loyal to his brothers. Wanted to wing him. He shot a mite too straight for it to go any other way. First one didn't give me any chance; that second one I wish I could have done different. Not so broke up I wish it was me there, but I didn't come here for trouble with anybody, Sheriff."

Dan Hill nodded. Killers said all sorts of things afterward. Most were still excited. They babbled. This one was cold and calm, as if somebody else had done the shooting and fighting. The calm itself made him think of a big cat he once saw in the hills watching a group of hunters—dangerous by the very fact of existing; confident nothing could hurt him.

"Crowleys got kin, son. They got friends. If you stay around, Gordon—the only one you didn't kill—is gonna heal. He and them are gonna find you if Double J don't find you first. I'm the only law there is in the valley. I only try to civilize this town so that it is safe for drunks, women, and kids. This land being what it is, men gettin' even for their kin bein' killed is nothin' any law anywhere is gonna stop."

"Thank you for your concern, Sheriff. Finding a man isn't the same as killing him."

Shaking his head at the stubbornness of one more man who was refusing to see the difference between right and foolishness, Dan Hill pushed himself away from the table. "There's a cell at the jail where you can spend the night if you need a place that's safe. Jed Owens runs the stable. If you want to stay there with the horses, tell him I told you it was all right."

"Thank you, Sheriff."

"Thank me by clearing out, son. Man gets old he starts becoming tired of burying the young."

"It does tire a soul to do that, Sheriff," Carrick said with a wistful voice born of experience. "It does do that indeed."

With words whose meanings were a mystery in his ears, Hill left the saloon for home. Elsie would be missing him. She'd been warning him about the job, that the wild men were getting

15

wilder and that nothing was worth all of this. Maybe, as he thought about the stranger, she was right.

# CHAPTER TWO

Carrick's gray stallion—called Beast for no other reason than it was the first name Carrick thought of when he stole him back in Texas—loped along the hard-packed dirt trail northwest out of Lincoln Springs. He had spent the night in the stable. The boy who stayed there nights had already heard about the gunfight, and treated Carrick like a hero. Silly kid.

He forgot about the night as he rode through the valley. He remembered his half-breed friend telling him in a quiet moment before he went away that he'd be back—the browns, yellows, and grays of the rugged land were in his soul. He'd wondered along the road if he had a soul. Guess he had. It was waking up.

The grasses growing wild in the fields around him bent before the wind. Antelope were jumping off to the right; if memory served, there should be a creek bed there that only filled up in the spring where he used to catch frogs. A stand of oaks he recalled as being giants were a lot smaller than he thought they ought to be. Everything seemed familiar, but nothing was the same. He had to keep reminding himself that even if it all felt familiar, it had been ten years—the war, the prison camp, the hospital, Texas, and then two years of doing things he'd rather forget. He had been young back in early 1861 when the old First Nebraska Infantry was raised to save the Union. He felt old now, old in the ways of life—and death. Then he came to Cougar Rock. It was weathered a bit. Maybe more than a bit. He had a lot harder time seeing the cougar in it than he did

17

when he was ten and Grandpa told him the Indian legend about the big cat turned into rocks. Not long now.

The white house was there, ahead. The old shack his folks had lived in was gone. Empty stood in its place. Everyone must live in the big house. Maybe there were kids and they added on to the big house in the back or built a new house on some piece of neighboring land. Maybe he was an uncle. He was getting nervous now. He wondered what they would look like, aged ten years from the day they waved good-bye when he rode this trail away from home. For a moment, he wondered what he would look like to them—a dusty man in a worn brown leather jacket, battered leather hat and trail-worn clothes, unkempt from the trail, riding back to tell them he was their son and nephew. What was left of him. What if everything changed? What if they were mad at him for not writing more? He swallowed hard and rode on. He hadn't been this nervous since before Shiloh.

Shade from the trees hid the details. Double J? Lazy F? This had been Bar C country then and the ranch house was spruced up to show that this ranch was a cut above the rest. Not now. There was no gate; no fence rails setting off the place. There used to be. He painted them every spring. Somebody lived in the place. Blue smoke rose from a chimney. The heavy shutters for the windows—a vestige of the days when Indian raids were frequent—were flung wide open. Beast rode on with little guidance. Carrick's eyes were working funny. He had to blink a spell. A woman was out front tending a fire. He'd ridden up to this house in his dreams 10,000 times. She was there in every one. His vision blurred again. He wiped his eyes with the back of his hand.

Everything was clear now. The young woman at the fire was not someone from the distant past. She wasn't wearing a blue dress. She wore a man's blue flannel shirt and pants. She was small framed and dark haired. She had also stepped back from the fire and was glaring back at him down the barrel of a rifle held in very steady hands. A faint breeze sent a rebellious strand of hair across her face. She was not distracted.

"You got business here?" she called as he and Beast ambled closer, moving slowly to avoid any misunderstanding.

"Not coming to make trouble for anyone. Looking to talk. Tell me, who lives here?" he called back, wishing he'd cleaned up before riding out. It was hard to see her face behind the rifle and the wind-whipped black hair, but the girl did not look familiar. Her family must ride for his. Despite her lack of courtesy, he would try to be friendly.

"I do," she replied. "Now git."

From the inside of the house, the voice of an older woman called, "Reb, who are you pointing a gun at now?"

"Some tramp, Aunt Jess. Maybe a spy from Double J. I'll send him on his way or shoot him."

Vexed but incoherent sounds of a female voice making its way to the front of the house came to Carrick. The rifle remained leveled.

"That thing might go off," he told her. He could not place any woman named Jess, and this was the second time a spread called Double J had been mentioned in a threatening way. Some kind of trouble had infiltrated the valley.

"Your worry, not mine," she replied.

He found himself unexpectedly grinning at the young woman's grit. He was wondering whether she would really shoot. He could find out. Then again, it might hurt. She didn't have the look of someone who would miss. Her face was a study in purpose. Yet she lacked the look that comes from killing on a regular basis; there was innocence amid the bravado. For a moment, he forgot about his family and all of his worries as he focused on her. "This the Wyoming brand of range hospitality?"

"Fit for Wyoming's brand of range bums."

He hooted out an uncontrolled laugh. Whatever had been in his head as he rode up to the place he lived seventeen years of his life, this had not been it. Maybe this was better. Time would certainly tell. Laughing at life's joke that was amusing him as much as it was infuriating her, he started to get down from the saddle.

"Don't." The girl did not relax an inch. She could have been carved from wood aiming down her rifle at the world.

He took up the challenge in her eyes and flung his leg over. "Are you hard of hearing, tramp? I said not to get down from that saddle."

He was still laughing as he dismounted and stood with his hand on the pommel of Beast's saddle. The other was raised over his head in mock surrender. The door to the house opened with a creak of old hinges. A woman a couple of handfuls of years older than the girl, with a streak of gray by her left temple, stood in the doorway, wiping her hands on a rag. "Reb, what on earth . . ."

As the girl turned and started to speak, Carrick moved fast and grabbed hard. She wasn't expecting it. The rifle was out of her hands and into his. As she sputtered, fumed, and swatted at him ineffectually, he handed it to the older woman, who had rushed up beside them. As she came closer, he saw that she was younger than the gray in her hair made her appear. There was a resemblance, but the older woman radiated kindness and peace, even amid the other's rage.

"Excuse my niece, Mr. . . ."

"Carrick." The older of the two women knew the name; he could see the look on her face. Whatever it was, it wasn't a welcome. Not a good sign. The younger one seemed to not know the name at all.

The older of the two women started speaking to him. "We've been troubled by range loafers here . . ."

". . . such as him," Reb muttered.

". . . and we're a bit on edge," the older one continued. "The way things are here, we don't get many riders passing through now who aren't working for Double J or Lazy F or on the run from the law. I don't know how you found your way here, but since you already got down, please do come in. Excuse the condition of the ranch; we're a working outfit, not a fancy one." Her eyes kept looking, as though they were turning over questions her mouth hadn't gotten around to asking yet. "Reb, I think that cowboys still drink coffee."

"No need, ma'am," Carrick replied.

"Good," shot back Reb. Her Aunt Jess's face turned even darker.

Carrick was fascinated by the girl. She didn't have much for manners, which put her about on a par with him. Bar C certainly had one loyal person. He looked at the older woman. "I have a couple of questions about this ranch. I'd like to talk to the owner."

"You're talkin' to 'em," the younger woman replied. "The answer is no. Only way you get your hands on my land is when you get buried in it. Now git."

There was a low whispered snarl from the older woman, who seemed to have gone pale after his question. The younger woman contented herself with a glare of disapproval that alternated from her aunt to Carrick. Carrick knew the older woman would have been cussing if she was a man. Or maybe if he wasn't around. She breathed in deeply and then spoke.

"Mr. Carrick, put your horse in the shade there and come in. We can talk." The woman's voice was a bit shaky. It was more a command than a request. "I am Jessie Lewis and this is my niece, Rebecca," she added with formal courtesy and the touch of a hill country Southern accent.

"You can call me Reb," the girl interjected. "Get that straight.

21

I don't let nobody call me Becky. I don't like that name. It's Reb, and it was like that before the silly war even though I had to be 'Rebecca' because we were Union in Tennessee and nobody understood. Then we came out here the first time somebody heard my name, they about fired at me until I set them straight." Carrick tried to stifle a snicker; the flash of anger in the girl's eyes told him he had not done a very thorough job.

Jessie continued as though there had not been an interruption. She seemed to disregard Reb's flashes of temper the way an experienced cowhand paid no attention to distant flashes of what they called heat lightning. "Rebecca and I would be happy to make you coffee and share what little we have. And, Reb, not another word! Not one more word, not one! We will behave as Christians even if we are the last ones in Wyoming!"

With obvious reluctance, Reb stalked toward the door. The door slammed and a couple of windows echoed the sound as they rattled. Carrick walked Beast into the shade of an oak and tied him. Nothing made sense, but once they got to talking he was sure he would get the straight of it. He wondered if his family had moved someplace else. He was pretty sure from the look of the big house there were only the two women around it. The way he recalled the ranch, there were always kids and dogs running around and hands who should have been doing something else taking a break. This ranch looked empty; the weather-beaten appearance of the house, now that he was up close, looked like a house that had not seen a repair in years. If these women bought the place when his family moved on, they could tell him where the Carrick clan now lived and he could be off. Then he smiled again at the reception from the younger woman. He'd grown up with some girls who were as wild as the boys, but never one like her.

"Oh, no," said the older of the two women, looking down the

trail and blanching. Four men on horseback were slowly plod-
ding down the dirt track to the house. "Francis Oliver and Lazy
F again. That man!" Reb had come back from the house at her
aunt's exclamation. She moved beside her Aunt Jess, reaching
for the rifle. Aunt Jess shifted it to her other side to keep the
weapon out of reach. Carrick wanted to laugh again, but the
women were deadly serious as they looked at the approaching
horsemen.

Two riders held rifles. One had two guns strapped to his
hips. They fanned out behind a distinguished, prosperous-
looking red-haired man whose beard marked the steadily
advancing gray tide of age. The man wore a white shirt—a rar-
ity on any range—and a hat that looked new. He had on a black
frock coat that looked clean. Talking clothes, Carrick thought.
Not fighting clothes. The man's gun was holstered. Something
else Carrick could not identify was in the hand loosely holding
the reins. Not an attack, then. A threat? Carrick remained in the
shade. Whatever this was about, if the women were running the
place, he guessed it was none of his affair. He'd wait and find
out.

"Good day to you, Jessie. I see you are looking as pretty as a
sunrise this fine day." The man took off his hat, revealing a
windswept face that might have been handsome before it was
lined with the tracks of age. He manufactured a broad smile
that didn't seem to fit with the tension in his body. His eyes,
untouched by the smile, went from one woman to the next.
"Reb, how do? Nice to see you without that gun in your hand. I
hope we can have us a nice talk here, ladies."

"Git," Reb spat back. Carrick snickered at the man's rebuff
and decided the girl hated everybody.

The older woman spoke as the younger one glared, something
Carrick figured she must do often. "Francis, please do not
bother to get down and please do not bother to ask. I do not

mean to be rude, but the answer is no today. It was no yesterday and it will be no tomorrow. I do not want to sell this land, not to anyone, not for any price." Reb muttered something so softly he only caught the edge in her tone, not the words.

"Jessie, listen to reason. You got no crew to speak of. You can't protect what land you got and what stock you might have left. Come winter, you won't be able to afford to eat, either of you. I'm making a generous offer. Jessie, I want you to listen to me. I'm tryin' to get you to do what's best for you for your own protection. I have been tryin' to show you two ladies how much I care for your welfare. Realize, don't you, woman, that land ain't worth nothin' when you get buried in it?"

"Fightin' talk."

The rider—surprised by a voice he had not expected—swung his head to face Carrick, who stepped from the shadow of the tree and, on impulse, tossed his Winchester to Reb. She caught it, chambered a round, and pointed it at the rider in one motion, despite an angry exclamation from her aunt. The riders in the background moved in response to the threat, but Carrick focused on the lead one.

Francis Oliver looked closely at Carrick's face. "Haven't had the pleasure."

"Too busy threatenin' women for courtesy?"

"My business, whoever you are. You got none here."

"I think I have a real good say in what happens next, partner."

"Says who?"

"Sam Colt." The gun was in his hand as though it lived there all of his life. These last two years, it had.

"Goin' off half-cocked like that fool girl there does is goin' to cost these ladies something awful. You're making a mistake, son. Whatever they hired you to do, don't make a mistake. Let's you and I talk this out."

"I've lived with a few thousand mistakes. You don't leave real

24

quick, you're gonna be making one right now. Bet the girl will get two riders in her first two shots; I'll get you certain sure with mine. How it is, the way I see things. Go ahead and play it out if you think the wind's on your side."

Carrick watched the rider calculate. Francis Oliver looked irritated, almost embarrassed. Something was here more than business. Maybe it was not the chances of success, but the loss of face that rankled. If there had been a threat, it was blunted for the time being. Maybe later it would make sense. Later had to happen, first. None of the Oliver fella's men had drawn guns. Time to stand down and walk away, if the rider would let it happen.

Carrick holstered the gun. "Guess this little pow-wow is over." Reb did not lower her gun until the older woman nonetoo-gently pushed the barrel downward.

The rider spoke with conviction as he looked at the two women and Carrick. "Jessie, I don't know who this man is, but no one humiliates me. Last thing you need is some hired gun to make things worse. Fightin' back is only gonna cost you what little you got left, cuz gunslingers never come cheap. You know your choices are to lose the ranch and go broke, sell to Double J, or sell to me. I can offer you something more than Double J. You got to see sense and see clear. You come and talk to me. You got to come and talk to me soon! Don't let Double J or this cowpoke make you do something stupid. Understand?" He jerked the horse's head around savagely and pounded away, his men following. Carrick saw him hurl something into the brush along the trail.

Carrick stood with the women. The riders grew smaller. The noise of the hooves faded in the wind.

"Guess that there hospitality of yours is catching, Miss Reb," he said to the girl, holding out his hand for the rifle. She slapped it hard into his hands.

25

"Well, thank you for making things worse!" she exclaimed. "Bad enough we got Double J and Lazy F scrapping over us like dogs for a bone. Now you got Francis Oliver wanting revenge personal-like and that means we have to either beg Double J for help, and I'd rather die, or we have to sell because everyone knows that there's dead men a plenty to say that Oliver never takes insults lying down. And I don't want to sell it or lose it because this is my home, no matter who tries to take it away!" The last few words dripped with sobs that overcame them. She rushed into the house and slammed the door once again.

Carrick, regrets running high as they always did after a showdown, spoke to the older woman. Questions flowed through him. How a woman could insist this was her home when it had been his; but they could wait.

"Sorry if this was some business deal I turned on its head," he said. "Didn't look like no social visit I ever saw—more like a man seeing how far he could push."

"Oh, with Francis one never really knows," Jessie said with a sigh. "He will die trying to wheedle God out of one last acre of Heaven. And as for Rebecca, don't worry. She has a little bit of a temper but she is a good girl. She is . . . well . . . very devoted to our ranch."

"Our?" Carrick guessed his family must have moved to a better range, but he could not imagine where that could be.

Jess Lewis was taller than the young woman, physically worn from the toll range work took on a body, but composed as if she was telling someone else's problems. Her hair was mostly gray with a little black, with dark eyes and an angular, cultured face that bespoke dignity and warmth. In her rush outside, she had not put her hair up and it flowed behind her in the breeze. Carrick could see similarities to the younger woman. There was no gleam of constant battle in her eye, though. She looked like someone who would feed everything from range bums to stray cats. She did.

"Buffalo Horn Creek flows all summer, mostly," she told Carrick as though he was talking about the land and not who owned it. "It's the most reliable water on the range. It goes a bit through Lazy F and some through Double J but the prime grazing is here, the old Bar C land from the old days. Each ranch wants to buy me out now, or push me out, and they are each trying to push each other around as well. Even though, after all that has happened, we don't have that much range land left, we have the best access to the creek. Francis tries to be charming on some days; on others he isn't very nice at all. He is the most baffling man I ever met. He has come by almost every week, and Reb is usually waiting for him. I think she enjoys scaring off the poor man. Double J offered more money; they can afford to, being so large. People like the Crowleys threaten our riders constantly. That's why most of them quit."

The words "old Bar C" struck a nerve. Carrick decided to wait and see. For all he knew, the girl had more rifles in the house and was watching him. But Carrick knew how big Bar C had been when he left. The valley could hold a dozen ranches the size it had been. "Don't you have lots of open range out here?"

Jessie laughed sourly. "In Wyoming, open range goes to the one who is the strongest. Double J pretty well pushed my men from the big old north pasture and Lazy F moved in some from the south after that when some of our riders left us, so we didn't really have much land left for grazing. What we have is prime, as I said, but there's not as much as we need to be a big ranch and give them the run for their money Reb wants. Of course, having a crew would help, but we lost most of them after the incident in town. One of the Double J men got drunk and shot my foreman. My crew fired back and, by the time we were done, I lost three men dead. Five more were wounded. Double J lost about the same, but they had the money to hire more hands. Gunslingers more than cowboys they were.

"It was Reb and I and a handful of riders until they figured Double J was going to come out on top. They left. Now it's Reb and I, one good hand who has been loyal, and a few broken-down old riders who ride for us because they had nowhere else to go. They can't do much but they try. The young men come and go. Sometimes they come for Rebecca; those leave quickly. Sometimes they are looking for a place to start over. Then they move on.

"We get a few horses to auction and sell a few head of cattle to the railroad, but it's barely gonna keep us alive. If I had a head for business, I'd have sold out. I hate to give in to either of them. The land has special meaning to Reb. She knows every rock and bush, and every inch of it is something worth fighting for, to her. Reb will never want to sell it. As you have seen, my niece is a woman of very strong convictions." Her smile blunted the meaning of the words. "It doesn't help that they keep coming after us. Next thing you know, those Crowley boys from Double J will come up with their own threats."

"Don't think so." The finality in his voice made her brow furrow.

"Why not?"

"Two of 'em are dead and the other got his head busted."

"When?" She almost shouted. "I hadn't heard. Now, wait. They rode by here the other day, talking about how the barn might burn in the next storm and saying things that are threats only you can never get them for it. How do you know?" As with all who knew range gossip's exaggerations, Jess Lewis was not going to be taken in by foolish chatter, especially from an unsettling newcomer who could hardly know the latest news.

"I did it."

There was a very long silence. He could hear the wind in the oaks. Jess Lewis was looking at him closely, as if she could see blood on him. He stared back, not the least ashamed. He was aware the door opened again. The younger woman must have been listening.

"What is it, Aunt Jess?" she said, approaching.

"Your friend says he killed a couple Crowleys."

"Nice if somebody did something around here." Intense eyes turned on him. "And you are not my friend but did you really or are you telling tall cowboy stories?"

"Killed 'em." He described the dead ones and told how it happened. Women were funny. Killin' sometimes made sense and sometimes not. He wanted them to know he didn't have much choice.

The women exchanged glances. "Jeff Crowley had his eye on Reb," Jessie said. "Not just his eye. He also said some things a man shouldn't say."

"He ain't ever gonna do 'em," Carrick replied.

"Oh!" Jessie exclaimed. "The bread is burning." She rushed inside.

Reb followed and stopped. "Coffee should be ready any minute so you might as well come in and drink it." Her expression was unreadable. "I didn't make it for the horse," she added. Her tone remained defiant, challenging. She went in.

Carrick was in no rush. The land held memories of wonder. The house was a different story. It was already plain that whatever homecoming he thought he might receive after ten years was not happening. Mulling over who these women could be related to from his family—he could not picture them selling this land to strangers, given how much the land meant to his uncle and family—and wondering where all of his own relations had gone, he put Beast in the barn, took off the saddle, and made sure the horse had fresh hay. Then a thought struck. He walked away from the buildings to where a few trees stood near a black wrought iron fence that stood askew. It was then that he saw what he should have expected.

Stone markers told the tale. Samuel and Virginia and their son Morris. Died 1862. Morris had been barely one year old when he left. Poor boy—gone before he ever knew he was here. Carrick had never seen him. Uncle Joshua and Aunt Pauline were there as well; it had been their land. So were Bert and Andrew, their children. All four of them had died in 1862 as well. His family was now nothing more than a row of stones that were in front of the ones from his grandfathers and grand-mothers. Nine long years ago. All gone. Like the family had never existed. He wondered if any of them had ever read the letters that were such a labor for him to scribble in pencil by the light of a campfire. Somebody could have found a way to write to him. Then again, if something happened to wipe out a family, there were probably other things to do than write letters to somebody away in the Civil War. Back then, there were no Olivers or Joneses with big ranches and bigger ambitions. No Lewis women talking about the "old" Bar C. Bar C was the king because the Carrick family worked the hardest as all the ranches shared the vast open range that was so endless nobody cared much about legal boundaries. Back then, there were no Eastern markets or railroad to offer the temptation to get rich by pushing out everyone else. Ranchers were rivals, but they were friends. Guess all that was gone. The land did not look much different, but everything on it had changed; he was a stranger on his home range.

He drew his gun and spun around at the noise behind him. The young woman gasped, dropping the tin cup and its coffee on the grass, already starting to burn in late June. She started to get angry, then checked her rage when she saw the lines of emotion etched upon his face. She looked over his shoulder.

Comprehension dawned.

"Carrick, you said you were?" Her eyes went from the stones to the man. She swallowed hard. She seemed uncharacteristically unsure of herself. "That's the same as them, isn't it? Was this your home you were coming back to?"

"My kin. My uncle's ranch back then. My father, his brother, was a carpenter and handyman. We lived in a little shack over there, by that big old oak. Gone now, like all of them. I left in '61 because I was afraid to miss out on all that excitement in the war. Biggest worry I had the day I left was that I'd be home quick because the war would be over so soon. Never knew goodbye would be forever."

"I'm sorry. We keep the graves as neat as we can. Don't seem right not to. I guess that's why the name sounded familiar; I couldn't quite recall. Guess it's good I didn't shoot you. Anyhow, my ma's there, too. So is my uncle, Aunt Jess's husband." He had noticed the small stones in the back he could not read from the edge of the plot.

"How'd my family die? Indians? Nobody wrote back, but I never knew if my letters even got through. I never knew they were gone until right now."

"Don't think so. I'd have heard about that. Aunt Jess would know. She moved out here when I was a girl. I think she knew the family. She already lived here when we moved from Tennessee. We moved out here in 1862. I was twelve years old. Your kin were already gone. Guess I never thought this was somebody else's home, even with the graves and all. I think it might have been sickness because Aunt Jess told me they had to burn a lot of things. The house and this range: I always thought of it as mine."

There was, again, a strong emphasis on the last word.

He took a minute. He knew he was as likely to see stones as family, but there was still sort of a hope for a scene like in some stage play or some story book. Even with all that happened in those years before he left, there was still a sense of loss. There should have been someone. With all that family he left behind, one of them should have survived. It wasn't fair. So many things he always wanted to tell them: the charge at Shiloh; riding for Sherman. Now, it would never matter to anyone. He always lived by himself; now he knew he was truly alone in the world.

Time to set that aside. Death was part of life. The war taught that. Hang all if he was going to cry in front of a girl that had wanted to shoot him a few minutes ago. Reb touched his arm lightly. He almost jumped with surprise. Her face looked softer.

Her deep brown eyes were large. A man could lose himself looking into them, he thought. "I'm sorry. I'm sure it hurts to find out everyone you loved is gone. I know I can't imagine what it would feel like to lose Aunt Jess. I lost all the rest and I can't ever lose her. Let's go ask Aunt Jess what happened; she'll know for sure."

"So you are indeed Joshua Carrick's nephew," Jessie Lewis remarked when Carrick's cup had been re-filled with strong cowboy coffee. "I thought when you rode up there was a resemblance, even though it's been a long time since I've heard that name on this range. He always said you'd be back. Think he called you too stubborn to get killed. There was a fever that passed through in the spring of 1862. Took them all in only three or four days. My husband, too. He and I came west in 1860 because we knew the war was coming and we wanted to be as far from it as we could get. We moved around a bit trying to find the right place. He came to ride for Josh in late '61. You were already gone. I never knew why the fever spared me. I stayed on to run the place. Someone had to. My brother Pete, Reb's pa, got killed at Shiloh. Reb and Libby, my sister-in-law, came out here after that. Libby died in '64. She was sickly. She never liked it out here; she never recovered from Pete's death. It's been me and Reb now these seven years. Reb turned into about the best rider west of the Mississippi. She can shoot better than about any man, too, even if she is a little too anxious to give everyone a live demonstration of that. We showed the boys women can run a ranch." She paused. "At least we did for a while."

For a minute Carrick thought she was going to cry. He wondered why. He was the one who just found out his entire family was dead and he didn't really have a home any more. She looked up at him, trying to be brave, though something was clearly eating at her heart. "I guess everything ends. Some dreams are too good to come true." There was a pause as her eyes searched his impassive face.

Apparently he gave nothing away, because she spoke again. "If you are a Carrick, the way that I remember things when they all died, I guess I need to ask you: What did you come back for? And I guess what matters most to Reb and me: What are you gonna do?"

His face showed his bafflement.

"Out here, Carrick, in '62 there weren't lawyers and papers. Josh maybe had fifty dollars in gold and silver. He had this ranch. He was the last to die. He told me it was my home as long as I liked. I stayed because I had no place else to go, and this range, this place, they had meaning for me. Josh never sold it to me or nothing like that. No papers. I told the hands Josh left it to me and they accepted it because the ranch needed someone to run it. So did everyone else. Don't think there was ever anyone asked a question except whether we were going to change the brand. I didn't because somebody wanted money for that and I wasn't going to waste it. What I mean to say is that I don't have a paper that says I own this. I guess the law would say it's yours by blood. I knew there was a Carrick in the war so the first few years I sort of figured this day would come, but when the war ended and nobody showed up, I figured it was gonna be Reb's and mine forever." She was fighting tears, blinking rapidly. Her hand tapped the table repeatedly to contain her emotions. "Guess that's never going to be."

"Aunt Jess! This belongs to us! You can't . . . give it away. Not to him!" Reb's outrage was building fast as Carrick put up a hand to stop the coming explosion.

"Your sweat, your range," Carrick said, slowly and clearly, looking Jess in the eyes to be sure she believed him. "Jess, Reb, last thing I'm going to do is tell you two ladies that you have to pack up and leave your home. Not now, not ever. It's yours. I came back here because there wasn't no place better to go. Not lookin' for nothin'. Not expectin' nothin'. Wouldn't be expectin' anything even if they were alive. World moved on fast after the war; some of us moved a mite slower. Home's where you go when there's no place else that matters, and nobody anywhere cares what you do and you're in a spot like that Prodigal Son fella in the Bible. I can see everything here is different from the way it was when I left. I don't know what I'm going to do, but I'm not taking your land away from you and Reb. You want something on a piece of paper, I'll sign it without readin' it. I'll sign a blank page. Don't matter now. It's yours. Got that?"

"Are you going to stay?"

"Jessie, ma'am, don't rightly know right now. I don't know at all. All of this—my family gone like that—is something I can't explain real well. I think I knew but I didn't want to know. It's like when a shell goes off near and you feel empty and floating and you're alive but you don't really feel anything yet and you don't know what's comin' because it's too soon for the pain to set in." He got up. The house felt confining. He needed to get outside.

"If you don't mind, since I guess I should ask your permission, I think maybe I'll take Beast and ride a bit. Been a while since I seen the land. You think, maybe, when you live out here that the land is ground and rocks and trees. You look at it every day, but you don't see it. Then you see it in your mind when there's flies around the dead or the guns are booming or all you want is some blizzard to turn the whole world clean, white, and silent. Been waitin' a while to see it. Nothin' like this range anywhere. Guess I need to be alone a while." He set down the drained cup, face averted to avoid letting anyone see what he knew were the beginnings of tears. "Thanks for the coffee."

"Stop back for dinner," said Reb in a conciliatory tone, something like a smile trying to make itself seen as she came around the table and impulsively touched his arm. "I'll make biscuits. I make good biscuits."

Carrick's head nodded as though he was having a conversation with someone other than her. There was that fool thing with his eyes getting wet again. In the silence, he eventually focused on her expectant face. Being there for dinner seemed to matter to her. "I will do that, Miss Reb. Thank you."

# CHAPTER THREE

The rugged beauty of the land filled him as he rode. He'd seen the ocean; seen New Orleans when he was in the hospital; seen the Texas plains where the wind never stopped and the cattle never ended. Nothing held a candle to this Wyoming wild prairie. Each hill was a memory. Their stories were once his. Hawks glided above him in the serenity that preceded their descent to kill. Groups of horses, as wild as the wind, grazed by the edge of the clumps of trees. Somewhere bears were sleeping the drowsy hours of daylight away; he recalled the time he woke some up wondering if they wanted to play. The wind ruffled Beast's mane. The horse seemed to like it. Wild Wyoming wind. Carrick dismounted and led the gray to some grass. Beast grazed.

It was peaceful, if not silent. Crows were complaining about something in the distance, but that was hardly unusual. They were only silent when there was danger near. The wind moaned a bit as it whipped through branches overhead. Carrick looked and felt and smelled. So long away had he been that it was foreign; so long had he lived there that the more he inhaled of the land, the more he felt himself becoming whole once again. He set the black, flat-crowned hat on a rock and let the sun sink into him, remembering to look for snakes that might also like to sun themselves on the rock. The Wyoming wind blew upon him. For a time, he drifted with it. He almost thought he could hear the hawks way up as they flapped before soaring. He was certain he could smell the mix of rocks and brush and dust that carried in the wind. The smell of the land. The smell of home.

He'd ridden it all as a kid. They had gone up as far as the Powder River country once, when the army and the Indians were more or less not at war with each other. Uncle Joshua had taken him past the canyons carved for the wind and rain; where there were more shades of red and brown in the layers of rock than in the colors artists used to make paintings. There was a waterfall a few miles north that sprang from a straight rock wall twenty feet high. He tried to climb it once as a kid and got about ten feet off the ground before giving up. He wondered now if it was a stream or a trickle. The mountains way to the west were something he never tired of seeing as a kid. Every day he'd go to Cougar Rock and look, to see the first day when snow would crown the tops of the mountains. He could never understand how it could be blazing hot on the ranch and the snow would be falling way up there, but that was Wyoming. It was a place that let a boy grow strong; it was a place where a boy needed to grow strong.

Nothing much better than being a boy on a ranch. The chores seemed to take forever, but they didn't. He recalled their faces. Dead faces. After ten years of killing and death, it didn't feel the way he thought it would to know they were gone. There was frustration that he would never get answers, and a hollow feeling that everything of the past he knew was so far long gone it didn't even matter anymore. He never did really cry. Too much death; too many things happened at the end. He drifted to a time and a place that were never going to appear again anywhere outside of his head.

Then he felt the present return. Moving only his eyes, he scanned the horizon. Across the way, there was a man on horseback who had emerged from the tree line. Watching. It had been ten years, but he knew the limits. That had been Bar C land; they had grazed horses almost a mile beyond that ridge. Whatever the women called their spread, the land should have been theirs now. He could picture it from what Jessie said. Double J and Lazy F like a pair of jaws clamping together, chewing up the old Bar C until it was gone.

He stood up, and for the first time since before Texas, he felt a flash of purpose. Maybe they would gobble it up. Maybe not.

Rebecca Lewis was trying to make sense of things as she watched Aunt Jess bustle to make stew. "Aunt Jess, I don't like this."

"The stew?"

"No, Aunt Jess! This Carrick rider. I feel sorry for him that his home is gone but how do you know he won't want it back and throw us off? Why did you tell him you didn't have some piece of paper? You don't even know if he is who he says he is. Did he seem to want to even look around the house? No! Trouble. That's all we've had the last year or two." She veered into a train of thought she always rejected. "Maybe we should sell and go someplace else, Aunt Jess. I never thought of this as somebody else's home before us and I guess it will be somebody else's after us. I thought this was ours forever, Aunt Jess. I know we can't hold off Double J forever without something that breaks our way for once instead of Jackson Jones winning all the time. Things are coming to a boil, Aunt Jess, and I don't know how it will end anymore. I don't want to end like that Carrick man with no home and no place and nobody cares. I guess I'm scared. Everything I feel inside is all mixed up, bumping into each other. Carrick. What do you think about him?"

Jessie Lewis paused. She had not recalled Reb ever showing much interest in a man past the moment of telling him to go away. Then again, Carrick's arrival was hardly normal.

"I won't tell you not to worry, child, because I worry, too.

Some folks, child, are born to attract trouble. I think this Carrick man is one of them. Man's got a lot of marks on his face, arms, and hands like he was in a lot of fights. Busted nose, too. Most of the men here have been cowed by those Crowleys, let alone stand up to them and kill a couple. Double J won't let that rest." She sighed and brushed a strand of gray hair from her brow. "That man's been drifting six years. If he wanted to be here when the war ended, he'd have come home. There's a lot to the story we don't know. He could be on the run; he could be anything. The best we can hope for, child, is that he will drift on by. And, girl, I brought you up to be honest. You can't pretend to own a ranch you don't own when someone turns up who does. As for sellin', I don't know, girl. Double J offered hardly anything; Lazy F offers more, but there's something up with Francis Oliver. Something sly, I think. What we need is a couple of hands that won't run at the first sign of a storm. You really want to sell, Reb? You?"

The girl shook her head. "Think Carrick might stay on and work? We could use a man like him."

"I thought you didn't like him?"

Reb blushed. "I didn't say that, Aunt Jess. We need . . . I think . . . I don't know!"

She did not see her Aunt Jess's smile. "I don't think he's likely to stay long, girl. I think the work that one does is with a gun. I suppose we can see what happens. My Good Book says the Lord works in very mysterious ways, child, but never to lose faith. Maybe we should trust that somehow the Lord will bring us through this, and get back to making dinner."

Reb could not help but smile. Since she was a child, Aunt Jess's answer to everything that was wrong had been the Good Book and a dose of hard work. She admitted she didn't have much to complain about, and a look at the world around her told her that everybody else's ways were not that much better.

★ ★ ★ ★ ★

The heat of the day was fading as she saw his silhouette approaching in the distance. He rode loosely in the saddle, as though it had been his home for many years. Reb pushed the glossy black hair back off of her shoulders and let it blow in the early evening breeze off of the distant mountains. She'd spent more time avoiding men than talking to them. Aunt Jess went through a spell when Reb was nineteen or so where she fussed over Reb's appearance and seemed determined to bump into every cowboy on the range in an effort to get Reb married. Some were interested. Reb wasn't. She'd lived a very free life with Aunt Jess, away from all the strictures society—even frontier society—put on women. She understood that in every family somebody had to cook, but could not imagine a life without roping and riding—let alone living all the time in pounds of heavy material that they called proper dresses that weighed down a body. Give her a horse and gun any day. Men didn't give her the respect she thought she deserved, but she was as good a shot as any of them—better because she was always sober and too many men were drunks. Pistols were a little heavy for her, but she was fast and accurate with a rifle. Carrick was one of the few who seemed to recognize that, although, truth be told, he all but laughed at her when she pointed the gun at him. For some reason that made her smile.

For a moment, she wondered how all of this appeared to him. It would be like her going back to Tennessee after all her time away and trying to set up life in the house that someone else had been living in since they fled back in 1861. Nothing as it should be. For a fleeting second she wondered what he thought of her. She wasn't really sure why it mattered, but it did. She understood she was not what the boys called pretty, although some of the boys called anything female that very word. Her eyebrows were strong and full; her face reflected a strong character more than sweetness. She had a small nose Jess used to call a button that still managed to get broken when she fell off the roof chasing that cat. Her nose never set straight. One cowboy teased her about it. Only one. When he got up, and could talk, he said something about a kick like a mule.

Reb and the world had been fighting each other so long it seemed like the way it was. She didn't ask for mercy and didn't give it, either. In Wyoming, the strong survived. She might have been small, but she was strong.

While she was lost in thought, Carrick had ridden close. He tipped his hat and dismounted, watching her face look past him. "Them biscuits out ridin' the range somewhere?" There looked to be a smile on his face; he seemed different, relaxed. The rough edges had been sanded down. "C'mon, Miss Reb, let's eat this dinner you been cookin' while watching the wind blow."

As they walked into the house, she sized him up. Medium height, lean like all cowboys. There were lines in his tanned face from the weather, the war, and something more. Sadness underlaid toughness. He was trail-rough and shaggy with brown hair that curled out from under the battered black flat-topped hat and a beard to match, raggedy cut like a man on his own. There were a couple of white marks on his face like scars that never healed. She guessed he was maybe somewhere around ten years older than she was, maybe less. Hard to tell. Unlike horses, men didn't let you check their teeth to see how old they were. Whatever road he came up on, it was a hard one.

"Wondered if I was going to have to eat all this myself," Aunt Jess scolded as they entered.

"Long time away, ma'am. You can recall what the range looked like, but not how it feels. Wind don't blow like this anywhere else. Hot or cold, sometimes both together, but always wild. Gets inside you and it scrubs you clean. Appreciate you

41

waitin' for me."

"You had better eat. Your food's getting cold," Reb interrupted gruffly. She, too, loved the wildness of the wind and knew what he meant. It got inside her soul until whatever had been wrong in the world was put back into its proper perspective. She didn't know anyone else felt it.

They hadn't had much like dinner in a while. There were always chores and food was something to hurry up and chew before the next thing went wrong.

They sat down. Reb looked over at Carrick. "Uh, in this house, it's a rule and it's the way we live, we always pray before we eat, um, that is, when we actually sit down and eat." Challenge flared in her face. "You want to say it?"

Facing armed men was nothing like the panic racing through Carrick. He had last seen church years back. He could not imagine what would be appropriate. Words said while buryin' folks was one thing. They'd done it enough in the war. This was a world of different. He had no idea what God would be saying to him after the last two years and what happened in Texas. Then the girl looked up at him as the silence started to get embarrassing.

"Um," he stammered. "Um, God, it's been, uh, a long time since I been here and along the trail maybe we forgot to think much about You, and all, and probably the way it came out we wouldn't be here if You didn't think about us. Um, I know You got my kin with You and I guess that's best even if it don't feel that way right now. And thank You for keeping Reb and her Aunt Jess here safe 'cuz things like that only happen if You say so, and hold all these folks in Your hand—and thank You for lettin' us have food this day. When you don't always have it you miss it. And keep Beast safe. Horses don't deserve to ever suffer. Amen."

He looked up at her quickly to see if the prayer—as bad as it was—was acceptable. Her eyes were closed. She opened them, looked over at him, and smiled. "Eat," she said. He did.

Jessie Lewis tried to remember the things Josh Carrick had said about the man at her table. Wild and headstrong. Something more. There was some kind of family problem, but she could not remember it. So much had happened and it was so long ago that she could remember pieces of memories, echoes of emotions, but not what actually had happened. It could come in its own time. She found herself watching the man less and Reb more. Her niece covertly watched the man throughout the meal, averting her eyes when he looked her way. Reb was a combination of the daughter and sister she never had. Never would, she told herself, now that she was near to forty and men only looked at younger women. The girl had the stoutest defenses of anyone she ever met when it came to people. Reb had brought home an endless array of wild animals to heal. Some made it; some were in the land next to Carrick's kin. She could ride horses five times her size; never met one she didn't like. But men? Jessie Lewis had been fifteen when she was married. Reb was now 21, more than of age, but nowhere near ready to settle down. Rich, poor, tall, short—she had no interest in any of them, and barely noticed them. Oddly enough, this stray rider seemed to have gotten closer to her in a couple of hours than probably all the suitors combined over all their years in the territory. They looked to her like flint and tinder, but she could hope. She wasn't going to live forever, and she knew that world could be lonely—and that for all the wild cowboys drifting through Wyoming, not many were men she wanted Reb to be seen with, let alone close to. She would keep an eye on them and see—and try to remember.

# CHAPTER FOUR

Carrick spent the night by the fireplace on the floor. When the women had gone to the room they shared, he stayed up. He could not have slept. There was only one thing remaining from anything that had been inside the house when he was a kid—a horse he had carved for his uncle's birthday. It wasn't finished. He had been forced to leave for Omaha to join his regiment before it was fully completed, but he had given it to Uncle Josh anyhow even though the old man's birthday had been weeks away. At least he knew his uncle had kept it.

Though the woman had rearranged the furniture, he could picture the way it had looked. Then there was the way it really was. The picture wasn't one serene still image. It talked. It argued and fought and screamed secrets, and even before Carrick left, Uncle Josh was barely speaking to his brother, Sam, Carrick's father. Carrick knew he was part of the trouble, but everyone had insisted it was nothing he had done.

His uncle had come the closest to telling him when he had arranged with Colonel Thayer for Carrick to march off with the First Nebraska Volunteers when they were mustered out to head East to fight in the Civil War. "Got to learn to make your own way in the world, son. I think of you as my son, like my own child. Understand, boy, it's not who you come from that makes you what you are; it's what you do. Make me proud, son!"

In the middle of vague ranch gossip that Uncle Josh had

44

children before he was married, and since that gossip was usually connected with Carrick, Carrick left wondering the truth of the matter. It was not something he could have asked in a letter. Now, he would never know.

When dawn came, after Carrick's sleepless night, the women were by turns horrified and downright angry at his plans, but Carrick had always lived straight up when he took on the world. He wasn't changing now.

"Your family cemetery is full," Reb had spat out. "You'll get buried on the range."

"Good a place as any," he had replied placidly, wondering how a girl like that ever expected to find a husband if all she did was argue. Then again, she was awfully pretty when she did; really came alive. Of course, it could have been concern, but it sure didn't sound that way. "Don't you worry, none, Miss Reb. Too fine a day for buryin' folks and I reckon I know what I'm doing. If I got to worry about some Double J back-shooter while I'm still trying to figure out my own self, it's more than my poor head can handle. Heard too much. I want to have a talk with this Jackson Jones man everybody makes sound like a huge and all-mighty king."

Aunt Jess said nothing. Men did what they did and never said why. Reasoning with them was like talking to cattle. Carrick had told them he wanted to learn about Jackson Jones and Double J because they had been very clear that Double J was the biggest threat to their land. He would certainly learn.

The old Johnson place had changed so much Carrick did not recognize it. Morning dimness hid him as he watched the ranch wake up. Two bunkhouses meant size. Not many men around meant a lot out riding. He'd need to be more careful on the trails. The ranch had changed. Of course. The new red-painted house stood two stories tall and looked about twice as big as anything he'd ever seen before. He watched a man walk from it to the small one-room old house—not much more than cabin—that was older than Carrick's memory. The size of the man, and his clear ownership of everything he examined on his walk—meant he could only be the fabled and feared Jackson Jones. Jones had visibly looked irritated upon leaving the house, but as he walked to the smaller house, his walk seemed stronger, more confident, as if leaving behind something bad and heading for something better. Carrick watched a while longer as the man walked to the smaller building, opened the front door, and let it shut with a slam. Men rode out. One stayed by the oak near the gate. Using the rough ground as his cover, Carrick walked Beast to a draw and tied him to a stunted oak. The horse didn't like it.

"I'll be back, horse," Carrick said soothingly, the same tone he used on the long, slow trek from Kansas when the thunder rolled and the high winds blew. Beast quieted, but watched Carrick closely.

He'd grown up on the land. Memory served him well. All he needed was a little luck. Anyone going into a den when the snakes were wrathy needed it. He'd always assumed it would be there; if not, he'd not know very long that it wasn't.

The back door showed signs of use. Somebody chewed and spit there. Worth a try. Powerful men don't always worry about locks. With no idea if the other side held a gun, he pushed it open, pulling his own weapon and leveling it at the bear of a man sitting behind a massive desk plunked down in the center of the room. For a big man, he was fast. He was turning to see who intruded into his lair while reaching for a fancy shotgun that lay across the desk.

"I wouldn't," Carrick said calmly. "Both hands where I can see them."

The man put two huge hands on the desk.

"S'pose you're Jackson Jones."

The giant of a man grunted derisively. "If you broke into my office here to tell me that, cowboy, you must have been kicked by a horse. You some gunslinger from Lazy F? Can't believe that miserable old skinflint would have parted with a nickel to hire you, but it would be like him to let someone else do his dirty work. You might kill me, but you'll never get out of here alive."

"Not here to kill you. Would have done it by now if I was. Understood? I'm only here to have us a conversation."

Jones nodded. Carrick closed the door and moved into what had been the Johnsons' house, which had been stripped of all furniture except for the desk, which Carrick saw allowed the man sitting there to see what happened outside, a couple of chairs near it, and a table and chair by the massive fireplace that filled up most of one wall. A crude map was across another wall by the main door. Across the way, a row of large, wide, curtainless, unshuttered windows looked over the land, giving the room its light. This was the den of a man who wanted nothing of the soft things of life cluttering up his mind or blocking his view of his empire. Whatever the big house was, this was the place where he was the master.

"Name's Carrick."

"I heard that name the other day for the first time. Not much good."

"Your boys wanted to push things."

"My men get paid to push things."

"Like the Lewis women at the old Bar C?"

"They hire you? Get paid first, son, because they got nothin'."

"Nope. Bar C was my family's range before the war. I'm back now."

Jones looked at Carrick with new interest, clearly surprised

47

that the rider before him who had killed his men had a connection to the valley. While he studied Carrick, Carrick studied Jones. The rancher was well over six feet tall, muscle starting to soften but he was still a man who looked like he could break a tree in half. There was loose skin along the lines of rock-hard jutting jaw; maybe age and maybe sickness. Gray hair marked his temples. His eyes truly defined his face; they were gray. They flashed from underneath bushy eyebrows that danced in anger as his gravel voice boomed in the confines of the room. Jones finished his inspection before Carrick finished his.

"Your problem, son. The War Between the States ended in 1865, and that is six long years in the past. You took your time coming back here. That's your business. Not my problem if the ranch fell apart and your family sold to those women."

"Never got sold. Nothing was ever filed with the territory. Name of Carrick will still be on the deed, wherever it is. That means it's mine because I'm the only one in the world that's got a legal claim to that land."

"Paper don't tell a man where to run his herd," Jones said angrily, spitting on the floor to punctuate his disgust. "Ink and paper don't mean a thing. Out here, a man has what a man takes in his own God-given hands and holds onto so tightly no one can pry it away. Not one inch more. You ought to know that."

"Wasn't always that way. Used to be there was land enough for everybody."

"That is not the way this range works now, Carrick. When I was in the ditches at Petersburg with flies and shells all around me, I told myself no man was going to make me live like that again. I had lived back in old New York State, where they figured people like me were made to work the mills or fix the wagons so somebody born in some family that had what they call breeding got to be fed from a silver spoon. I was not going back to that life. I made some fast money in Virginia selling things the rebels left behind in Richmond. Then I came out here." He fidgeted in his chair and started to get up. Carrick moved the gun.

"Shot in the leg. Bothers me to sit too long. Put it away. I won't call anyone and you ain't gonna kill an unarmed man or you would have done it by now." Jones stood with some difficulty, braced himself on the desk, and walked around the room. Carrick holstered the gun.

Jones stopped by the huge set of windows. The light shone full on his face as he looked out at the land. "Out here, Carrick, a man can reach out and grab onto a dream like an Easterner reaches out and picks an apple off a tree. It's that easy. All you got to do is reach hard and hang on. I came out here; this place was a ruin. Look at it now! I built that house next to this one; it's got more furniture and trimmings than the rest of the range combined. Once the army pushed out those Indians, this land was there for the taking. Them women want to build a ranch, more power to them. They won't ever do it because they don't know how. They're women. It takes a man.

"You know how many nights I spent in a saddle; how many days on a horse? I built this by the right of my own work, and I will grow it as big as I want. I'm not going to be cut up and hemmed in by whiny women or an old weasel like Francis Oliver or pestered by the thieves in the badlands. Not many times in history, Carrick, can a man walk out in God's good sunshine and build an empire out of his own hard work and nothing else. This is one of those times. One of these days real soon I'm going to have me a son. He will own land beyond anyone's wildest dreams because I won't let anyone or anything stop me." As Jones talked, his hands waved and his voice rose with the fervor of a tent revival preacher.

Jones stopped and put down his hands. "The Crowleys mean nothing to me, Carrick. They've already been replaced. Heard

49

what happened. Their bad luck. A man makes his own luck. The old Bar C and the old range you knew before the war got as much to do with the future as the Indians. It's a new world, Carrick. This Wyoming we're living in is for the strong, not the weak. I'm not gonna tell a man where to ride, but them women had their time, and it's over. Sell or not, they're done. Ride their range and tell me what you see. The place is sagging and ready to go under. What's meant to go under should go under, so the rest of us can thrive. That's the law of the land, Carrick. That's the law of the range, the law of nature. Wolves don't feed the weak; they kill the weak. I want to build this valley, Carrick. I want it strong. You can't build strong and tolerate weakness. I will not allow it in my own ranch, and I refuse to countenance others taking up land to no purpose."

Jones limped back toward Carrick. "You want a job, you come to me. I respect a man with the iron to come straight up and face me. A man who lives that way should be working with me, not against me. You want to fight for some silly dream about the world you left behind you, it's gonna buy you nothin' but trouble. In the end, Carrick, you're going to lose. Even Bobby Lee found that out when he faced Grant: It's not how good you fight; it's how big you are. Double J is bigger than anything you've ever seen. Ride around and see. I built it, Carrick; I built it to last. Nothing is going to stop me."

His oration finished, Jones landed behind the desk with an audible grunt.

Carrick put his palms on the edge of the desk and leaned in close to Jones. "Don't think I can let you swallow Bar C."

The bushy brows twitched but Jones's glare never wavered. "Don't think you can stop me."

Carrick looked across the gulf that separated him from Jones. He felt a tinge of regret. In another place, he'd have gladly worked for a man like Jones. Not here. "Guess we won't be talkin' much more, then."

"Not much to say. Change your mind, you're welcome here, Carrick. One more thing to tell you: I got rules. I don't backshoot or lie or steal. That Oliver is a whiny man who moves like a worm in the light when he gets cornered. That's not me, Carrick. I live this life straight with the Lord, and straight with every man. I don't shoot women. If I did, I'd have their range by now. But let me tell you it's not being mealy-mouthed that builds dreams, Carrick." They looked at each other across Jones's desk—poker players dealing with lives and land instead of cards and chips.

Jones slapped his hand on the desk again with the sound like a .45 going off. "Tell them stubborn fools to sell, Carrick. Tell them I'll double the last offer. I'll triple it. There! You got that? Triple it. But if they don't take what they can get, they got a fair chance to end up with nothin'. Understood?" Lions did not roar louder.

Carrick understood. The war had sent thousands of men West with dreams and ambitions. He'd seen a hundred men like Jones who were ruthless in building their dreams, regardless of what they did to anyone else's. Men with a code they lived by. Greed was too simple a word for it. They were driven by pride, by glory, by something Carrick knew could make a man say all kinds of noble things and hire folks to do the things that got the job done any way that made the boss happy.

"We'll be seeing each other," Carrick said, impulsively holding out his hand.

Jones took it. The door burst open. A man Carrick's age came in, stunned to see Jones talking to anyone in the stronghold that was his private sanctum. Carrick thought he focused on the handshake and got very pale very fast. The man, tall and thin with what looked like a boiled collar on his shirt, started to call for help.

"Get back in here, Henry!" Jones roared. "This is Carrick. Family used to run that old Bar C range before the war; the range the Lewis women are running into the ground. Carrick and I have been talking. Carrick, this here's Henry Petersen, my ranch manager. Never thought I'd see the day I got too big to remember all the numbers but it came and Henry keeps track of it all for me."

Jones may not have known the history of the name, but the ranch manager reacted when he was introduced. He tried hard to hide it. Petersen was nervous. Carrick wondered how much Jones knew about the details of running his empire. A big man with a bad leg might not ride as much as he might, Carrick thought.

"If you want that job, and I'm not here, see Henry," Jones added, telling his manager Carrick had free run of the range. Then he turned the full power of his gaze on Carrick. "I think we understand each other." Carrick knew he was being dismissed. He'd come to learn. He had. Jackson Jones was going to die grasping for one more acre, and nothing short of death would stop him.

Carrick was restless, or maybe he was putting off the bad news he would bring to the women. He rode up to Black Wind Pass. The name itself was from an old Cheyenne legend that when the hot, wild winds blew through the pass and into Buffalo Horn Valley, they brought a black wind of doom. Because the worst storms had an east wind that would come from that direction there was the usual level of practical information in the legend.

Crazy Uncle Charlie's cabin—he recalled being told from the time he could remember—would never last another winter and the old fool would freeze to death when the snow buried it. He'd lived there a lot in his teens when the Carrick ranch house was nothing but fights; Charlie didn't care about much, told good stories, and enjoyed going any way the rest of the world wasn't headed. There it stood. The place was an odd mix of decay and decorum. Somebody had planted a few flowers; a wood pile not far away had rotted over the years. The roof had a patch on it that looked new. He guessed the shack was some place people went when they had no place else. At least that much had not changed.

The pass was the one place where the valley was visible. Shaped like a buffalo horn, it curved around from the narrow east end to the wider west end. Carrick thought about making camp near the shack. He'd been lucky last night. No sleep meant no screaming wide awake in the middle of the night when it all came back. They all screamed at the hospital, all the ones that survived Andersonville. No one cared there. No one cared when he was in jail. Some nights on the plains he'd awakened to find Beast looking down at him. It was getting better, but he wasn't taking chances. He was not having the women look at him the way folks did with pity when men got crazy. He'd tell them it wasn't right for a man to camp with two women like that. It wasn't his home. He wasn't their rider. Folks would say things if he stayed any time at all. Not right for Miss Reb. They'd see that. The house brought back memories. Too many. Nope. Staying there would give the nightmares the chance to ambush him and humiliate him. The cabin was safer.

The more he thought about it, the more he liked the idea of staying at the shack. The wind felt clean. Putting distance from the old place reflected his state of mind. He did not know what he would do next. Ride on if the women sold? Stay if they didn't and stand up to Jones the way he wanted to? Maybe he'd hole up here and see what happened. After all, he wouldn't be the first man who made a fool decision because there was a woman involved whose face kept wandering into thoughts when it probably shouldn't.

He took his time riding back to the old Bar C. He'd eaten enough the night before to go without for a day at least, so there was no rush on that score. Beast picked his way over rocks and along trails that had held untold wonders when he had been a boy. He remembered Georgia boys trying to tell the Union army that they didn't care about slavery; they were fighting for the land. He could understand that better now that he had come back. He had no reason to stay; but even after a day, he was starting to feel that no one was going to make him leave. Not again. Not ever again. Man needed air and food and a horse and gun, but above all, a man needed a place to belong. This was his.

Predictably, Jessie Lewis took the news of Jones's offer calmly and without comment while her niece peppered her speech with anger.

"I hope you told him I'll shoot his head off before I move out for the likes of him," Reb scolded. "I hope you stood up to him like a man. That wife of his who thinks she's so important. She cheated in that contest where she got the sharpshooting ribbon. You remember, Aunt Jess? The judges were against me. Both of them, those high and mighty Double J people. Why, I'd like to . . ."

"Rebecca Lewis! Less violence in your language, please. There must be a way to resolve this that will not result in violence."

Reb looked at Carrick. "Not my range; not my fight," Carrick observed. "Don't like seein' Bar C carved up and gone, don't like it at all, but unless you got a hole card I don't see, Jessie, he's got all the aces. He can wait you out until you go under. Unless . . ."

"Gutless like all of them," Reb shot back. "If you wanted your old range back, you could have it by standing up to him.

What's the matter with you? Another man who is all talk but no action?"

Reb eventually calmed down. She even, with only moderate prompting, apologized if Carrick took anything she said the wrong way. Since Carrick figured there was only one way to take it, it wasn't very contrite, but her obvious clumsiness in having to apologize at all was worth a smile Carrick made sure was hidden.

"What I was sayin', Jessie, was that the only thing you can do, if you don't want to cave and you don't want to sell, is find a way to make the ranch pay. Jones thinks you are going to fail and wants to be the first to scoop up the land. If you can make the ranch pay, Jones might decide to back off. He doesn't respect anything but strength. Don't like to be the bearer of bad news, but the man knows the ranch isn't runnin' like it needs to if you want to survive. If you can't find a way to make this land pay for you, Jess, I don't see how there's a good ending in all of this for you and Reb. Might not be today or even this year, but if nothing happens, you end up losing."

"Not without a fight," Reb spat out. "Nobody gets this while I'm breathing."

"I think what Rebecca might be trying to say, Mr. Carrick, is that we will do anything we must to keep the ranch," Jess Lewis interjected. "You lived here when it did pay. If you can think of something we have not tried, we would be most grateful."

Carrick could not imagine what they had not done in the past 10 years, but made noises that he would try to think of something. Not likely. He's probably forgotten all he ever knew these past years. Everything except guns. Those he knew too well.

Neither woman liked his idea to stay at the pass for the time being while he was trying to figure out his own plans. It didn't help that he was trying not to explain that the house wasn't really his home—it was the place where the ghosts of the past lived. He wasn't going to explain the nightmares. Never. If they sold, which he figured they would because it was the only sensible thing to do, they might be gone before that ever came up.

Reb was, as always, the more vocal; wondered what deal Carrick had cut that he didn't want to be seen at the ranch. Carrick lost his temper.

"Well, what do men say about a girl when a man who likes a girl stays with that girl in the same house when they're not married, Reb?" he asked, stung into bluntly bringing up one of the main reasons he didn't want to be there right now while avoiding what he did not want to say. She looked like she had been slapped as her face went red. Jessie seemed to be stifling a laugh, but Carrick could not imagine what was funny. There were no further objections.

"I'm not runnin' off. I don't rightly know what to make of everything, and I need to figure this out in my own time in my own way. I slept in that shack plenty with my Uncle Charlie before the war and I want to sleep there again." It was true. It didn't say why he had to be there, but that was fine.

Reb brightened a bit when he asked her to show him the range in the morning so that he could learn where the stock was. "If I'm supposed to help out until you get a real crew or until you figure out what you want to do, it might be useful for me to know where you got your critters hid," he said.

" 'Bout time you said something that made sense," Reb grumbled.

Carrick rode off to the shack with conflicting emotions. The fight wasn't his. The land wasn't his—not anymore. But the truth was, Carrick wanted to fight. It was all he knew how to do. Although it stuck in his craw to give in to anyone, the safest thing for Reb and Jessie was to sell and move along. Women weren't made to be dragged into a range war. Even when they wanted one.

# CHAPTER FIVE

Reb was waiting for him, mounted, when he and Beast rode up early. She was sitting atop a black stallion; not a ladylike horse, but one born for saddle work. Her black hair spilled out from under a tan, broad-brimmed hat. She was wearing an old brown leather jacket that was work-stained. Her pants were tucked into a pair of high-top boots. Her posture radiated contentment. She informed him the horse's name was Arthur, after some legend about a king who could never be conquered.

"Thought you were sleeping the day away," she chided as he approached. "Arthur is the fastest horse around Buffalo Horn Valley except for that wild stallion Jackson Jones thinks is his but can't ever catch. See if you can keep up." She and the stallion were gone in a wink. Carrick found himself with that dumbfool smile on his face only the girl seemed to cause. There was only one thing to do. Follow!

He caught up with Reb under the shade of an oak that had been cut in half by lightning when Carrick was a boy. It had regrown itself in a crooked fashion, looking like a tree that should blow over in a breeze.

"They never teach you how to ride?" she challenged.

"Bein' polite to a helpless little woman," he jibed back.

Reb's lips compressed. Her good intentions were warring with her instincts to fight back until she realized the man was trying to incite an explosion. "For the sake of behaving the way Aunt Jess says a lady is supposed to behave when dealing with a range bum, I will declare a truce for the moment, Carrick," she said. "Now, do you want to see the range?"

They rode side by side as the morning drifted past. Each took turns pointing out features of the range. Cougar Rock had so eroded Reb didn't recognize it; other changes that were new to him were favorite haunts of hers. The creek road had spots near the water that were overgrown—places where she hid from the world.

She had made some biscuits that served as their lunch. They ate in the shade of a giant pine. He asked a question about the land and her attachment to it. "Most folks, dirt is dirt. Maybe they fight back to save a house. You don't give an inch, Reb. Curious."

She was quiet a moment. "We were a Union family in Tennessee before the war. We lived not far from Nashville. We pretty much got run out of our home when Lincoln won in 1860. By 1861, there wasn't any place that was really safe. We ended up on the run over to East Tennessee, where my Pa had some friends. They took us in but they didn't really want to. When the Union army re-took Nashville, we thought we'd go back to the old house, but it had been ransacked and burned after we left. The army decided to use the land for some fort or other. We were in Nashville when Pa died at Shiloh."

"I was there," he interjected.

"Then you know," she said. "Aunt Jess wanted us to come out here all along. She said that all the places we had ever seen were nothing compared to the wide open range out here. She said nobody here cared about the stupid war and we could start fresh. My parents wanted to stay in Tennessee. After Shiloh, there wasn't much left to stay for, so Ma gave in to Aunt Jess and agreed to come out here, but she didn't ever like it. She grew up in the woods, and all this wide open was like some foreign place to her. I thought it was the greatest place in the world, especially when the wind whips across the mountains and it blows away whatever is wrong inside your head. Watch a bear walk one of these meadows, you forget there's a pack of people crying for more money or more something out there. I lost the first home I had; I got kicked around from place to place when no one in Tennessee wanted to take in a Union family; I had to leave there when the people who were supposed to protect me took over my home. I'm not getting pushed around and pushed out—not ever again. Not by Jackson Jones or Francis Oliver or anyone else. If I die here fighting for this, then I'll take that, Carrick. Then I'll haunt whoever kills me until the eagles stop flyin'. I'm not running ever again. Ever."

Carrick could feel the intensity of her dream. He recalled Jackson Jones. The same dream, different dreamers on a road bound for a collision. "It can't be easy out here. You and your aunt taking on the world."

" 'Cuz we're women?"

"That don't make it easier."

She shrugged. "Not marryin' some range rider who can't do a day's work without whining because tongues wag in town about two women livin' alone out here. One of the Lincoln Springs gossips said something to Aunt Jess once she didn't like; she never repeated it, and Aunt Jess dunked her in a horse trough."

Carrick grinned.

"I don't complain, Carrick. When it gets hard, I got all this to see and feel. It don't get a lot better. People come out and talk about this city or that river. I thought Tennessee was perfect, Carrick, but then I came out here. Give me this, Carrick, until I die. It's mine! I don't know about ink and paper and laws. It's part of me and I'm part of it. No one can tell someone where to go and where not to go. I don't understand Jackson Jones. How can a man think he owns all of this for himself?"

Whatever he was going to say was cut off by her exclamation of rage. "Look at that!"

Carrick looked. One rider, by a small pond. He had a sack of something in his hands that he stopped dumping and dropped as he saw Reb and Carrick. A cloud of white was puffing up around him.

"Our land!" she called. "Our pond. Somebody's up to something!" She kicked her heels to the horse and was gone. "Stop, you!" she was screaming.

Beast had not flat-out run in a long time. He was rested and well-fed. In a moment, he had caught up to Reb and Arthur. The rider up ahead had mounted, but he was losing the race. The man turned in his saddle to look back. He pulled a long gun from his saddle. Reb did not slow down or act like she saw the action. She was yelling. Carrick urged Beast forward faster, pulling his own rifle as he did.

The rider was aiming at Reb. Carrick put the rifle to his shoulder and fired, as he had learned in the war. Five quick spaced shots. At this range, they might miss, but they would upset the aim of the man drawing a bead on Reb. He shoved the rifle back into the sheath and drew his pistol.

The rider had lowered the rifle. If he fired, he had missed. Carrick called to him to drop the weapon. The rider didn't respond. Then he slumped against the neck of his horse. The animal bucked. The rider limply flopped back and forth in the saddle as the horse tried to dislodge the burden on its back. Reb grabbed the frightened animal by the bridle. She saw three red holes in the man's chest. Three hits out of five shots at fifty yards on horseback. She could do that on a good day at targets, but not on the back of a horse. Maybe there was something more to this Carrick than she had thought.

"Know him?" asked Carrick.

"Larry Gordon. Rode for us; went to Double J when the

ranch started having tough times."

"Sure this is your land?"

"Beyond the trees and that hill, we can't keep an eye on everything. Not enough stock to fill up all the land any more, Carrick. It's ours but Double J uses it. We don't even try any more, Carrick, without riders willing to stand up for themselves. This, this is ours, Carrick. Double J never tried to push us out all at once; they gnaw off a piece at a time. We got maybe thirty, forty horses running out here. There are about twenty-five cattle in the southern pasture below the creek that borders Lazy F; that is, unless Oliver stole them all. Aunt Jess feels different but I hate that man! Crazy fool that still rides for us must be down there today. Half-breed Cheyenne; about the only one not scared of Double J. What was Larry doing here?"

Carrick went to the sack. Salt. Simple enough. Dump enough into any standing water and it would ruin the pond until nature flushed the salt away. Nothing permanent; only a water hole out of commission as the hot season of Wyoming was starting. Clever. Devious. Double J meant Jackson Jones, but ruining water holes didn't strike him as Jones's style. One way to find out. He looked over the land as he tried to plan the next move. The man appeared to have been out on his own. He had killed another Double J rider. If the ball was going to be opened, he had done it. Better play out what had to happen next.

Carrick unhooked the dead rider's legs from the stirrups and tossed the man limply across the saddle. The horse was unhappy, but Reb had it under control. "You ready to go callin' or you want to sit this dance out?"

"What are you talkin' about?"

"Time to tell Jackson Jones that what he says and what his riders do are two different things."

Reb spent half the ride to Double J explaining to Carrick that he was crazy and that they were on their way to be killed. The rest of it was in silence after he told her if she had nothing better to say to be quiet and let him alone. After he lost his temper with her, she was quiet so long riding behind him that he half wondered what the odds were that she would shoot him if Double J didn't.

"They guard the gate, so ride hard behind me when we go in," he told her when they stopped out of sight behind a rise. "I got words to say with Jackson Jones, and I don't want some rider with a gun to get in the way." He looked her over. Fear and resolution were both plain. "You don't have to join the party, Miss Reb. You can wait here."

" 'Fraid to find out you shoot second-best to a girl if it comes to that?"

"Nope. Man has to protect his biscuit supply." He grinned. Grit and spark were good things to have on your side. "Watch my back, Reb."

"Someone has to and this is my lucky day."

With a whoop he was off, leading the reins of the dead rider's horse. She galloped to catch up. Soon they were at the Double J gate. A man under the tree moved to bar their way, but three running horses coming straight at him convinced him that it was not the best idea he'd had that day.

When they reached the ranch's yard, in front of the stone house, Carrick fired once in the air and called out for Jackson Jones. In a moment, the Double J owner filled the doorway, almost having to stoop to walk through.

"Miss Lewis," he said, lifting his hat. The tone hardened. "Carrick. Again. Something that can't wait?"

"Want to talk to you about men who make war on women, Jones. Men who send men to poison waterholes, Jones. Men who push too hard too often. Men like you."

Jones, limping, stalked closer with a face contorted by anger. "No man talks to me that way," he called. "Not in private, not with my men listening, and above all not on my ranch. Get down, Carrick. Man to man."

Carrick got down, but turned his back on Jones to cut the leather strips that bound Larry Gordon to his horse. He all but threw the man at Jones's feet.

"Explain why you sent a rider with a twenty-pound bag of salt to the water hole on Bar C range," Carrick accused. "That's not a man who's about buildin' dreams. That's a sneak coward who deserves to get his face slapped hard and maybe that's what I ought to do." He took a step toward Jones, who stood tall and held up a hand. Carrick stopped.

"Miss Lewis, is this story true?"

"It is," she called out. "Your rider was near the watering hole by where those three red oaks grow. You never graze there—ever. We caught him. I was showing Carrick here the range limits and we were barely a mile from our house. He tried to run and he tried to kill me. Carrick got him first."

"She doesn't lie, Jones. You know that."

"I didn't send him," Jones declared, chin outthrust, cords of his neck standing out in anger. He turned to Petersen, the ranch manager having scurried over when the fuss was building. "Where's Easy Thompson?"

"The main crew went north because there were reports of Indians coming down from the Powder River country. He won't be back for a few days."

"What do you know about this?" Jones's voice took on a threatening edge. "Did you send this rider to salt a water hole?"

"No. Never. I know nothing," said Petersen, visibly shaken by the rage Jones was radiating. He stopped fidgeting with the boiled collar and cuffs he wore under his Eastern-style jacket and looked down at the ground. "I don't know anything." At that minute, Jones reminded Carrick of ancient kings of legend whose rages tore their own clothes and rent their own skin in their savagery. When Petersen spoke again, his oily tone was very subservient. "I never order the men without your approval. You know that."

Jones swung back to Carrick. "I gave no orders. Last I saw you, I told you I'd pay them women more than their place was worth. If they'd come right back and said they'd sell, the way they should have, nobody would have no trouble, Carrick! Guess they're thinkin' it over. When they stop eating, maybe they'll start thinkin' straight. This is the kind of trouble that happens when people don't do what they ought!"

"I am thinking straight," Rebecca Lewis shot back, leaning down from horseback and glaring into Jones's eyes. "I am doing what I should. I am protecting what is mine and you had better get used to it!" In the return glare that followed, Reb felt herself very thoroughly assayed and weighed. "No one takes what is mine," she added, flicking back the hair that blew past her face and staring straight back into Jones's angry face.

The wind gusted and dust swirled, but no one moved. Carrick looked for one twitch that would signal a fight. He wanted to move his hand to his gun. Get Jones first. Reb's eyes bored into the big man. Carrick waited. After a long silence, Jones turned back to Carrick. His face was unreadable. His tone was lower; the words barely carried to Carrick through the wind. "You come back here in a week, Carrick. I'll get Easy and the crew back from the north ranges. We'll get this figured."

Jones focused up at Reb. "Miss Lewis, you have my word that I have never ordered anything like this. I made no secret that I want your range. It's business. Nothing personal. You ladies want to live your lives, you can have the house. I want the land. I need the land! You are not using this range to its full potential and I can. I will!" Jones stopped and made an effort to control himself. "I apologize that anyone from Double J acted in a way that is not worthy of this range. When I know more about this—and you can trust me that I will determine why this man was acting without my orders—I will inform you and your Aunt Jess. I wish you a good day. Do you need protection on your ride home?"

Reb's snappish manner had been blunted; she was clearly awed by Jones's fervor and intensity. "Thank you, Mr. Jones," she said, sounding to Carrick like she was dragging out manners learned for receiving company but not used very much since. "I, um, I appreciate your saying you had nothing to do with it, but it would be a sight easier to believe if Double J was not practically in my house every day. And I got all the protection I need with Carrick here and my Winchester. Your rider got what he deserved, and I guess it's high time to put you on notice that I'm not going to warn the next Double J rider who trespasses on my land. I'm going to kill him—whoever he is." Her eyes made the threat very clear and very personal.

Jones frowned. Carrick again made ready to go for his gun. Jones had clearly been holding on to his temper. Reb's final outburst may have pushed him over the boundary. Jones had a very odd look on his face. It was a moment before Carrick recognized it as a smile.

"Miss Lewis, I commend your Aunt Jess for her efforts. I hope that when the day comes and I have a son, that he is as devoted to this land as you are. Perhaps we can come to an agreement based upon mutual respect. When Easy returns, we will all sit down together—you, me, your Aunt Jess, and Easy— and we will talk about the future of this valley. I believe that it is the responsibility of the strong to be wise. Perhaps—no, I say, as sure as the rocks below us—I need to know you and your aunt better."

"Mr. Jones . . ."

The ranch manager was stopped in his tracks by a baleful stare. "Petersen, I do not need interference! I am running this range, and that means it will be run as it should be, not—as it seems today—as it is. Until we meet again, Miss Lewis. Please send my warmest regards to your aunt. You have my word your passage and your home range will be unmolested." Jones raised his hat.

His eyes locked with Carrick's. "You are a stone that has rippled the waters, Mr. Carrick," he said. "May I remind you that no matter how great the ripples, they dash themselves against the rocks and fade away. The stone, inevitably, ends up sinking to the bottom to be forgotten. You may be passing through; you may be from one of those syndicates trying to get a foothold in this range for some other purpose. I shot one of those men who came around last year, but I know there are more. You may even have told me the truth. In any case, Carrick, tread softly. I respect a fighter, but those who fight without honor deserve the punishment that shall fall to them. If you have misled the Lewis women, woe betide you. Good day, Mr. Carrick."

With that troubling valediction, Jones limped back to the stone lair where he dreamed his dreams of empire. "Petersen!" he bellowed. The ranch manager scurried to follow. The door slammed shut like a cannon's blast.

"Probably time to leave," Carrick told Reb as he swung up into the saddle. "Follow close. Eyes front. They're looking for an excuse."

"I'll lead," she said. Up close he could see tiny cracks in the mask of her pride, but she would show defiance to the world. He let her. Carrick mounted and rode behind her as they left the crowded farmyard amid a few whispers and mutterings, but without anything that resembled a challenge.

They were out of sight of the Double J when Reb pulled her mount to the right by a small stand of pines. Carrick waited a minute, then followed. The interaction at the ranch was nagging at him, but he could not put his finger on what was bothering him. Jones was Jones. Reb was Reb. Strong people don't get along until they yell a lot first. Something else. He'd seen curtains move inside the big house and knew they were being watched. Petersen had been glancing toward the house a few times, but the man was a nervous wreck trying to escape Jones's wrath. He set that aside. Something was wrong with Reb, and that's what mattered. The girl was pale when he reached her.

"Carrick, what happened? Did I say what I think I said to that man?"

"You did. Surprised a man who guards against surprises. That you did. We stuck our heads in the lion's mouth, Reb, and lived to tell about it," he replied calmly. "Don't you folks have this kind of fun without me?"

"Did I really threaten Jones?"

"All you did was talk plain talk to a man who doesn't understand anything else," he replied. "Seemed to work well. Had you ever met the man before?"

"We met a couple of times at places where we nodded and said nothing more than what Aunt Jess says are pleasantries and I think are nothing but a waste of hot air."

"So Jones never knew who he was really dealing with. He thought he was dealing with two women running a ranch that was more than they could handle. That's interesting," remarked Carrick.

"I thought they were going to kill us."

"No," he said with calm authority, drawing a look. "Nobody is going to hurt you, Reb. Nobody is going to push you off your home. Not today; not any time soon. Not while I'm here and breathin'. Anyone who wants to get at you has to come through me, first."

"You expect me to believe it's that simple, cowboy?"

"Long as you talk like that and shoot like I hear tell you do, it's that simple, Reb."

"Carrick, who are you? You ride in here, tell us you're kin from the folks who had the ranch before us, but you barely took five minutes to look around the house. That doesn't set right with me. You find trouble like a hound on a scent, and when you don't find it you make it. And if it is there, you mix it up and make it worse. What are you doing here? What are you *really* doing? Jones talked about syndicates buying land; are you with one of them? And don't give me this story about a wounded soldier who took six years to ride home after the war. Other men came back from the war. I've seen a few who moved out here after the war. They talk about the old days and the war like it was an adventure they're glad they survived. They're settled. You are different. I can see it in your eyes. They're done fighting and you're not. And you let me do it! You let me threaten a man who could wipe us off the earth if he chose. Oh, what have I gotten myself into?" Her voice was breaking as the strong front she put forth to face the world started to dissolve and tremble.

"All that don't really matter, Miss Reb." He had no idea what to tell her in place of the truth. At the end, he was welcome anywhere on Bar C except that old house. As for the war and what came after, that was not a story to share—at least not yet. Probably not ever. "Ancient history and family history are chimney smoke in the wind. There's stuff nobody wants to hear and I don't want to say. Land has more memories for me than the house, if you need to know. What matters is that you got nobody else and I'm here. And nobody is gonna hurt you while I'm here because that's plain simple and true the way it is! I'll protect you and I'll protect your Aunt Jess. I'm not good at much, but I been in tight places and I came away alive. Like I told you: Nobody is going to get to you while I'm in the way." He leaned over the space between their horses and enfolded the trembling girl in his arms. At first he could feel the tension; the instinctive reaction of a wild thing to struggle and break free. Then she jammed her head on his shoulder, and he could feel her small body shaking with sobs.

Late afternoon was fading as they approached the white house, now guarded by a very suspicious woman with a rifle. Carrick had lifted Reb onto Beast—she was small enough the weight wouldn't much matter. They had ridden slowly until the tears had stopped. Carrick had seen it before—folks who fought like lions in a battle and then were scared of what they had done. He guessed Reb had threatened more than fought. Now she knew what it was like. She would learn. She would live.

They still rode together on Beast with Arthur being led by the reins looped around Beast's saddle. Jessie Lewis inspected the sight of her niece in an unfamiliar posture as she held the rifle by the barrel and leaned against it.

"Will I get a satisfactory explanation from either of you?" she asked as they approached in silence, the arch in her voice fueled by anger and fear.

Reb hopped down and led the horses away in silence. Jess followed her niece with her eyes, concerned.

"What did you do?" she gritted.

Carrick boiled it down to the big issues and assured Jess that no one was hurt. "I know you got troubles, Jess, but Reb maybe isn't used to goin' places where folks are itchin' to kill you and you stand a few feet away and dare them to give it a try," he finished lamely. "I tried to warn her but until you know what it's like, you don't know."

"And you know?"

"Yes, ma'am. Lot I don't know. That much, I know real well, Jessie. What matters most, Jess, is that Jackson Jones knows he's not going to walk all over your range. Maybe he'll have that there talk with you folks; maybe not. Your niece opened his eyes, Jess. You ought to be proud of her. Real proud. I'll help Reb stable the horses."

Dinner was the remains of the stew and some hard bread. Nobody talked. Jess slapped food on the plate hard enough to break it. Reb looked by turns defiant and shaken. The women had clearly had something happen that shook them. Carrick could feel the change. He wondered if maybe they wanted him to ride on. To him it was simple: Meet violence with more violence. Maybe that was more than they were prepared to do. Nothing ever works out the way it should. He ate as fast as possible and got up to leave when it was done.

"Carrick?" He already had his hat on to go.

"Miss Reb."

"Is Jackson Jones afraid of you?"

"A bit."

"Are you afraid of him?"

"Silly not to be."

"Can we beat him?"

"Depends on how much he wants to lose; how much you want to risk. If you take him on, girl, straight up, it's likely to be a fight to the last ranch standing. Go in knowin' that. Can he wipe you out if he attacks one fine day and throws everything at you? He can. He's that big and that strong. But he can't do that without losing something it's taken him years to build. The more he realizes how high that price is gonna be, the more he might think twice about pushing too hard. Wouldn't think too much about it."

"Can we hold out?" Reb insisted.

"Maybe, depends on what happens next. You're safer tonight than you were yesterday. Not many folks stand up to Jackson Jones. He's going to think that out a while. Only a fool fights someone not afraid to fight back. He's no fool. You bought time, girl, if nothing else."

"Did you mean it? What you said back there?"

"I did."

"Men lie a lot to women."

"They do."

"Do you?"

"Not lately. You'd shoot me." He nodded, said good-night to Jessie and walked out through the doorway into the blackness beyond. A falling-down cabin was a refuge for a man on a day like this.

Reb watched him go. "I still might," she said softly to herself, pursing her lips as the door closed. She realized he never said he would never lie to her. "I still might!"

# CHAPTER SIX

By morning, Carrick was convinced he had made the biggest mistake of his life setting foot on the old Bar C range. Rebecca Lewis refused to leave his thoughts, and yet when he added it all up, it wasn't even certain the girl liked anyone, let alone him. There was no good reason to stay but he was committed to staying. Fool!

Probably Jackson Jones was keeping him here more than anything else. There was something grand and noble in the man, and yet he was also dangerous because greed and ambition were so intertwined, Jones himself would never know when his dream of an empire turned into a nightmare for everyone else.

He'd made a promise to Reb he probably couldn't keep. The last one he made he kept, no matter what it cost. For a moment, he wondered what this one might cost him. Too late now.

Nothing had changed from when he was young. People. Nope, he never could quite figure them out. The land, though. He recalled the kid he grew up with—half Cheyenne, half white. He talked a lot about the connection between the land and man. Without it, men wandered forever in search of their home. There were certainly enough people wandering. He looked at the splendid ruggedness of the landscape from Uncle Charlie's shack. There wasn't any Double J or Bar C or Lazy F—only land, sun, and wind. Carrick never figured out much about religion, for all that he'd listened to preachers. They found God in churches and books and arguments and such. He found Him out on the badlands or up in the mountains when the loudest sound was the wind in the trees.

Something moved. Way out there. There was a reflection of sun on metal. He scanned the edge of the woods across the way. Gone now, if it was really there. Could be nothing. Could be someone seeing how tough he really was, waiting and watching. Something to remember.

His reverie shattered, he rode south, where the cattle were supposed to be. If the Lewis women had one good, trusted hand who didn't leave them when others panicked, maybe the hand would know Carrick and he could get a better sense of the range. If nothing else, anyone who could work for Rebecca Lewis was worth meeting.

He stayed to the open plains. He didn't want any mistakes about his intentions. The range was on edge. When that happened, shooting accidents followed—even intentional accidents. There was a pasture with some rough rail fences to keep cattle from heading down into the rocky lands to the west. He rode for it.

A rider on a white horse, wearing a floppy hat and carrying a rifle, riding so loosely in the saddle he seemed half-asleep, came down a hill behind Carrick, acting ready to shoot, talk, chase, or run as need be. Carrick stopped. His hands stayed on the pommel. His eyes probed the shadow under the hat brim. One corner of his mouth twitched. The rider drew nigh.

"What's your business here, friend?"

Now he was home.

"Hello, Bad Weather."

Randolph Morgan was his white name. No one knew where it came from any more than they knew his real home or family. Most likely he was a soldier's child by an Indian woman. They guessed he was the product of some raid where a white soldier

74

or rancher couldn't kill a child after killing the parents. Since, as a boy, he was the best liar on the range, no one would ever know. Carrick had known him since he was twelve. As a boy, he had always been full of stories about making the clouds rain. Carrick named him after that.

"Clawing Wolf." Randy had been obliged to give a name back, and Carrick's notorious temper had made it simple. If he was surprised at Carrick's materialization on the range, it did not show. "I heard that you were dead. Until this moment I thought I was the last of the old Bar C."

"Tried gettin' dead but it didn't work."

"Surviving in spite of yourself was always one of your talents. Why are you here? You get lost riding home? Didn't you know they were gone?"

"Unfinished war business."

"Did you kill him?"

Bad Weather had always understood Carrick. Carrick nodded.

"Are you here to claim all this? Do the ladies know?"

Carrick shook his head. "Not takin' anything. Wouldn't know what to do with it. Ran out of places to go and reasons to put off coming back."

Bad Weather nodded. He knew all the Carrick family's troubles. Carrick's final years had been troubled by it all. That was what Bad Weather had long suspected kept Carrick from coming back. Carrick had either never understood that half-breed children were a lower class than everyone else, or didn't care. They had been inseparable as boys throughout the final years before Carrick left.

"Welcome to the old Bar C, which is what everyone calls it. The new owners use the old brand, but they never really named it or registered a new brand. So it has been the old Bar C for a while, now. Have you met the ladies?"

Bad Weather's laugh screeched and rolled as he looked at Carrick's face. "You have met Reb!"

"I have."

"She threaten to shoot you?"

"That's what she was doin' when I met her."

Bad Weather laughed again, like the crazy shrill barking of a wild dog. "She likes to do that. Threaten. Far as I know she never actually shot anyone. But she knows how to shoot. I taught her, and then she would shoot for hours. Her Aunt Jess is a gem, Carrick. When your family died from the sickness, she kept the ranch going. I sometimes thought she took it over for them more than for herself. She takes care of anything and everything. She should have sold out years ago when they first died. I think she saw this as a gift from your family. Now, Reb would never let her sell, even though they could be comfortable for many years with what Double J is offering. What do you plan to do? How can I help?"

On the pretense of coming up with an answer, Carrick studied his friend. Bad Weather's face was lined from wind, but there was serenity about him as though he was doing what he was born to do and would do until the day he died. He had a rifle in his scabbard, but no pistol. The half-Cheyenne's long black hair reached halfway down the back in a braid. He looked little different than the seventeen-year-old Carrick had left— maybe a little bigger in the body, but the same smile and the same loyalty.

"Bad Weather, answer is I don't know. Never knew they were gone until the other day when I come back. Tryin' to take all of this in—Double J, this Lazy F fella. The land looks the same, but everything on it has changed. I feel like I belong; like the land is mine, but when I deal with the people it all goes wrong."

"The changes have only started, Carrick," said Bad Weather, who at a fairly young age had been a servant to a passing preacher who thought an Indian slave was a bonus for attempting to convert the heathen Cheyenne. Bad Weather had slipped away one night. He was the most imaginative story teller Carrick had ever met. Carrick assumed most of the legends Bad Weather told him were stories created out of his head. "The army comes out here more and more each year to guard the settlers. That means more horses for the cavalry. The railroad runs more trains every year. More trains mean more people and more demand for horses and beef. A few more settlers stop every year on their way to somewhere else, or end up here when they've been run out of Kansas. Lincoln Springs gets bigger and bigger. Have you met Jackson Jones?"

Carrick nodded.

"An interesting man. I met him in town. It's hard not to like him, unless you work for an outfit that is in his way. He hasn't bothered me down here very much, but ever since there was a fight between cowboys that had more to do with liquor than anything else, he has grown stronger at the women's expense. I'd like to work for him and ride for him, from what I know of the man, but the Lewis women were here first. Jess Lewis is the kind of person you stick by no matter what."

"What about Lazy F and this Francis Oliver?"

"He bought the old MacRorie place, and grew it. He and Jones hate each other. They have been competing with each other since the day they arrived. Oliver is a clever man, and he survives by outsmarting Jones. He was the first to get a railroad contract Jones wanted. He has two problems, and they both relate to the land. Sooner or later, Jones will want what he has, of course. Oliver is also almost at his limit of what he can raise on the land he has—and especially at the limit of the water he has. With me here pretty much all the time he can't move out onto Bar C range, but he'd like to be able to water his stock at the creek. He pushes at the edges. If I was not here, he'd be here taking this in a minute. That said, he hasn't pushed very hard. He's more like a vulture than a hawk. I can't say the man has ever done anything to me, or really anything to the Lewis women except pester them to sell, but there is still something I don't like about him, Carrick. He had a partner when they first moved out here, but the partner died. There was talk that there was something shady about the man's death, but there's always talk. A lot of the people who came out since the war ended want to be rich, and are not too concerned with who they step on along the way."

"Never got infected with that disease."

"From the way you look," joked Bad Weather, "it is very easy to tell."

Carrick recounted what had happened since his arrival. Randy was not convinced Jones was the only one after their range.

"That salt trick sounds more like something Oliver would do than Jones, but he would never ride through Double J land to get there or dare to hire a Double J rider. He hates Jones, but he's afraid of him."

"What's this about syndicates?" Carrick asked. "Jones asked me if I was with one and I never heard of one."

Bad Weather laughed. "Your knowledge has been neglected. Everyone knows there is money to be made out here. Cattle and horses, of course. Mines are popping up. There is coal here, and I don't know what else. Ever since California, there are people who think there is gold everywhere. Syndicates are groups of business people in the East who buy up the land and then use it for whatever makes them the most money. There is a world of difference between them and Jones. Jackson Jones wants this to be his, but he really does care about it. A syndicate would buy it and not care about what they did. We keep hearing about syndicate men looking to buy up the valley, but we never actually see them. Of course, that could be because Jones shot the last one to come around publicly."

Carrick asked about the rail fence. "You turning home-steader?"

"I'm trying to make sure the ladies' cattle doesn't become somebody else's breakfast," Randy replied. "If they get much past the fence, I have to chase them down right away or they never come back."

"Rustlers?"

Bad Weather frowned and waited a minute, choosing his words. "Out west of the range there's that heavy wooded country; you remember? That is where your old friend Colt Ramsay lives, along with a collection of people who don't work as hard for their food as I do. I don't know that they rustle as much as they take anything that they can claim might have been theirs. The women thought about asking Jones for help once in running them out, but in the end Jess Lewis got soft and let them stay. Lazy F tolerates them, and they are closest to their land. If there is anyone who would know about something going on that isn't quite breaking the law but isn't legal either, Colton Ramsay is your man."

Colton Ramsay had been in trouble from the day he was born. Carrick recalled the boy as having the best ideas to cause trouble of anyone he ever knew. Colt was range-smart. He'd come up with a lot of schemes that should have gotten them both somewhere between severely punished and more or less dead. They never got caught. The Ramsay land was west of Bar C, near where Buffalo Horn Creek emerged from Brown Break Rocks. There was a small rough cabin tucked way back in the trees. Lazy blue smoke filtered through the trees. Carrick rode slowly. There was an air about the cabin that strangers were unwelcome. He was pretty sure he'd been the object of curiosity for more than a mile. The click of the gun came as little surprise when he reached a clearing that was about ten yards from the cabin.

"Hands up! Who are you and what do you want?"

Carrick was smiling. Times change. Voices don't. "Colt, you are getting sloppy in your old age. I could have killed you when you looked out from behind that pine tree a ways back. Bet you ain't stole a pie off a window in years, slow as you move now."

"Get down! Who are you? Get down and turn around so I can see you."

Colton Ramsay was thin and bearded. The worn hat on his head matched the disrepair of the rest of his clothes. The new shotgun in his hand was steady. Carrick could hear noises from the cabin. A kid was being shushed.

"You marry that Brown girl, Colt? The one kicked you in the mud right before the fair? Got kids now?"

"Three. Who are you that you know me and I don't know you? Turn this way." Carrick turned. Colton Ramsay moved closer, never letting the gun shift its aim. "Carrick! Rory Carrick, home at last! When the rest of the men came back and said you stayed with Sherman we figured you were gone. When the war ended and you never wrote or came home, we figured you either had stayed or more likely were dead—I could never see a renegade like you settling down. Guess you know about your kin. Sorry. If it helps, the sickness that took them was quick. My folks went, too. How long you been back? Eileen! Eileen! Rory Carrick is back from the dead. Bring the kids and come out to say hello!"

Eileen Brown and Carrick had been rough and tumble friends as kids. She was the only girl on the range who not only relished rock fights with the boys, she often won them. She and Colt had been together when he left for the war. Carrick had had a fool notion about her at one time, but his long-time friend thought the world revolved around her and that meant nothing went very far in that direction for Carrick. She was smiling as she came from the house, followed by a boy and two girls. She wore a simple brown dress; her chestnut hair was loose. She was thin, Carrick thought. Thin and too pale, like she never got out as much as a woman on the range should have. Back beyond the cabin, he noted, two other men with rifles were watching.

"Carrick?" She stopped and studied him. "Rory! God, it is good to see you. It is so good to see a friendly face on this range for once. We thought you were dead. I'm sorry about your family." She wrapped her bony arms around him, felt bones underneath the worn trail clothing, and wondered what had kept Carrick away so long. Even at a glance, it was easy to see that the wild exuberant boy who rode the range as though every moment of life needed to be lived to the fullest had been replaced by a man who saw and heard everything around him with a caution that could only have been learned through experience. She knew that the hard way.

"Hello, Eileen. Nice kids. Hope they behave better than a pack of kids I used to know who roamed this place a long time back."

" 'Course they do, Carrick. Their ma knows all the tricks," she replied. "When did you get back? It's been years since the war."

"Took a while to get here. There were some things that got in the way." It was enough. He looked around. His friends had settled themselves with a family and a place to be. He was still a long way from feeling at home anywhere. Suddenly, he did not want to talk about the past any more. It brought that feeling he tried to keep down. The past was dead. Let it rest in peace. The range around his was a contentious, angry sea. He promised Reb and her aunt he'd make things right. Time to forget what was and figure out what came next.

He turned to his old friend. "Colt? You act like you got suspicions any company coming down your trail isn't friendly. And I hear range talk that maybe things go on out in these here woods that the law wouldn't smile at. Maybe you can set me straight. Lot of changes took place since I left and I don't understand it all."

Colton Ramsay explained that after a bad bout of fever, and some Indians who took advantage of the war to raid farther south than usual, the valley ranches all shriveled to bare bones. Oliver and Jones arrived at about the same time, and had been rivals from the start. Oliver had fought for the South, and Jones, the North. Jones wanted an empire from the beginning; Oliver started wanting more land to spite Jones. When the Carrick family died off, Jessie Lewis kept the ranch limping along in the war, riding the range herself with her kid niece. They had kept the same brands, being too poor for much that was new. Other ranchers helped some, in admiration of their spirit. When the war ended, the Lewis women were starting to get the old Bar C to rights as a working ranch when Lazy F and Double J began their duel and started encroaching on the old Bar C lands. The women were not tough enough, in Colt's eyes, to fight back hard. They gave ground, tried to stave off a showdown, and in the end the other ranches nibbled away until the once-sprawling Bar C was down to its home range and nothing more.

Carrick touched his old friend's arm and steered him over by the fire for some words beyond the earshot of Ramsay's children. He kept his voice low.

"And when did you start shadin' the law?"

Ramsay's face had a wry look on it. "Law's funny, Carrick. Range law out here became what men like Jones and Oliver say it is. Dan Hill over in Lincoln Springs is Jones's man. He was a drunk until they put a star on him. Jones says it's the law, Hill agrees. This was my family's land. You know that. Not much, but ours. Anything goes through it, it's mine. Horses, cows, anything. You know that what other people can't hold becomes somebody else's. Way it's always been. When the railroad men came, they didn't care about anything more than getting what they needed. So if timber came from Double J, or steaks from Lazy F, they didn't care. Me and the railroad, we got what you might call a business deal. They want it, I get it. Lincoln Springs store sells things for a lot of money. I sell them for less. No questions. New Winchester cost you twice in that town what I sell it for, but I don't exactly advertise. Riders find me. Maybe we live on the edges, Carrick, but it's more honest than tryin' to squeeze them women off their land."

Carrick frowned. Behind the smokescreen of words that didn't really add up to anything, his friend had all but admitted being a thief. That wasn't kids being kids; that was real trouble. He thought about saying something, decided against it. Ramsay was old enough to know how to live his life without Carrick's help.

"Oliver keeps pesterin' Jessie Lewis to sell," Carrick said, both wanting to change the subject and get some questions answered in his own mind. "I understand Double J. Jackson Jones wants to rule the world. Oliver seems like he's got enough land for him. Asked Randy and he said Oliver's getting near what his range can hold. Man's making money. What's his game?"

Colton Ramsay laughed so hard the whiskey he was drinking sprayed all over him. The liquor fanned the flames of the fire for a brief flaring moment and illuminated his crafty face. "For one, as soon as Jones gets Bar C, he'll be right next to Lazy F and that will push Lazy F off the range like it never existed. So, Oliver knows once Bar C goes, he's as good as gone. It gets real personal, too, Carrick. Oliver would do anything to stop Jackson Jones from getting what Jones wants. He ain't had much luck in that department to date, you might say." He kept laughing.

"Gonna share the joke, Colt?"

"Remember Lucinda Callahan?"

It was a face he could never forget. He had almost at one time thought about staying behind from the war for that face, even though it was very clear that her family had plans for their daughter that went above marrying a boy like him. It was like a fever. He had it briefly. Then it passed and he was cured.

"She's Lucinda Jones now. She married Jackson Jones. The man made her father his ranch manager until old man Callahan died. One version of the trouble between Jones and Oliver is that she picked Jones over Oliver even though Oliver did everything he could to win her, and Oliver never forgave them. None of them are people you can ask about that, so it could be nothing more than smoke. Jones has a temper you don't want to set fire to. Oliver never told the truth a day in his life. Lucy acts like she's the Queen of Wyoming, now, and doesn't speak to folks who knew her when she had patches on her one and only dress. What drives Oliver? No idea, Carrick. It could be personal. He may think he can out-smart everyone and scheme his way ahead of Jones. He's a shrewd man; be careful. With Jones, you see it coming. With Oliver, you don't."

Jessie Lewis eyed Carrick critically as he returned to the old Bar C's ranch house. With her arms folded and her right foot tapping out impatience, she was waiting in front of the door, with something clearly on her mind. It had never dawned on him to stop by the ranch first thing. Until he saw the firm set of her jaw.

She barely let him dismount. "Mr. Carrick, after yesterday's adventure with my niece, it is time to get some things clear around here," she said authoritatively. "Do you know if you are going to stay with us, or go your own way here, or simply ride on?"

"You are direct, ma'am."

"My niece's influence. That is not an answer. I deserve an answer. Reb deserves an answer. I do not approve of windy promises made to her if there is nothing to back them up."

Carrick tried to frame the words.

"I am waiting," she said.

"Got nowhere to go, Jessie. Land kind of seeps into your bones. Not quite sure why, but I figger I'll be around a while. Got myself knee-deep in all this already so I might as well go in all the way, don't you think? Why?"

"I like things settled." Her posture and tone eased. "I thought you were staying from what Reb told me, but I wanted to be clear. I know all this must confuse you, but the ranch needs attention and if you plan to help, I needed to know because there are things we need you to do. By the way, if you are going to work for us for nothing, the least we can do is buy you some decent clothing. The rags you are wearing should be burned. Go into Lincoln Springs and get what you need. We have an account at Godfrey's store. You are not obligated to pay for provisions."

"From my non-existent wages?"

"If you have been wanting more coffee, Mr. Carrick, you must speak up and ask. It is not my fault if I don't know your needs!" a grin of mischief played across Jessie's face. Jessie Lewis sure must have been a fire-breather in her day, Carrick thought. Then he reflected: She was still one now.

Reb appeared at her Aunt Jess's side. She saw the smirks on two faces. "What did I miss?"

"Mr. Carrick has decided he's staying, Reb, and that he will be working for us on wages that amount to coffee and beans."

"Aunt Jess, does that mean he's going to do real work one of

85

these days instead of riding around and eating us out of house and home? And if he's a hand, then isn't it one of us—like maybe me—that gives him his orders?" A vaguely evil smile danced briefly on her lips, then vanished, replaced by the poker face he was beginning to know well.

"I said I promised, Reb." Eyes met eyes. She looked away first.

The flustered young woman told them abruptly dinner was cooked and led the way inside. Jessie Lewis went last, smiling. She had noticed that Carrick looked for Rebecca every time he entered the house or barn—or even outside. Reb was doing the same. Jess was aware that neither of them knew she was watching them watch each other. She wondered a moment whether what was going to come would end well or badly, but she decided that whatever emerged, it was part of a plan in which she, like all the rest, were only players. She did find herself humming. That hadn't happened in a while. One man alone would not stop Lazy F and Double J, but she had a feeling that at last she had found a hand who would not run when either ranch, or both, tried to push her and Reb off their land. It was a start.

# CHAPTER SEVEN

Lincoln Springs, Wyoming, enjoyed an unsteady existence. It was a quiet place tending to a few needs of local ranchers when Dave Jackson built his first store and named the place Jackson's Springs. It all but dried up during the Civil War years. Reconstruction brought a new name and new settlers. Fire destroyed the building where the post office had been. The old store and saloon were joined by a stable and a few other buildings. A hotel was built that had eight rooms. There was endless talk of bigger and better, better and bigger. The telegraph line was supposed to be connecting Lincoln Springs with the world around it, or so the town's residents were told. After that, the railroad might come and all of the things that lingered in the bright, indefinite dreams of frontier families might come true.

As Wyoming grew more ranches, when boys from the war started coming home and new men with big dreams came west, a few farms took the land nearest the hills while others took land around the town itself, where the water flowed all year except in the worst of droughts. Other folks drifted and stayed. Some small ranches raised stock, a few horses. Indians roamed from the west now and again. Every so often, a few wild young men disturbed the peace, but that was as often true with whites as it was Cheyenne. The days of the big raids were over, or so it seemed. To the north, the Sioux were giving the army fits, but along the southern towns of Wyoming, Indian wars were a thing of the past, or so the army insisted. That meant towns started sinking roots. Some had churches; some, schools. All had saloons. Lincoln Springs had hired itself a sheriff to keep the cowboys in line.

Despite the pretensions of those who gathered in town meetings to talk of a future that would be something more, the present was gritty and often harsh. To Carrick, Lincoln Springs was as dirty and dusty as any other frontier town he had seen. Someone had compared frontier towns to seeds that would sprout given sufficient time and enough water; they looked more to him like scars than seeds.

Jed Owens at the stable remembered him.

"How are the Lewis ladies?" he asked.

"Not giving an inch," Carrick replied.

Hughes looked quickly both ways to see if anyone was listening. "Bully for them," he said. "They've got grit."

Hughes would not take any money. Carrick wondered if the town was giving charity to the Lewis women out of respect for an underdog or plain Western defiance of anyone who seemed too powerful.

Charity ended at Willard Godfrey's dry goods store.

"I deeply respect the ladies for their efforts, but they no longer have credit at this store," said Godfrey, a skinny man who wore a vest, a gartered long-sleeve white shirt, and wiped his hands time after time on the black pants he wore. His thinning red hair was plastered over the bald spot that dominated his white skull. In a place where almost everyone looked as though they lived outdoors, the whiteness and softness of his skin gave him almost a prison pallor. His prominent nose and small eyes gave the appearance of shrewdness; the yellowed bad teeth gave a sickly cast to the false and fleeting smiles with which he peppered his speech to Carrick.

"You tell the ladies that?" asked Carrick lazily.

"I have not yet done so. It is very busy here. On their next trip to town we will discuss this. I am certain of that."

"You cut off their credit because they didn't pay?"

"Oh, no! No! I never said that."

"Then why?"

"Well, um, I, um, with all of this, um, uncertainty, um, all of this talk about the anticipated failure of the ranch, of course, you know, I could not afford, if things turned for the worse as I hear is expected . . ."

"Somebody told you to do it."

"No! No. I never said that."

"Crowleys maybe? Before I killed them the other day?"

"That was you who did that? I value Double J as a customer, sir, and . . ."

The bell over the door announced the arrival of other customers. Audibly exhaling his relief, Godfrey turned away from an encounter he obviously found unpleasant and a discussion he was clearly losing.

Jackson Jones strode through, with the former Lucinda Callahan on his arm. She had been beautiful ten years ago. Now, she was regal. Wearing a royal blue dress with endless folds of expensive looking fabric bedecked with ribbons and white lace at the cuffs and throat like some Eastern lady's fashionable outfit, her auburn hair was tucked up under a blue hat precariously perched atop her head. There was neither mud nor dust upon her, as though the elements most common to Wyoming were banned from such a grand personage. Her eyes were bold, green, and direct. Her skin was pale the way ladies who were supposedly proper kept it. She was tall for a woman, standing almost eye to eye with Carrick, which left her still half a head shorter than her husband. She was busy barely acknowledging the near-bow from Godfrey when Carrick spoke.

"Luce." He nodded.

Suspicious eyes moved from Godfrey to Carrick. She clearly

did not know him. For a moment, a look of annoyance passed across her face. Her nose went up and her eyes looked down at him.

"Mr. Carrick," rumbled Jones, giving Carrick a look of suspicion that matched hers. "You are acquainted with my wife?"

"Carrick?" she asked, eyes wide, the mask she was wearing shattered by surprise. "Rory Carrick? Are you really alive after all this time? Heard you were dead or living in the East. Is it really you?"

He took a step towards her. After all around the fall of 1860 when the fever he was certain was love was burning in him, they had been about as close as two ranch kids could get while still being proper. He saw the panic emerge in her eyes as they took inventory of the grime on his jacket and the crusted dirt on his pants. He stopped.

"Mrs. Jones," he said, taking off his hat. He turned to her husband. "Valley this size only had so many girls when I was a kid," he explained. "Everybody knew everybody. Luce and I were friends as kids—long, long time ago. Guess you found yourself the pick of the litter for a bride."

"I believe she understood, as I hope you will understand at some time to come, that the future is best when one partners with a winner, Mr. Carrick." Jones was not wearing one of the silly fancy suits men wore when they came into town. He had on range clothes, but they were clean and looked like they were made from much better cloth than anything Carrick had ever worn. "As I have said, there is in nature as well as in the affairs of men an established and preordained order in which those who are the best able to survive must do so. In nature this is to weed out the unfit. In society, it is to discourage from business and industry those who should not seek to waste resources. The rewards of success should only belong to those who deserve it, not those to whom some accident has bestowed riches beyond what they may deserve. Your emotions may cloud your judgment, Carrick, but there is no doubt that I can do much more for this range by uniting all of the ranches as the Double J than anyone else can do by fumbling and stumbling and surviving by nothing more than the nearest blind good fortune."

As Carrick looked at Jackson and Lucinda Jones looking down upon him, his temper flared. "Guess you ordered your man here to shut off the women's credit, Jones, so they couldn't buy anything. Man who goes straight up at the world wouldn't do that. Would you? Or do you talk one way and live another?"

The reaction was not what Carrick expected. "What is this?" Jackson Jones roared at Godfrey, stepping forward and pounding his open palm on a shelf, spilling the bolts of cloth that had been neatly piled upon it.

"Gordon Crowley, Mr. Jones, came to me and told me that they were not getting any more credit. You didn't want them to get it." Godfrey was scurrying to pick up what had been dropped. "That's what he said, Mr. Jones, so that's what I did, Mr. Jones. Double J is my best customer."

"I did not send Gordon Crowley to tell you to do any such thing. The man will be fired the next time he sets foot on Double J land!" Jones looked at Carrick. The big man seemed overly large in the confines of the store, which was packed with goods. "Buy what you will, Carrick. Put it on my bill, Godfrey!" He then turned to his wife. "I must see Easy Thompson. These cowhands are getting out of hand." The door slammed behind him.

"You still have your ability to make people angry merely by walking into a room," Lucinda Jones chuckled, shaking her head at him as one would at a naughty child that had done something both bad and amusing. Her posture relaxed after her husband stomped his way out. "The rest of us all grew up. You don't act any differently than ever. You didn't have to say that to

Jackson. You like making trouble!" She moved closer. Godfrey fled to some back room where, Carrick guessed, he could hear but not be seen to eavesdrop on Jones's wife. Her eyes studied Carrick from bedraggled head to toe. "What did keep you so long? Didn't you know what happened back here? With your family? Or were you so occupied back East that you didn't care about us?"

Lucinda Callahan had, through the odd chance of being born with a beautiful face in a world of common ones, been accorded special status all her life. Between the influence of her parents, who knew that marriageable girls were few in the rugged wilds of the West, and her own keenly developed sense of her own worth that manifested itself in a flirtatious manner with every male she met, she managed to have about all the boys after her at some point or other while she kept enough distance that she could preserve her options for the best chance. Carrick, who was neither physically impressive, rich, nor temperamentally suited to play the games girls played with suitors, had mostly watched from a distance in his final months at home after the brief spell of affection he was sure he had felt for her had run its course like a fever he had been happy to shake.

World-wise and world-weary, he could sense the act in her now. He thought of how much more enjoyable it was to have Rebecca Lewis point a gun at him than hear the phony talk of a woman who had grown up to be every bit as beautiful as her childhood promised, but without real warmth animating her features. He wondered what, beyond beauty, Jones saw in her.

"Life goes sideways on us sometimes, Luce. I better go. I'm sure old Godfrey there won't want interruptions while waitin' on his best customer. I'll come back later and grab what I needed."

"I heard about your visit the other day, Rory. You should really get to know Jackson. He is a great man who will make

92

this range something better than anyone ever dreamed possible. I am sure he could give you a job. You were a carpenter for your old ranch, weren't you? You made the coffins around here, as I recall. You used to carve things, too. The ranch could use someone else who has some skills. Most of the cowboys can only handle guns. I can speak to Jackson for you if you want to. Maybe once we take over that old place you lived in, you could live there again without those annoying Lewis women."

"No thanks, Luce. I like it where I am. Haven't been a carpenter in years. And I wouldn't make too many plans for the old Bar C house. Don't rightly think anyone else 'ceptin' Reb Lewis and her aunt are gonna live there for a long, long time to come. I'll see you some other time, Luce."

"Good day, Rory." She moved her hand out an inch or two in front of her at waist level. If she was a man, Carrick knew he'd be expected to shake it. Maybe she moved it so he could kiss it? Hang it all! He stuck his hat back on and fled, the sound of the bell over the door laughing at his discomfort.

He had been silently cursing every fool decision he had made that brought him back to Wyoming as he walked down the streets of Lincoln Springs. He all but ran over a man in an Eastern suit who was stepping down from the wooden duck-boards outside the hotel.

The man roughly shoved Carrick away. Two men material-ized behind the man in the suit to back his play.

"No offense, gents," said Carrick, knowing the last thing he needed was a fight on this trip to town. "Range business makes a man powerful puzzled."

"Watch where you walk the next time, cowhand," said the man in the suit. Carrick tried to place what kind of man he could be. Some kind of tough; big burly men with weather-worn faces and rough hands didn't look like businessmen when they put on a silly suit. He was trying to think who the man could be as he walked—a little more carefully—down the street. One sign made him stop: ROY DANIELS SADDLES. There could not be two of them.

"Howdy, Roy."

The old man looked him over. Roy Daniels had once been as straight as a pine. Now he was bent. His white hair was ragged, and his face had sagged into the despair of age. Carrick recalled that Daniels had never had children. He did not seem impressed with Carrick, giving him a glance before turning back to the piece of leather in his hands. "I am too old for games," he replied. "Names are a nuisance to me. Tell me yours and we can get on with our business. If you are new to Double J, you need to tell Easy what you want and he will let you know if I can do it and when."

"Rory Carrick."

If Carrick had hoped for a smile, he was disappointed. A grimace of distaste flashed across the old man's face. "I thought you were dead. Your family died. The Royal Family." This last was said with heavy sarcasm.

"Roy, as I recall you were friends with my family."

"Your family had a big ranch, Carrick. You were customers, nothing more. Your uncle, Joshua, he thought he was important. Thought the range revolved around him. You were nothing more than a stupid kid. What would you know? You were the one who was always on the range or out with that crazy uncle of yours or your wild friends. You and that Ramsay boy once stole my horse and left him tied to a tree. You were twelve. I remember that and that half-breed friend of yours. I suppose you two had something in common, didn't you?" Daniels sneered. "Bar C is long gone and we're doing fine without it. At least we were until you came back to stir up trouble. Oh, I have heard all about you. I suppose you started this war to get your land back? Too late. Jackson Jones will be taking over that range soon, or that

94

jackal Oliver."

"Didn't start a war, Roy. Tried to stop somebody from push-ing too far. Not lettin' the Lewis ladies get stampeded out of their home."

"Noble talk from a Carrick, but you are like them all. You can't fool me. You want to own what your family used to own. I don't know how that woman sharped your uncle out of the land when he died but more power to her. Joshua Carrick never talked as big and wide as Jackson Jones, but he knew how to throw his weight around. Now, are you here to discuss the past or buy a saddle? I won't be making too many more of them so if you want one made, better ask now. If you do, I want the cash up front. The way you're going, you're likely to get shot before you need a new one."

Carrick said a curt good-bye and left. More questions! He'd never considered whether, in its day, Bar C had pushed people the way Double J pushed now. Was this the law of the range— that one outfit grew big at the expense of all the rest, and then died away to be followed by another and then another, each pushing everyone else aside like a bully in a saloon? Nobody ever said anything, but why would they tell him anyhow? He recalled the way his uncle had whatever connections it took to get him into the 1st Nebraska at a time when every boy and man was scrambling to get in and become a hero. Maybe there was truth in there. Or maybe Roy Daniels was a bitter old man. He was so lost in trying to look at the past with the eyes of the present he almost knocked over the sheriff.

Dan Hill did not look glad to see him. Then again, the last time he ran into Hill he had killed two men. Lawmen didn't like that sort of thing. It always seemed a town that had one or two men killed ended up being one that had more men killed on a regular basis as the would-be gunslingers came to show how fast they were. Carrick wasn't that fast; just fast enough.

"Carrick." They exchanged hat tips. "Staying long?"

"Nope. Got to get some new clothes. Women think I look like a tramp."

"Women notice things like that, Carrick. Won't say that I disagree. Go on. Don't want you here any longer than necessary. Don't want some Double J cowboy thinking they have to kill you to even the score."

"Can't do much right now in the way of shopping, Sheriff, not meaning to be contrary."

Hill inhaled and shook his head. "Carrick, you were born to be contrary. Why in the name of common sense can't you simply walk over to Godfrey's and buy a pair of trousers and a shirt and whatever else you need and then get out of my town before anyone knows you were here? Do I need to escort you there?"

"Lucinda Jones is in there now, Sheriff."

Even Hill's dour visage could not restrain a smile. "I can see where that might make two customers a crowd in that place, Carrick. I suppose you might have a point there. I bet old Godfrey is more than occupied and is like to be that way a while. Maybe you might want to see Chuck at the barber shop. Sure them women won't mind if you don't look like a mountain man and you can even get a bath, if you care for that kind of thing."

Carrick was loath to end a rare moment of camaraderie with anyone. There had been few of them. But he touched the hair hanging down and rubbed his hand through the beard that was last shaved in the spring some time. He figured the sheriff was right. Mostly. "Never understood, Sheriff."

"Understood what?"

"When you're a kid, there's always a woman tellin' you to come in out of the rain and stay dry. You get to be a man, you always got to get all soaking wet for 'em. Fine mystery if you ask me."

Hill was smiling again. "You find the answer, Carrick, you

share it. Now maybe I'll go sit outside Chuck's shop in case any Double J boys want to make themselves pretty. Chuck hates blood in his bath water."

With Dan Hill trailing, Carrick walked off to the barber, chuckling.

Carrick's welcome at the Lewis ranch consisted of Jessie Lewis proclaiming that she no longer felt like she was harboring a fugitive, once she was assured there were no gunfights or other hostilities. Reb looked more than she spoke. He felt odd to have her study him that way, not realizing the complete nature of the transformation that came from shaving off his beard and cutting several inches of hair. He mentioned Lucinda Jones. Whatever Reb growled made her Aunt Jess smile impishly before telling the girl to mind her manners.

She was less than pleased about Jones ordering the purchases to be on his bill, despite Reb's claim that the man owed them at least that.

"I'm not taking charity," Jess grumbled.

"You aren't, auntie," Reb replied. "Carrick is. Let him worry about it. We have enough to worry over."

Jess let it go. For the moment. "Mr. Carrick, I hope you found something against the rain, because from the looks of the sky, we're going to have a good one." Carrick recalled the storms of his childhood; Eastern weather seemed mild in comparison, pale and tame. Instead of the sensible reaction, he found himself looking forward to seeing the thick black clouds swoop down on the hills, bands of rain obliterate the landscape from time to time, and when it was done and the world was mud where there had been dirt, it would paradoxically be the cleanest air a man could breathe aside from the day after a blizzard.

Morning brought the east wind that presaged a storm, and low dark clouds that were soon obscuring the distant mountains.

Carrick rode to the southern pasture to be with Randy; cattle were always worse in storms than horses. Spook one, spook them all. "I am not having what may be my last decent herd run off to be breakfast for somebody else," Jessie gritted. She and Reb would ride the northern slice of their lands to be sure that their horses didn't range so far they never came back.

It was a day without daybreak; the night's black simply changed to a deep gray as the storm's heavy clouds of looming destruction grew thicker and lower in a sky that grew heavy with tension. On the ground, everything from rabbits to wolves moved into places of relative safety, for survival told them to do so. Birds nestled near the trunks of thick trees, and the omnipresent hawks left the skies for some less dangerous perch.

Randy and Carrick had the last of the coffee; strong enough to last until whenever there would be time for a next meal.

Carrick asked Randy a question that was nagging at the back of his mind.

"No," Randy answered at last. "Bar C was a huge outfit for its day, especially on paper, but your uncle never had the iron in him that Jones does. He would get angry over people squatting on the range and ride out to threaten them, but by the time he was through he would hire them for his crew or let them stay a season before moving on. He liked to be important, of course. We all do. But he was a good man, Carrick. Daniels is one of those sour men who always wish men who succeed would stumble and fall so they are down at his level. I am sure there were things that happened when we were kids that we never fully understood, but as a half-breed kid who was almost a part of the family, I can't say anything bad about him."

Carrick still wondered. Randy was a friend. Friends tell you what you want to hear, he thought. Maybe they also tell you what you ought to believe.

His thoughts were broken by the shattering crack of an oak's limb tumbling down a few feet from where they stood. There would be time for thinking later. Now, as the storm lowered its fury on the Wyoming landscape, it was time to survive.

For a moment, Carrick thought he was back on the battlefield. Ball lightning struck the ground, leaving the smell of sulfur behind. Beast whinnied and shied as the eruptions sent dirt flying ten feet in the air and scattered sparks around. The cattle milled about. There were only about forty of them, but with only he and Randy to control them, any stampede could get beyond control in a second.

A shot of lightning like the blast of a canister erupted in front of him. One steer plowed into another, and the milling mass moved faster and faster, the outside animals swirling around those in the center. Then a bolt struck a dead tree, toppling sparking pieces of wood everywhere and sending the maddened herd into a frenzy.

They had each taken one side. Now, as the rain swept down and pounded on the cattle, he could not see Randy at all. The cattle were moving too fast. He needed to find his friend.

Randy had been shrilly yipping at the cattle to keep them in some type of compact group as long as he could. Sooner or later the storm would spook them, but the longer he held out, the less likely he would be to lose a steer. The shower of sparks was his undoing. As he turned to look, his hold on the reins loosened, his horse turned with him, and he was now facing against the tide of steers. He jerked the horse's head to the left, but the animal, now as frightened as the steers, bucked unexpectedly. Randy was barely hanging on. The dilemma was clear: hang on the horse and hope they moved out of the way, or let go and take his chances with the steers.

He leaped. The horse galloped off behind a curtain of rain and into a flash of lightning that hurt Randy's eyes when he tried to follow which way the frightened animal had run. No time to look more. There were fifteen yards between him and nearest steer. A tree was ten feet away; if he could make it he could take shelter behind it or try to climb.

The steer was moving faster than he was. The animal was going to run straight over him in an instant.

Gunfire echoed in his ears. The charging animal staggered. A hand grabbed Randy by his shoulder and hauled him up into the air.

"Hang on!" It was a command Carrick did not need to give. Randy grabbed his friend's jacket and hung on, swinging a leg over the saddle until he was riding double on the saddle behind Carrick.

Randy felt the horse jerk to a halt. They were near the rail fence. "Get up a tree; get behind the fence," Carrick yelled. "Beast can't carry us both for what I got to do!" Randy, with Carrick's rifle, jumped down and Carrick took off into the driving rain. The downpour screened his friend from view as Randy waited, the sounds of lightning crackling, thunder booming, and panicked steers sounding to him what he imagined would be the chaos of Judgment Day.

There they were! Coming toward him. They'd lost one steer today. The women could not afford to lose more. He fired the rifle into the air several times. The animals turned away from the sharp reports and stampeded back the way they had come. For a moment, Randy breathed in relief. Then a new wave of driving rain assaulted the plains. The sounds of panicked animals began to crescendo again. But the storm was losing its punch. The rain fell, but not as hard. Flashes lit the sky, but forks of yellow no longer split the blackness. He could hear the world around him over the sounds of the thunder. The herd, winded from its panic, was tiring. They came to the barrier of the fence, and all but pushed against it, then moved along, some running but some—at last—walking.

Carrick, riding on the outside edge of the herd, sent them in endless circles around the pasture land. He waved his hat to Randy as he rode by. They were both grinning like fools. It wasn't over, not yet, but the worst of the storm had tested them, and they had survived.

Jackson Jones was always up before dawn; today, the energy in the air brought him outdoors long before the black night could give way to the deep gray of day. He could feel the size of the storm in the air. The power of Wyoming's storms fascinated him while also prompting him to be vigilant. One storm could send livestock all over. He knew any Double J stock that drifted to Lazy F range would never be seen on his ranch again. Bar C was less of a threat, but with Carrick around, anything was possible.

The cattle he raised were off to the north end of the valley, hemmed in from running too wild because of the topography of the land. Wooded broken sections would funnel any stampede back down the valley. The horses grazed out in the wider flat lands. They might spook. Those horses could not be lost. In addition to selling horses good enough for cavalry mounts, he was now raising blood stock that would be sold at auction to men like him—men who only wanted the best in everything because they worked for it and deserved it. Those prize horses were not going to end up in the wild lands to the west.

He looked at his wife, still in bed, before he left. She never felt the wonder of the land, even though she had been bred to it. Too bad. Then again, she was a woman. A woman's job was to have children. Jones was getting impatient about that. They had been married two years and Lucinda had not yet given birth. He would not live forever, and he wanted to be sure he had a son who was old enough to inherit his empire before he died. He had spoken to her about it, as delicately as a plain-speaking man could do, and she had gotten into some female state of nerves and tears over it. The problem was very simple to him: If his wife could not perform her function, he would divorce her and find another wife. He had told her this in his usual brusque manner. Wives, like cowhands, needed to be told when they were not pulling their weight. After first resorting to the female ploy of tears—something he found insufferable—she assured him she would have a child soon. She was a woman, after all, and women were supposed to know. Since that ultimatum was delivered, she had been more agreeable and less likely to argue, confirming in his mind that a strong hand was required, whether it was leading a household or guiding a ranch into an empire.

Jones saddled Fergus, a massive white stallion that cost Jones more than his hands earned in a month. The horse could ride all day through any weather. His stature and status made Jones feel every inch a king. There was none like him on the range. He sat the horse as the wild wind blew, a precursor to the arrival of the rain. He could see forks of lightning striking across the valley. The thunder rolled and swelled—louder than the guns at Petersburg and majestic in its own way.

Something raw and elemental was awakened in Jones by the storms. The wild, unconquerable weather of Wyoming was all that was left to test his mettle and challenge his spirit. The storm that could break him had never been brewed. He sat the horse and watched as the gray line of rain advanced upon Double J, meeting Jones and then pounding upon him as if daring him to break. He threw back his head, shook the rain off his hat, and rode out to check on the horses.

To the west, streak after streak of lightning crackled from the black sky to the gray-tinged ground. He rode that way. Where the greatest danger was, there he should be. As he passed a wooded area along the rough pastureland the Lewis women had failed to use properly, one jagged line of lightning streaked to within ten yards of him, snapping down half of a tree in seconds. Jones felt a surge of energy as though it had passed through his bones. As the limbs and trunk fell, a shape darted from where it had been standing, under cover.

The stallion!

For more than a year, a black stallion that was faster than any other animal in the valley had lived with a herd of mares and other wild horses along the intersection of the old Bar C and the Double J. He was the only horse that could leave every rider behind—including Jones. Jones had tried at various times to trap him and catch him. The horse was as clever as he was powerful, and always eluded Jones. Now, the horse was only a few yards away from Jones, running with fear-induced frenzy. This was his chance!

His own stock forgotten, Jones gave chase. Fergus started to gain. Then the stallion leaped the rain-swollen creek with ease. Jones followed, splashing through it as if the rising, muddy water was not there. Another bolt sent the stallion back over the creek. Back and forth they went. Jones felt his confidence grow. The animal was wild and untamed, but it was in fear of the storm. Jackson Jones feared nothing and no one. He had his rope coiled and ready. Soon, even an animal as magnificent as the stallion would have to tire.

Sparks flew from the rock ahead as another bolt struck. Jones could barely believe what he saw. The stallion turned back the way he had run, pivoting in an impossibly fast turn, passing Jones and leaving the rancher to rein in his mount and gallop hard to make up the ground.

"No!"

Jones saw the animal stagger. It almost fell. It could not die! He had to have the stallion! He spurred his own mount to gallop faster. So intent was he on reaching the animal he failed to see the rider at the edge of the trees. Then the lightning flashed brightly and he saw the rope against the horse's neck.

Jones was angered at first. His men should know that this horse was his business. He, Jackson Jones, should be the one to catch this animal. Then he decided, as he approached the snorting, angry horse, that his riders must have wanted to help. There is, he thought, something to be said for loyalty—even in a cowhand who should have been somewhere else doing what he had been ordered to do.

"I had him cold," Jones blustered as he rode up. The storm was slacking. It was almost as spent as the winded animals. Jones did not recognize the rider at first. "Here, I can take him back to the house."

"What makes you think he's your horse?" A slack-jawed Jackson Jones beheld the drenched, diminutive form of Rebecca Lewis, broad grin splitting the mud covering her face. "This is our land here, Mr. Jones! You're more than a mile from your land. Gave us a chase, didn't he?"

Jones was silent, open-mouthed. A woman had captured his stallion? Impossible! And to boot, it was one of the Lewis women whom he held in such contempt. He was more shocked at that than to find he had lost track of his bearings, so intent had he been upon the chase.

Reb was enjoying herself. She had been riding to check on the horses when the storm rolled through. She had seen Jones cross onto her land but didn't know why, so she followed, galloping through the mud to keep pace with the chase. At the end, the stallion, focused on running away from the lightning and Jones, had galloped away from Jones and straight toward her. The animal was almost past her before she saw her opportunity. She caught up to the stallion almost before he knew she was there. It was no effort to drop the lasso over the animal's neck and snare him.

Still grinning, she rode closer to Jones, keeping tight grip on the rope that the stallion was trying to pull out of her hands. "Know you been chasin' him a long time, Mr. Jones. We don't have a bronc buster to tame him, so he's all yours." She tied the rope tight on the pommel of the dumbfounded man's saddle as he watched, seemingly unable to comprehend what had happened. "Better hang on, Mr. Jones, or he's gonna drag you to Denver!" The exhilaration of the storm and the chase were in her, and she was radiating joy. Her laugh was like a bell amid the thunder. She loved the battle with nature that was part of Wyoming life. She loved to win!

"Miss Lewis, I . . . I do not know what to say. Thank you," he said gruffly. The concept that this small woman could capture a horse he could not was so at variance with his view of the world that no words could emerge from his stupefaction. He knew range manners required something. The stallion was trying to escape and Jones would not suffer the indignity of the horse escaping in front of the girl. The stallion needed to be in the corral Jones had built for him. "This is not the time or place, but if I may call upon you and your Aunt Jess at a time in the near future, perhaps we can talk about the range limits and allow you to continue to operate your ranch." The stallion tugged again. Jones hauled in the rope. He needed to get back to the corral with the animal before the rope broke. "I shall call upon you later." He jerked the rope and turned the head of his horse back toward the Double J.

Rebecca Lewis watched the struggling figure and the pulling horse ride away with glee. She didn't care whether Jackson Jones ever acknowledged how his stallion was captured or ever remembered a promise made in humiliation and anxiety. People always said things they didn't mean. She had caught the fabled stallion of Buffalo Horn Valley, by herself and in the teeth of a storm. She looked up. Patches of blue were appearing. Sun was poking out to the west. There was work and chores. But for a moment she smelled the clean smells of the land and enjoyed her triumph. The King of the Range learned there was somebody better! She whooped because it was too much to keep inside, then rode back to the ranch house. Wait until Aunt Jess and Carrick heard this.

The Lewis family, such as it was, was celebrating, with such that they had. Reb's days of joy were never as many as Jessie wanted them to be—some days she wondered if the price of their choices had been too high. Tonight, the girl was about as happy as Jessie had ever seen her. Catching a stallion Jackson Jones wanted made the achievement much larger than it would have been otherwise. Carrick barely mentioned the stampede he and Randy had endured. He reported the one dead steer to Jess, since it would be meals for a while and leather in the winter, but he was happy to let Reb have her day as the center of attention. The girl deserved it. She chattered all through supper, and never seemed to notice that everyone else did the cleaning-up chores. In time, it was dark and time for folks with animals that needed tending to get to bed.

"I will see you in a minute, young lady," Jess said with mock severity as she headed off the main room to their bedroom.

"Yes, Aunt Jess," said Reb, suddenly feeling awkward at the silence and being alone with Carrick. They were standing a few inches apart.

"Never did feel quite like this before, Carrick," said Reb. "I can't explain it. I won't really try. But it's good—real good."

"Good to know next time I don't want to get soaked in a storm," he said. "I can let you soak your head and be all happy as can be. Reb, we don't talk much, but you know Jess is real proud of you and I . . ."

"Well?" she asked, the first coy look on her face he had seen.

"I um, um, was wondering," he said, looking her in the eyes and fidgeting. "Um . . . I don't know what you feel, but . . ."

Muttering some exclamation of disgust he didn't really hear, she closed the gap between them and wrapped her arms around him. Carrick wanted to tell her a thousand things that didn't fit into words he knew, but he held on. Reb understood somehow in a way she could not explain, that the man needed her; she already knew she needed him. It seemed right, and if she waited for him it would take forever.

They were still kissing when Jessie stepped into the front room, then retreated into the hallway. She need not have worried about interrupting them. It took several loud steps and noises from repeatedly clearing her throat before Jessie heard the shuffling of feet that told her she could go back through the front of the house again. She had wondered what would happen when Reb found someone. Now she knew.

By the time she reached the front room of the cabin, Carrick was heading out the door—he still maintained his vigil at the shack by Black Wind Pass. He and Reb's eyes were dancing with each other. Reb's emotions were plain to see. After all the men and boys who brought her flowers or poems or promises, and a couple who sang poorly but with great gusto, her niece fell in love with a hard-bitten cowboy who had no prospects at all. It was, she reflected, the sort of thing to be expected from the daughter of a man who never listened a day in his life to sound advice. What God willed would be. Jessie didn't know whether to be glad or sad. She believed there was an iron core of goodness in Carrick that had not been ruined by the war or whatever came after it, but she also knew—the hard way—that ten years was time for a lot of secrets to build up. There was no telling what they were and when they would spill across the Wyoming landscape.

★ ★ ★ ★ ★

The next morning, Carrick rode south from the pass toward the Lazy F. In the past few days, he'd learned a lot more about Jackson Jones, and understood the rancher. Jones might still want to gobble up the old Bar C range to suit his ambitions, but he was pretty sure the man behind the ranch had come to respect the Lewis women. The incident with the stallion was the clincher, Carrick thought. In a way, Reb had saved the ranch. Whatever Jones did, which Carrick figured at most would give the women their place to live while Jones took as much land as he wanted, it would not end all the threats in Buffalo Horn Valley. He needed to speak with Francis Oliver.

Unlike Jackson Jones, who was clearly drawn by everyone who knew him, Oliver was less clear-cut. A man with a smaller outfit had to bend to the winds to survive. Boldness was often rashness. It was not certain to Carrick whether Oliver was the kind of man who was by nature the shifty sort trying to maneuver his way to get what he wanted, or whether he was so pressured by Double J that it was the way he came to operate. Maybe talking would help Carrick figure it out. Jessie had been kind of nudging him in that direction. For some reason she didn't see Oliver in the same light as Jones, but she didn't really spell it out to Carrick. He'd half wondered when he thought over his introduction to Oliver if there was something more than land on the man's mind, but it was also clear the man was pushing the Lewis women pretty hard. No matter. He'd learn what he could.

Before he rode into Lazy F, he gave the place a look over. The ranch was noticeably poorer than Double J. Lots of cracked paint. Stuff was lying around. A working ranch; no female touch. One bunkhouse. No guards. That was good.

Luck was with him, too. No one contested his slow approach to the ranch, or seemed to care when he entered in through the gate. In fact, no one seemed to be there. He followed the noise and found out why. The man who had spoken to Jessie the other day was by the corral, watching a rider breaking a new horse. Carrick waited. Francis Oliver was in his 50s, maybe. Maybe an officer in the war; nothing to go home to. The man and his crew were laughing and back-slapping as the man in the corral made progress, and shouting encouragement when he did not.

Some men led from above through a combination of power and fear. That was Jones. Oliver led by getting dirty with the rest of his men, working right beside them, and pushing them forward with him. That was clear to see. Something made the man turn. He started when he saw Carrick. He spoke to one of his men and then moved to meet Carrick, who dismounted and tossed Beast's reins over a hitching rail.

"Can't say you're welcome here," said Oliver, "but I'll give a man the chance to explain himself before he gets thrown off my ranch."

"Name's Carrick."

"Bar C. Josh Carrick. Either a great man or the first of the cattle kings or nothing more than a lucky rancher who got to the land first, depending upon who tells the tale. Now it makes sense you bein' all fired up the other day. I know that was Bar C's place before Jess and her firebrand there moved in. War's been over a long, long time, friend. Where you been?"

"Texas. Other places. My business."

"Whatever business it was, son, you got no right walkin' back into Buffalo Horn Valley and pokin' your nose in a man's affairs."

"It was my family's land. Thought you knew that."

"Who is talkin' about land, son?" The baffled expression on Carrick's face made Oliver guffaw. "I been trying for an ever-livin' month of Sundays to ask Jessie Lewis to marry me, you fool. That woman is everything a man could dream of, and she's so busy with all her work she never lets a man get her attention. Why does she think I been over there so much askin' and askin' and askin' again?"

"Don't think she knows you been thinkin' of anything but land."

"How can she not know it? I been offering to protect her from Double J by combining the ranches. If that ain't marriage, what is?"

"The flowers; the ones that grow down by the creek. There was a bunch of 'em by the trail. That's what you threw away the other day when you came a'courtin' Jess Lewis with guns and riders."

"A man gets desperate at my age, son. And there you were all flint and tinder and that niece of hers that would rather shoot a body than eat. What's a man to do? Every time I come near the place that Reb's got a rifle in her hands and she can shoot. Not a fence on her land without holes in it from her practicing. Girl's like a grass fire in May. Don't snicker. Wrote this here poem for Jess. Never got to give it to her. See?"

He reached into his jacket and pulled a piece of paper with florid, bold writing upon it. Carrick started to read the words closely but Oliver pulled it back and jammed it in his coat pocket. The humor of the situation touched Carrick. "I knew somethin' was goin' on but I didn't know what. Never thought about marriage." Now he had to laugh.

"Laugh at the old man, son, but if Double J keeps creepin' down, it's gonna be all over for those two before long. Maybe I don't know pretty words and I don't have a pretty face because I been riding the range too long, but I bet if I can get some time to talk with Jessie, she can make up her own mind."

Carrick thought about it. Ramsay and Bad Weather distrusted Oliver, but the story could be true. Bad Weather characterized

Lazy F as mostly making sure Double J didn't get what it wanted more than pushing out the Lewis women. He'd take a chance. Maybe Jessie understood all this and that's why she didn't feel threatened? If Jessie Lewis, who probably knew all the range gossip better than he did and knew the man to boot, wanted Oliver as a husband that was her life and none of his affair.

"Do this," he told Oliver. "Come by the next day or so maybe afternoon some time. I'll ask Reb to show me something out on the range; get us out of the house for a short time. Best I can do. Jessie don't want to get married there's nothin' I can do about it. And if I regret doin' this because you say or do somethin' that upsets Jessie, we won't be talkin' next time I see you."

" 'Course she wants to get married. All women want that! What else do they ever want?" Oliver said. "I never got me a chance to tell her . . . well, you know, Carrick . . . that I love her! Hard to talk that way when there's someone with a gun six feet away with an itchy finger listenin' for some word she don't like."

Carrick could understand that! "Oliver, I'll do my part to help you."

"This isn't some trick to get Bar C back for yourself is it? Texas is a long way to come for nothin'." Suspicion as a response to friendship was nothing more than plain common sense. Carrick wasn't offended.

"Left Texas for other reasons," Carrick said, dismissively. "Don't know that I want the range for myself. Don't want it taken away from them ladies."

"Good man!" Oliver clapped him on the back. "Now, promise me even if that girl won't ride, you'll hog tie her and git her out of that house this once. If only for a couple of hours. For an old man!"

Carrick promised he would find an excuse to forward the

courting and rode back out after shaking hands with Oliver.

The shack was about a half-hour ride from the Bar C house; about an hour from Double J and the same from Lazy F. Carrick had made it plain to the ladies: He needed some place that was his. He'd lived alone the past two years, and indoors wasn't always comfortable. Even though he hadn't had a nightmare in two nights, he didn't want one when they were around. He was glad for the solitude. He needed time and space to sort out everything he had learned.

He was thinking of the cabin as his, even though there were some odd things in the cupboards—two fancy glasses and fancy lace things stashed in a wooden box in one corner that was cleaner than anywhere else. Whoever was using the cabin would have to find some other place.

Carrick gathered some sticks to start a fire after cleaning out what he could from the chimney. It was askew, but it worked. He'd need to build a shelter for Beast. There was lumber at the Lewis ranch. Maybe he could borrow some.

He was wondering if he should make the shack into something a little more permanent. If Oliver was successful, and Carrick figured the conniving old rancher would probably get his way, the old house would be no place for Carrick. He wondered what would happen to Reb if Oliver moved in as Jessie's husband. Maybe Jess would move to Lazy F and Reb could continue living where she was. Like Oliver or not, what he said made sense. Probably Lazy F wouldn't hold off Double J forever, but only a reckless man would start a range war with a ranch the size of Bar C and Lazy F combined—and Jackson Jones was far more calculating than reckless.

Would Reb hang onto the house alone? His past was in the place, but her roots were there, deep. Would she want someone to share it with? Fool! She was excited from catching the stallion. That's all it was. He was putting the wagon ahead of the

112

horses. First, they needed to find out what the day would bring when Francis Oliver asked Jess Lewis to be his wife. Then, maybe he could figure out what he was going to do, and if there was something like a future in the Buffalo Horn Valley.

Jessie Lewis was also thinking about the future. She had walked outside as the day dimmed and the breeze picked up. Introspection was rare in her life. There was work to do; Reb to watch; a life to live. With her hand on the iron railing by the family plot, she looked at the stones of her family and Carrick's and thought for once about her own future. Clawing a living from the land was a challenge she had accepted, and surmounted. Carrick's arrival had her thinking. If he and Reb ever married—she laughed at how unthinkable Reb and marriage might have been only a few days ago—she would be in their way, no matter how much they would say otherwise. She thought about Francis Oliver. Funny man. By turns delicate and devious. There was something on his mind other than land, she was sure of it. Reb would never hear of it, but she did like the man; anyone who was a survivor could admire another of the same breed.

She looked off across the land towards Double J. Easy Thompson sprang to mind. The rumbling giant of a man was probably the only reason riders never quit Double J, she mused. He was about the biggest man in the valley. He was about her age; the last time she saw him there were bits of gray in his huge brown mustache. His face proclaimed he had lived outdoors most of his life. His past was lost down the trail, but she always felt that, unlike his boss, he was an honest man. His smile was kind.

She recalled him when they met in town. Every time she said hello to him as part of her effort to teach Reb to be courteous even to the enemy, he blushed and stammered like a little boy in church. He took off his hat to her, as though she were a lady.

He had been there that time the drunken cowboy thought she was his sister, and was so overly solicitous Jess was afraid Reb was going to shoot him!

She thought about Carrick. Much like Jackson Jones, he threw his will against what stood in his way. Much like Reb. Sooner or later, they would all collide. Sooner or later. She looked at the stones and the graves. May it be later, Lord, she prayed silently. Much later.

# CHAPTER EIGHT

Carrick sat up. A blanket had curled over his legs. He frantically kicked it off. Beads of sweat dotted his face. His hand was at his right hip, reaching for what wasn't there. He was not in the Abilene street. It was his shack near Black Wind Pass, in the hilly country no one cared about between the ranches.

As wakefulness returned, the panic eased. He had been sure there was a shot—a booming sound that penetrated the shrouds of sleep. He listened. Silence. Not even birds. Trouble.

Another shot; then one after. The big booms of a powerful long gun. Then silence.

Hunters were in the hill country all the time. Deer. Big cats. That was the other way. This was out toward the range, the flatlands, where trouble in the form of men lived. Trouble had found him. He tossed off the blanket.

Late summer daylight was filtering in the shack. There were piles here, stuff there. He got up from the floor. He'd lost the bed habit in the war, and never recovered it.

It was still silent outside. Beast looked back from the tree where he'd been loosely tied. Carrick walked to the thin flow of water that dripped from the rocks and splashed himself fully awake. He looked across Buffalo Horn Valley. Somebody was out there. Not moving. He thought he heard a rider moving north, toward Double J, but with the wind in his ears it could have been any kind of noise.

He saddled Beast. They loped down the path between the

trees. Long before he reached the flatland, he could see a horse standing in the middle of the field. It wasn't until they were fifty feet away he could see the lump by the side of a giant white horse. Whoever the rider was, he had a faithful animal.

Beautiful horse, thought Carrick. Beast snorted, as if reading his thoughts. Beast was not beautiful. He was long-legged all right, but his gray coat had so much brown in it he looked mud-splattered on the best of days. But the horse was Carrick's, and, for weeks on end making their way from Kansas to Wyoming, he had been Carrick's sole friend in the world. He never chided Beast for any real or imagined shortcomings in the area of looks because he figured the horse might have noted a few of his shortcomings, too—like the beard and hair that didn't get trimmed much, the old clothes that got washed every so often or not maybe that much, and the face with the scars on the outside that showed and on the inside that didn't.

They reached the corpse. The shape and the size looked familiar. Carrick rolled him over. Jackson Jones. Double J land was over the hill about a mile or so. They were on the old Bar C's land, if it belonged to anyone other than the bears and wolves.

He wondered where Jones would have been going, but it didn't really matter now. The man whose dreams were larger than life had come to the end of his. Too soon, thought Carrick. Jones had been changing, he thought. The man was going to have an empire, but he reckoned that the Lewis women would be allowed a part of it thanks to Reb catching the stallion. Now, it was all up for grabs again. Was this Oliver's work? Hard to see who else would benefit.

Three bullets. Good shooting. One in the front. Two in the back. Probably one riding and the other two when he was down. There wasn't as much blood by the second ones. Second wounds never bled as much as first ones. Jones had fought and fought against the world, thought Carrick as he struggled and stumbled until he eventually lifted the big man into his horse's saddle. The man's fight was now over. The white horse didn't like the feel of a man draped across his saddle, and it took Carrick a minute to calm him. He had the feeling Beast was watching closely, as if a horse could get jealous. Didn't the fool horse know there weren't anyone in the whole world but each other would know if either of them died? Silly horse.

"Good boy, Beast, you contrary beast," chided Carrick. "Now c'mon. We got to take this here fella into town. Sheriff'll have to figure this out. No way after these last few days am I riding to Double J with their boss's body on his horse."

Lincoln Springs Sheriff Dan Hill went whiter than a blizzard when Carrick told him the news. Dan was pushing sixty. He was a big man who could wrestle a drunk and was old in the ways of the young and wild. Murder was not in his line. He retreated into the limits of his job as Carrick demanded Hill take charge of Jones.

He shook his head sadly as he looked at Jones's body. "Best take him home, son. His, not yours. I feel bad for the kin, and I guess it's all gonna blaze up out of control, but my job's keeping the boys from wrecking the town here, not riding any range. I'll see what Wally Perkins and Sam Johnson want done—they're such of a town council as we got—but I don't think they want me interfering with this, because the only reason anyone would kill old Jackson Jones is to stop him grabbing land. Man was planning to build a school and church here next year. Now that's gone. It's none of our business. Town hired me to keep cowboys in line within the town limits. You better take him home to his ranch, Carrick; then you better tell them women to fort up their place because whatever happened before today is gonna be nothin' to what comes after. 'Spose someone ought to

117

tell Oliver, if he don't already know."

"Sheriff, ain't there an undertaker here?"

"Sam Morris builds the coffins; he don't hold the dead. Church never got built. Sorry, Carrick, you're on your own." Hill turned away.

Carrick was disheartened and more than a little irked the lawman was able to wriggle out of what should be his job. He half wanted to leave Jackson Jones right there. Not his business. Not his fight. But he knew he could not do that. A man couldn't leave a dead man lying around to start smelling bad.

"C'mon, Beast. Double J it is. Maybe they won't shoot first. Least maybe we can get you a bag of oats out of this." The horse looked back. Carrick wondered what he thought. At least he never said.

They rode slowly across the range. Perfect place for horses and cattle. Dry. Grass grew no matter what anyone did; nothing much else grew no matter what they did, except for the places where the trees grew thick. Wyoming weather meant that if you traveled five miles you could be in a different world. Not the kind of land they had in Kansas, where the plains went on forever, or down South, where the land was thick and rich.

The rough open terrain was all Carrick's as he rode slowly, trying to find a good way to tell this story on the Double J ranch. Most days, Carrick thought, there would be someone riding around—someone who maybe he could have pawned off this trip on. Today, of course, no such luck.

He swung off the wide trail that led toward the town and onto the one straight for Double J. He figured there were eyes in the distant hills. As he had learned, Double J was vigilant. He was right. Too much dust for one rider was coming toward him. Carrick hated talking on the good days. Today, he hated it worse.

He plodded along. Beast could run if he had to, and if things got ugly, that was the plan. He had been hoping to avoid a war with Double J, not start one. Still, he eased his gun in its holster. A man had to be ready.

Six riders spread out as they came nearer. Carrick stopped and let them know they were in charge. Easy Thompson was the Double J foreman and his unmistakable figure was in the lead as they rode up to Carrick, surrounding him with a cloud of dust that filtered through the air and came to rest on everything from Carrick's face to the cold body of Jackson Jones.

"Got bad news, Easy!" Carrick called out, trying to size up the legend he had only met through range talk. "Found your boss shot about a mile south of the pass. Lincoln Springs didn't want anything to do with it. Ask the sheriff. I'm coming from there now. I'm taking him back to Double J."

Two riders, hands near their guns, suspecting something, anything, came closer. One nodded. The other grabbed the reins.

"You're Carrick," rumbled Easy. "Man who came up in my boss's face when I wasn't there. Man who killed those Crowleys and Larry Gordon. Heard about you."

"Man who doesn't back down, Easy. You want to talk about history or you want to talk about your boss?"

"Tell me about it," said Easy, who seemed to be blinking a lot after taking a long, close look at the body of his boss.

"I did," replied Carrick. "I'm done."

"You're done talkin' when I'm done askin'," Easy replied curtly with the voice of a man whose authority is so solid that no man ever questioned it. "Bring him, boys. Shoot him if he doesn't cooperate."

For a moment, defiance flared in Carrick. Easy Thompson's massive shoulders tensed as he watched it spark. They relaxed as he watched it die. Carrick's eyes locked onto the foreman's a mite longer than necessary. Then he let it slide. Man finds his boss dead, a man's likely to be touchy. Range gossip had nothing bad to say about Easy. Only thing Carrick had heard was that he had some kind of interest in Jessie Lewis, but Easy didn't look or act like the marrying kind.

Thompson turned the horse to lead the group back to the ranch. Two riders kept to the back behind Carrick. He could kill them and probably get away, but where would there be to run? He had to play this out.

Easy Thompson spurred ahead as they reached the ranch. The rest of the riders accompanied Jones's body to the stone house he had used as his headquarters. Carrick saw them struggle to carry the man from his horse. Easy watched, then went into the big ranch house.

Carrick was riding behind the rest. Grief was private. He'd had his. Never shared it. Didn't need a share in anyone else's. He thought about riding out now that the riders had all dismounted and seemed to have forgotten him, but Easy's language had been definite and it was not a day to rile a man.

He dismounted and took Beast off to the side of the growing crowd. Maybe he could get food for the horse; oats were a treat the poor animal didn't get often. Double J was bound to have some.

"Where are you goin'?"

Ken Billings had his gun out and pointed at Carrick. "Horse has been ridin' all day. I'm gonna take off his saddle, get him some oats. Animal didn't do nothing to deserve to suffer."

"And Jones did?"

"Fella, all I did was find him. I don't like it either, but I didn't shoot him, didn't have a thing against any of you. You know that. I been standin' up for some women who needed a hand. Nothin' more. What happened to your boss hurts kind of raw now but let it alone. Easy wants me around, so I'm around."

He didn't wait for a reply but kept walking. Soon, Beast was in a stall Carrick liked for him; it was by the big door and the breeze. Wally, the stable boy, would look after him and feed him. Beast would be fine. Carrick was less sure about his own fate.

Carrick watched Billings watch him. He rubbed his neck. The need to show Double J he was not going to be watched and hemmed in was like an itch that had to be scratched. A cowboy needed to eat. Carrick went out the far entrance of the barn, where Billings could not see, then hopped the rail fence to cut through the corral. In a moment, he was in the farmhouse's pantry, then the kitchen.

"Are you here to steal coffee again? Or did you sneak in the back door to steal something else?" a female voice called coyly. Lucinda Jones walked into the kitchen with a playful smile on her face that transformed into something a lot more wooden as soon as she saw Carrick standing there.

"Luce?"

"Carrick? What are you doing here? Did you decide to come and work for Jackson? Oh, wonderful! He rode out this morning but I'm sure he will be back soon." She moved close enough for him to smell that she had on some perfume that was probably supposed to smell good. She walked funny, though. She held herself like something hurt and she wanted to hide it. Her right shoulder was off; it hung low a little. For a fleeting moment he wondered if she and Jones ever had physical battles and she had been hurt. Anything was possible with people. He could defend her it that's what she needed. She was looking at him with curiosity. He was trying to decide how to tell her the worst news a wife could hear.

Feet came stomping into the kitchen. Easy Thompson filled the doorway, measuring the closeness between Carrick and this woman that until a few hours ago was his boss's wife. On a good day, it might have planted the seed for some range gossip.

Today, it was grounds for even more trouble.

"What are you up to, Carrick?" growled Easy. "You kill him to get to her?"

Lucinda's face contorted in the image of anguish. "Kill?" she shrieked. "Kill? Carrick, what did you do to my husband? Easy, where is Jackson?"

"Sorry, Luce, to be the bearer of bad news," Carrick explained. He told her about the shots and finding her husband. "He was gone when I found him. No idea where the shots came from except the hills give a lot of cover. Tried to tell the law back in Lincoln Springs but the law don't want to be caught up in anything out here on the range. I was on my way here when your riders met me."

Black eyes looking back at him were dry. "Did he say anything?"

It was a funny question. People ask strange things about the dead. "He was gone when I got there, Luce. Sorry." He touched Lucinda's shoulder; she winced and pulled away.

"Why do they think you killed him?"

"Me and Jackson had a full airing of our differences that day I came here. Not sure we parted friends, Lucy."

"Did you kill my husband?"

"No, Luce, no. I don't sniper shoot. I don't kill people unless I have to. Your man was a man trying to build a dream and it was colliding with some other folks' dreams. I think we might have figured out a way to let everyone have what they wanted. He was a good man, Luce, and he was starting to understand that this valley could be more than one man's empire; that it could be everybody's home."

"Those Lewis people paid you to kill Jackson?"

"Luce, I didn't kill him. I got no reason to kill him. Them Lewis women gonna have their own protection and it ain't me. Anyhow, your husband was going to sit down and talk range limits with them. Why would they hurt him when they were waitin' for that to happen?"

Her eyes were snapping angry; not a trace of a tear or mourning. She turned to Easy. "Well? Is he telling me the truth or not, Easy? What's this about range limits?"

"I don't know, ma'am. The boss and one of them Lewis women met the other day in the storm; he was telling me something about it yesterday. Don't know what he was thinkin' on that, ma'am. Had a look at your husband, ma'am. No proof this man did it; no proof he didn't other than his word, whatever that's worth. Don't think nobody's enough of a fool to kill a man and bring his body to his ranch. You that much a fool, Carrick? You figure maybe she'd protect you? That how it is?"

"Mr. Thompson!" Carrick watched Lucinda Jones, whom he knew as a flirty, almost giggly, girl, stand tall and proud. Her voice ripped through the house. It could flay a man's soul from the sound alone. "If you have something to say about me and my conduct as Jackson's wife and now his widow, say it now! Then I can remind you who, as of this very moment, is now running Double J."

Easy Thompson hemmed and hawed and looked a lot at the floor. "Didn't mean nothin', ma'am. Sorry."

"I want to be alone," she said. "Go! Both of you! Get out of my sight!" The men left. They passed Petersen on the way, pasty-faced and sweating. "You, too!" they heard her roar a moment later.

Easy Thompson gripped Carrick's arm hard as they stepped back outside. In the distance, someone was calling out his name. Not a good sign. "I want to hear the whole story."

"Told you the whole story, Easy. Woke up. Heard shots. No idea where they came from. None at all. Found your boss."

"Was he riding to see you?"

"Me?" The skepticism in Carrick's voice was genuine. "Don't

know he knew where I lived."

"He did," Thompson said. "He was talking about riding up to the pass near you a couple days ago. Talked about seeing what was going on at that old shack. Maybe he came to see you and you shot him dead and you're trying to cover it up with some tale."

"Not me, Easy. Boss and I didn't walk away friends the other day, but I respected the man. Sounded like he and Reb had some kind of understanding the other day, but I can't say I got the straight of it. I don't take a gun like the one that killed him and hide out like some sniper and take pot shots. Not much sign to read where I found him. If you say he was heading out that way, maybe he was, but I can't say for certain sure which direction he was facing when he was shot, or where he was go-ing. The horse had wandered a bit. He was blown clear off it. Somebody hit him, then hit him after he was dead and down. Hit him twice like that. Look at the holes in him, Easy. Big holes. Everything I own is on me. Somebody had a buffalo gun or some such. Not me. I never had one. I killed your men when they pushed it, Easy. Jackson pushed everybody, but he hadn't pushed me yet."

Easy Thompson's glare examined every inch of Carrick, as if there would be evidence of a lie seeping through somewhere. He breathed in and out, as if there was a whiff of a lie he could catch on the wind. "Don't trust you. You come and go like some ghost. You got to the boss the other day without anyone seeing you. No trick at all to get him on the open range. He's been changin' about them Lewis women and I don't know why."

"And if I wanted him dead I could have done it the day I first came here and left with none of you the wiser."

Easy Thompson was not quite convinced. He had been loyal to Jackson Jones since the day Jackson picked him to run Double J, and he gave his life to the ranch. The man in front of him was a threat. He was sure of that. Carrick watched Easy judge him, weigh him, and measure him.

"Longer you stay, longer I got to worry about a hangin'," Easy grumbled. "Better git. Take the back road out the pasture. Don't want the men to know until you're gone. I hate vigilantes. Jackson Jones gave me everything, Carrick. I was about as far down and out as a man can get, and long past the age when a man gets second chances, Carrick. The boss hired me and made me his foreman because he trusted me to do the right thing; the thing he would want done. That's the only reason you're breathin' now. He would not want me to kill you if you didn't do it. But I'm not convinced. Gonna have a few boys go out and see what there is to see, Carrick, and if I see you anywhere near the place where he was shot, I'll take that as an admission of guilt and you hang. They come up to that shack of yours, they got the right to look around. Clear?"

Carrick bristled. He had nothing to hide, but he had his rights.

"Lookin's one thing, Easy. Touchin's another. They come when I'm not there, they're thieves and I got the right to shoot them. Hear?"

Two wills collided in silence.

"Don't think about ridin' off," Easy threatened, looming closely into Carrick's face. "If you leave this range, Carrick, you can't go far enough I won't hunt you down."

"Not leavin', Easy. Not yet, anyhow. Got work to do first." Defiance glared back.

"Git then."

Easy Thompson called the riders to the bunkhouse. While they were going one way, Carrick saddled a well-fed Beast and rode slowly out of Double J. Now that he was, for the moment, safe, he felt the regrets flow through him. Jackson Jones was a giant of a personality, a man who was going to stamp Wyoming

125

in his image. It might have been for the better; it might have been for the worse. At the end, he thought Jones was starting to understand the character of the Lewis women and respect them. Now, he would never know.

He wondered what Jones's death would do to the rivalry with Lazy F. Lazy F? He'd forgotten Francis Oliver entirely. He rubbed the back of his neck and shook his head from side to side. He'd probably managed to get all the ranches in the valley mad at him the same day, but he might as well play it out. Anyhow, Reb and Jessie needed to know that with Jackson Jones dead, anything could happen next.

# CHAPTER NINE

Rebecca Lewis never much liked milking the cows, but with the few hands they had out checking to see what animals they still had, she was the entire crew to do all the chores. Aunt Jess did what she could, but Aunt Jess also did all the cooking. She had hoped Carrick would help, since he was supposed to be working for them even if all he got were meals, but like all men he'd rather ride a horse than get off of it and work. Usually, he at least showed up, but today he hadn't even ridden in from the shack where he was holing himself up. Things between them were not really clear. She knew he cared about her; she cared about him. But what was that compared with everything going on around them? It wasn't the time for talking about all that. Maybe when the ranch was safe, if it was ever safe.

She was grumbling to the cows about men and their foolishness and such when she saw the rider coming fast up the trail. Francis Oliver plain as day, alone. He never rode alone. With Double J trying to push him out, and men like the Crowleys riding around, it was only common sense that he went about armed and escorted. Alone? He must be up to something sneaky; must have thought one rider would never be spotted, whoever it was he was trying to hide from.

Reb fumed. She had one more cow, and a cow won't give milk any faster than it will. She finished, dumped the milk in the buckets they used to store it until they made cheese and butter, and ran to the house. Nobody was going to bother Aunt

Jess when Reb was around—especially Francis Oliver.

She burst into the door and stopped cold. Francis Oliver was not only alone, he was wearing a suit—a real Eastern style suit with a vest—and was holding a bunch of flowers. His hair was slicked down with something to the point where it looked silly. He had a patch of dirt on one knee of the pants of the suit. Aunt Jess had a look on her face that Reb had never seen before. At first, she was afraid Aunt Jess was really sick, maybe apoplexy caused by something Oliver said to her.

Reb strode over to confront him. She wished she had grabbed her rifle on the way. "What are you doing to Aunt Jess? Get out of here before I kick you back to your own range where you belong."

"What are you doing here?" Oliver replied. "Carrick promised me that he would . . . Drat the man!"

"I live here and what did Carrick say about me? And what are you two in cahoots about? Get off my land!"

"Reb!" Aunt Jess was shouting. Aunt Jess never shouted. "Could we sit, please? Francis? Rebecca? Please?"

They went into what passed for the parlor. It had a padded chair Aunt Jess used for her Good Book reading and two other delicate ones that had come with them from Tennessee and two big solid ones that had been there. Reb wondered for the first time if Carrick had made them. Aunt Jess took the padded chair. Oliver sat on a delicate one. Reb perched in one of the heavy ones, wondering if the fragile wooden chair could handle Oliver's bulk and hoping that it couldn't.

"Now," said Aunt Jess, with finality in her voice. "Reb should understand what is being discussed, Francis. This is her home. I am the only family she has in the world, and this is a very important decision."

"As long as she don't point no guns."

"No guns, I promise."

"She can stay."

"Well, thank you for letting me stay in my own home!" Aunt Jess held up a hand. Reb stopped, chastened.

Aunt Jess turned to face Reb, who did not notice the slight tears in Aunt Jess's eyes and the almost dazed look that was still on her face. "Mr. Oliver has asked me to marry him, Reb. What do you think of that?"

"You'd do anything to get this land, you conniver!"

"Rebecca Lewis!" Jessie could not restrain her impatience. Did Reb know how insulting it was to assume that no one could want to marry her for herself but only for the land of which she more or less had custody for the past nine years? She realized again how true it was that the young never understood anything except themselves. Even her Reb. She would not allow sadness to tarnish this moment, this day. "Reb, I know that you have suspected Francis of many things and that you are looking out for my best interests. I think that while the land may be important to Francis, I think that Mr. Oliver and I have perhaps not understood one another in these recent weeks. Am I right, Francis?"

"Ma'am, I've wanted to find the right way to say it so you wouldn't laugh. I ain't a spring chicken and I don't have fancy stuff around the house but it gets awful lonely over there and I guess it does here, too, and it ain't right that two people are lonely when we can do somethin' about it."

Reb was spellbound. Aunt Jess looked like a silly girl at a county fair. But she looked happy. Very happy. Happy in a funny way Reb had never seen before. Reb was irrationally angry. How could Francis Oliver make Aunt Jess this happy when Reb couldn't? How come no man ever said or did anything that made *her* feel this way? She wanted to throw the man out, but she couldn't do that to Aunt Jess. She sat and fumed. It was a while before she understood what they were saying.

"Reb, I have told Francis I will marry him, but I do not know that we have yet settled at a date." Jess did not tell Reb about the lonely nights. About wondering if her life had a purpose once Reb married. About her quiet thoughts she never shared with her niece. She could not explain that Oliver's proposal seemed like fate intervening.

"Been waitin' a long time, Jessie," spoke up Oliver. "June, now. Summer's good for weddin's."

Hoofbeats drummed outside. Reb rose to see what else could possibly be going wrong. Carrick burst in.

"Done it myself!" said Oliver. "Fat lot of help you were."

"Jessie?" asked Carrick.

"Everything is fine, Mr. Carrick!"

"It is not," burst out Reb, who turned on Carrick. "Is this some plan of yours? Pretending about me? Is that snake paying you?"

"Reb," Jess interjected, "I know this is a very sudden announcement, but I think I knew what Francis was trying to say, but I wasn't really sure because, like a man, until today he never actually said it!"

Anger overflowed restraint. "You get married. What about me? We live here, Aunt Jess! Lazy F's run down. That house is a shack. I'm not getting run out of here. This is mine!"

"Reb, let me think! Never thought at my age I would be asked to get married again. Now, girl, let an old woman enjoy herself." Carrick wanted to remind her that she wasn't old, but figured keeping his mouth shut would be in his best interests.

Reb stalked out of the house, slamming the door behind her.

"I got to see to her," Carrick said. Looking at Oliver, he said commandingly, "No weddin' dates. Nothin'. Not until Reb is settled."

"Mr. Carrick? I've been all of her family for so long, she needs some time. You might want to wait a while until she cools off. Francis, we can wait for her to come around and understand."

Oliver's smile was forced. "Of course, Jessie," he said. He glared at Carrick. "Go ahead, son. I won't abduct her!"

Reb was standing at the edge of the horse barn. "What do you get out of this?" she flung at him as he approached. "I should have known you were up to something. Trying to pretend you liked me when you were partners with him! Another one like him, are you? Trying to get your range any way you can?"

"Reb, listen for a minute!"

"Why are you helping him?"

"Not helpin' him. I went to Lazy F the other day. Your aunt knew. He told me about this. He said he was embarrassed to ask in front of you. I was supposed to take you ridin', let him have his say. That's all. What if he means it?"

"Aunt Jess should hit him over the head with his flowers."

"That would do a lot of damage," Carrick remarked drily.

Reb's eyes were wet. "Maybe you think all of this is funny, but how would you feel, cowboy, if some old geezer was proposing to your aunt and you can't even get a decent cowboy to come around and then you come around and now . . . I don't know what you are up to now! How do you think that makes me feel? The girl that nobody wants! What do you know about feeling that way? And now I'm going to lose everything I ever had and end up with nothing."

"That ain't the way it is. Listen, Reb, you . . . I mean you got to see, girl. Can't you understand, Reb? I . . . I mean . . . you . . . I . . ."

"You what?" Snapping mad eyes bored holes through any good intentions he may have had.

There were things Carrick didn't have a clue how to express about feelings for a woman, and being face to face with the woman herself while she was so angry she was about spitting

131

nails didn't make it easier. Her glare could have melted iron. Carrick did what all cowboys do in the face of a woman's wrath—change the subject.

"Um, Oliver claimed he was after your Aunt Jess, not the land. He said it over and over. Maybe . . . Look! I figger we tell him you want a paper with writing saying you control the land when your Aunt Jess marries him; maybe we see if he meant it. Then you are protected."

Mistrust was plain on Reb's face. She knew he had something else he was going to say. She was mad at him. He could have said something nice that men say to girls, whatever that was. No! She really didn't want to hear anything he had to say. Then she thought about it. If Aunt Jess was off her feet because Francis Oliver surprised her, she'd protect Aunt Jess better than ever. She was sure Oliver was a sneak and a liar, but Aunt Jess was lonesome and Carrick was every bit as much a sentimental fool as every other cowboy on the range—either that or he was Oliver's partner in trying to fool both women into giving up their ranch. It was up to her to do the thinking.

Leaving Carrick to follow in her wake, Reb stalked back into the house. Carrick all but snickered when Reb announced the very specific terms under which she would allow her Aunt Jess to be married. Francis Oliver was not very happy, but once Jessie instantly agreed he had no choice.

When all of the angry words were over, Carrick dropped the news. "Jackson Jones is dead," he said, looking straight at Oliver, who seemed as surprised by the news as the rest.

"How?" said Reb. "He was fine the other day in the storm."

"Shot down. Cold-blooded murder. Killed this morning."

"I was on the ranch until I came here, Carrick. Ask my men. Ask any of them. Ask all of them! Never went near his ranch."

"He wasn't killed there; he was killed out on the range in the open. Anyone could have done it. Not me you got to answer to,

132

Oliver. You got to answer to Double J. Bet they're going to come calling real soon."

Francis Oliver was pale and shaking. Alibi or not, he would be the major suspect unless he could prove otherwise, prove it fast and prove it well. With expressed regrets he left the ranch. As Oliver rode away, Carrick noticed the wistful look on Jess's face and the sad and angry look on Reb's visage. Maybe there was something he ought to do about it, that is, if the range didn't erupt in violence.

Even when the struggle for who owns a piece of land is waged at its fullest, the demands of a ranch can distract all comers. Despite fears that Jones's killing would launch a war, days went by with no new provocations from Double J—no answers either, Reb remarked archly on yet another unsuccessful attempt by Carrick to talk to her. Francis Oliver had stopped by to say that Easy Thompson had been there to see him, and accepted Oliver's alibi. There had been a railroad man at the Lazy F that same morning, and, if the man was telling the truth, there would not have been time for Oliver to ride to the hills and back to Lazy F.

Francis Oliver had agreed to let Reb write the terms of the agreement for the land, amazed a woman could write and seemingly more than a little afraid of words on a paper. Reb had labored on the words that would protect her. She thought about asking Carrick, once, but decided she wasn't sure she could trust what he might say. She was, as usual, on her own.

Jessie had last been on Lazy F land some five years previously, so the day after Jackson Jones was killed, when it seemed that there would be a time of relative peace until his funeral in a few days, it was agreed she would go—unchaperoned, by her own very firm statement to Reb—to see the ranch. She would stay three days and return. Reb glowered at this latest affront to all she held dear, but said little. She barely had words for Carrick, although from the looks she threw him, there was much on her mind. He once thought about trying to breach the wall growing between them, but decided in the end that he didn't have the right words and that Reb would do what she wanted no matter what.

For Carrick, the rhythm of ranch life was a welcome return to the life he had not known in ten years. He stayed close to the house, fixing broken things that hadn't had a carpenter's attention in many years. It felt good. The work may not have been physically demanding, but it was engrossing. He did not scan the horizon for riders every time he left the barn or walked around the corner of the house.

Even when he should have.

This time he came out of the barn after putting new wood on the roof so it wouldn't leak—much. Instead of unbroken landscape, a man stood there, waiting. Not any man. A man who had come a long way on a mission of revenge, and who now radiated the feral pleasure a predator feels when its prey has entered a carefully prepared trap. Carrick had known that feeling. Now it was his turn to be on the receiving end.

"Hello, Uriah."

"Carrick."

Uriah Saunders was taller and thinner than Carrick with a narrow face behind a full mustache. Malice glittered in dark eyes; satisfaction in the slight smile that revealed yellow teeth. Greasy brown hair flowed neatly from under a black hat. The man's face was trail-worn. A soft leather holster around his hips was black, as was the richly tailored suit he wore, with black boots and a shiny silver and black vest. The star he wore shone in the morning sunlight.

"Biggest star you could find, Uriah?"

"Glad you noticed it, Carrick. Star means I'm the law. Sworn by the town of Carmichael, Texas, to find you."

"Carrick? Are you so busy with whatever you're doing that you can't answer when I ask you a simple question?" Reb's querulous voice reached him as she rounded the corner from behind the barn.

The man in black pulled two long-barreled revolvers. One covered Carrick; the other, an exasperated and now-stunned Reb, who carried a pail of milk. "Cozy, ain't we?"

"Keep her out of this, Uriah."

"Man has a wife, man should protect her. That's the way it is. Man has a brother, man should do right by his brother. That's also the way it is, you murderer."

"Man's brother deserved to die, Uriah. World's a better place without him."

"Abigail and the kids don't think so."

"She marries anybody it will be a better life. He would have done dirt to her in the end. How'd you find me?"

"Kansas folks wired me back in the winter after that little to-do in Abilene. Somebody knew you. I went up there. Lost you a while after that. Winter set in. Wyoming Territory was about my last hope. Knew you came from up here somewhere. Came up in the spring. I was at Fort Laramie when a man at Lincoln Springs sent word to them, sayin' some hard case rode into the valley. The man wanted to know if there was an outlaw named Carrick with a price on his head. Told myself there ain't two Carricks in Wyoming, so I came to see what I could see. Soon, there ain't gonna be one. Alive."

Carrick reached out his arms in front of him, joined his hands and cracked his knuckles. It ended here. Two years on the run; now it was ending. One way or the other. It was like the feeling that day at Shiloh. Enough waiting. Get it over with. His hands swung at his sides, inches from his holstered pistol. He had wondered how fast he was. Now, he'd find out.

Uriah waited, clearly hoping Carrick would reach for a gun. They waited each other out in silence until the pressure of the stillness made Reb speak. "Carrick, what's this about?" Reb had been restrained, for her. Uriah's deadly presence dominated even her.

"You never told your woman?"

"I work for her; she's not my wife."

"Carrick, I bet she'd like to know the story anyhow." He turned to Reb. "Uriah Saunders, miss. My brother Zekeriah was in the proud service of the Confederate States of America. When the war ended and he was honorably paroled, he came back, peacefully, to our ranch in Carmichael, Texas. He married. Had a family. About two years ago, he was murdered."

"Not murder to kill the likes of him. Call it justice. I promised my men I'd even it and I did."

The gun pointed at Carrick trembled. "What you did . . . was unholy."

"Me and God don't think so." The gun traveled down Carrick's body.

"In the guts. One shot. How long will it take, Carrick?"

"Long enough for me to have time to kill you and you know it. Start the ball, Uriah. It's a good day for it."

Uriah's gun clicked. "What . . . what happened? I don't know what any of this is about!" Reb wanted to keep Uriah talking. Carrick was acting like a fool. As long as the man in black talked, he could be distracted. Carrick was acting as though he wanted to be shot!

"This man . . ." the gun gestured again, but was no longer cocked. "This man rode up to my brother's farm. He dragged the man in front of his wife and children and forced him to tell lies."

"The truth, Uriah! The things he did at Andersonville that were unspeakable! How much he enjoyed his work! How he watched men die and bet with the guards who would die on which day!"

Uriah's face was contorted in hatred. Reb despaired. Carrick was all but dead. She cleared her throat. The man in black focused on her again and resumed the story. "When it was done, he shot him to death right through the belly and let him die slowly. The man died hearing his wife and kids screaming!"

Reb was revolted. Carrick looked defiant. "Guess I was a mite easy on him, now that you tell it so pretty," he said.

The hammer clicked. "No!" screamed Reb.

The man's eyes shifted back, focusing on Reb. She had never felt so much evil in a man; and now it was focused on her. She froze. This was death.

"Maybe you're right, little lady. Maybe you should die first, so he can see everything he loves die. That would be a better punishment than him dying. Maybe . . ."

Carrick reached for his gun. Uriah turned back to Carrick and fired once before a pail of warm cloudy liquid spread across him, blinding him. He fired both guns. Carrick's weapon blasted. One shot clanged off of the milk pail. One or both men exclaimed in pain as shots hit home. Reb rolled on the ground after throwing the milk pail at Uriah, the way Aunt Jess taught her to do if she was ever in town when drunk cowboys started shooting. A few seconds and a lot more shots later, it was quiet.

Reb rose, shaking. The white pool around Uriah's twitching body was deeply tinged with red. Reb kicked the gun from his hand; he had been struggling to thumb back the hammer in the final moments of his life. The man had four red holes in him. She ran to Carrick. He was slumped up against the barn in a position of the badly injured. Three holes in the wood above his head showed where Uriah had missed. Not all the shots had gone wide. There was red at Carrick's lips. He was breathing hard. The gun in his hand, though, was steady and trained on Uriah.

"Dead?" Blood sprayed. It dripped down Carrick's chin. Some sprayed onto Reb's face, inches away.

"He's dead, Carrick. He's dead!" Reb felt hysteria rising. Carrick looked to be dying as well. "Where are you hit?"

"Andersonville."

"What? Carrick. Don't move. Sit here and do nothing. I got to find the bullets. Don't talk. It doesn't matter."

His hand gripped her forearm. "Brother. Guard. At Andersonville. Two years to find him. I owed my men." Carrick's head sagged and reeled. "What he did. He had to pay. Don't think bad . . . of me . . . Reb? It ain't that big a sin to rid the world of a killer. Remind God, will you, Reb?"

"Shush, Carrick."

"Storm comin' Reb. Cold wind. It's getting' dark."

"Carrick, I said it don't matter. Where are you shot?"

"Reb." It was a whisper. The hand still gripped. "I . . . for you. Sweet . . . L-l—"

He slid even further down the wall of the barn until he was limp. She could see behind him the red trail on the unpainted barn that a bullet near his ribs had passed through him, taking a chunk of muscle with it before lodging in the wood. His face had been grazed. That was the source of the blood in his mouth. She kept looking.

The other trail of blood was lower. She took off his shirt and threw the soggy mess by the dead Texan.

A bullet was in Carrick's abdomen. The red, oozing crater was not deep. She thought she could see the bullet when she pushed apart the muscle. He moaned but otherwise did not react as she probed. Aunt Jess knew about treating gunshot wounds, but she wasn't here. There was nobody else. She had dug bullets out of the fence posts more than a few times but the wood didn't bleed all over. It couldn't be that much different. She started hauling him indoors. She lit a lantern to see.

Carrick watched as the moon danced. Up and down. Around. Carrick always wanted to see it do something different than just hang in the sky. He wondered if it was standing still and he was flying. He recalled looking up when they told him, as a child, someone was heading to heaven. Never did see anyone. It was hot; he was burning. There was fire. Fire everywhere. From his arms to his hips, there was fire. The angel bending over him must have kissed him. Angels did that. Too much fire. Everything tinged red. He tried to move and tell her. She was saying something. A formless noise surrounded him. He was starting to recognize it was his voice when it was swallowed in black.

Rebecca Lewis looked at the lump on the floor that refused to die or live. For three days, since she had operated on him by the light of the lantern, Carrick had breathed in and breathed out, barely. The scream that came from the depths of his pain when she dug out the bullet had been the last noise he made. It made it easier sewing him up to know he wasn't going to move. Then the long wait began. She milked the cows, fed the animals, and watched Carrick. She had ate something yesterday. Or the day before.

Foolish cowboy, she thought, pushing back that lock of hair that always fell into her eyes. Taking on a man with a gun drawn because he threatened her. Fool! Half of her said she could have talked her way out; the other half reminded her how close she had been to evil and death. She realized that Carrick had not cared about his own survival, but had risked his life to save her. She didn't like thinking that way. It made her cry, and she hated crying. She touched his face. It was cold. She put another blanket over him. The wound on his face was superficial; the one in his side would hurt, if he lived. The one in his gut was the one that worried her. That must have been the first shot; Carrick had not missed after that—the other man had.

She'd buried the Texas lawman in the yard where the dirt and debris were piled. He had a fat wallet. That made her about as cash rich as she had ever been in her life. He also had a letter. It was soggy with milk and blood, but it said a man named Carrick was in the valley and that he might be wanted for something. She did not know who wrote it. It was a puzzle for either after she buried Carrick or after he lived. She watched him again. If there was a change, she couldn't see it. She had been praying so long she had run out of words beyond "Please." And he was going to die!

In that moment, she felt filthy with blood and death and failure. She needed to be clean; she needed to be in the daylight. She needed the touch of the Wyoming wind and to feel the waters of the creek. She looked again at Carrick. She stood up, grabbed a few things from the room she shared with Aunt Jess, and strode out. He could sleep forever or die the next second. She needed what she needed right then. She did the best she could for a man who had never said if she mattered to him. "God, you watch him until I get back," she said. "I tried. I can't watch him die. I can't watch."

She saddled Arthur and rode.

Her hair was wet, still, when she returned. The blood-fouled shirt was past cleaning, so she left it by the creek. She wore a new one—one Aunt Jess gave her to wear at some silly thing when she wanted her to meet cowboys. Look how that was turning out. With the sun and wind and clean water on her head she felt closer to alive. She'd make something to eat. Maybe smelling food would wake him up. She'd make coffee. That brought cowboys to life.

She flung open the door. The hammer of a gun greeted her with its telltale click.

She froze. The darkness of the house was too dim for her eyes. "Carrick?" A noise. "Carrick?"

"Reb?" It was a croaking half-dead voice, but it was her name he croaked. Carrick was not on the floor. She walked in.

"It's me, Carrick. Reb. I had to breathe something that wasn't dyin'."

"Not dead. Not yet. Promised. Reb?"

Her eyes were adjusting. She found him in a corner, propped against the walls, .45 in his hands. Two very unsteady hands.

"Cowboy, if that goes off you'll kill the only one around here that's been nursing you. Come on. Lie on the blankets."

"You? Hurt?" There was panic in the wavy tones of his cracked voice. His legs tried to get up.

She touched his cheek softly. "Shhh," she said. "I'm fine. He's dead. Shhh." He stopped struggling. "Everything would be fine if some fool cowboy would lie down and not point a gun at me. Girl never likes that kind of thing in a man. Now, put that down or give it to me and get back to the bed I made for you."

How a half-dead man could make a pile of blankets disappear, she could not imagine. He had. After gingerly taking the gun away from him, she helped him struggle to his feet. He staggered sideways and then collapsed across Aunt Jess's bed with a moan. He kept reaching for a gun on his hip. He was alive and ready to kill. Guess that's about normal, she thought, smiling at the man as he went to sleep almost as soon as he hit the bed.

Carrick slept the rest of the day and the night. She heard him stumbling in the morning while she was hanging a pot by the fire to boil water.

"Carrick, would you stay in one place and not bleed all over the floor? Somebody has to clean the place."

A grin from a swaying figure in the doorway answered her. He would live. "Uriah?"

"Dead and buried. I told you but you didn't hear." She read his face. "No. Not with your kin. Over by the manure pile."

"Good place. Talk later," he said. "I need coffee."

"Lie down, you fool!" He would not. He insisted on walking into the kitchen, wobbly as a foal. He groaned when he more fell than sat. Then he got up and went to the door, opened it, and looked outside, leaning on the door frame. He stood unaided for a moment.

"Never looked better."

"The land or you? Got me some thoughts on that second subject if you're of a mind to hear them."

There was a grin as he turned. "Not fair, pesterin' a man when he's been almost dead." A pause. "Maybe I was talkin' about you, Reb. We got things to say. I recall hearin' stuff when I was out I don't rightly know if I heard or not."

"Think real careful about what to say unless you want to get shot again, cowboy." She knew how often she had told him she needed him to live, and how often she urged him not to die. "Girl doesn't want to hear about what a man thinks he heard. Girl doesn't want to waste time digging graves when she's got the work of two people to do because one of 'em's lying around bleedin'." But she was smiling.

When there was coffee and the biscuits were ready, he ate. She could see life returning to his eyes and his manner.

"Guess I need to thank you."

"Always wanted to dig bullets out of someone, and never had me a volunteer before, so no need to mention it." She grinned.

"You got questions?"

"You really do what that man said?"

Carrick looked uncomfortable. He stared down at his hands a long, silent moment. "I did. Uriah's brother was an officer at Andersonville. He ordered men shot; let men die of thirst; starvation; disease. Some fellas there had a conscience. Uriah's brother was one of those men who likes to see other men suffer. Evil. After the war ended, I was in the hospital until almost '66. Weighed ninety-one pounds when Andersonville was liberated. Some disease; forget the name. Probably should have been dead. Once I could walk, I tracked him. I promised the men I was captured with—a lot of 'em died—I would make him pay.

"Caught up with him in Texas in '68. I killed him in front of everyone that mattered to him, to show them what he really was. All I could think of was killing. It was wrong. I know it was wrong. That's what obsession does to a man—makes him think wrong is right. When it was done, I had no purpose. I wasn't even smart enough to light out. Uriah was the town sheriff. I got arrested and locked up. I escaped—well, I pretty much walked away from the room they had as a jail—because he was going to make sure I hung. Don't think Uriah's brother was too popular or I would have gotten hung right away. Uriah has looked for me ever since I escaped."

"What did you do afterwards?"

"Nothin' I'm very proud to talk about," he said. "All that time I was gonna even the score and when it was done, all I did was kill somebody else. I tried to give up carin' after that. Made my way in the world as a man with a gun. Not much of a way to live but I wasn't askin' for much. I got out of Texas and spent most of the time in Kansas. There was always work for a man with a gun in Kansas what with all the wild cowboys coming up the trail. Abilene last fall. Fella wanted to fight. We went out in the street. Little kid got away from his mom. Got killed by a stray bullet. Not mine, but when that happened, I got sick of it—sick of it all. Hadn't thought about this place more than stray thoughts on bad days. Afterwards, I couldn't stop thinking about it. So I rode out for here. Winter slowed me down, but I got here."

"You were a gunslinger?"

He made a face. "I didn't ride for people stomping other people. I didn't kill people for money, or the way some gunslingers do only to show they can. But when the ranches were fighting, they wanted a gun. When the cattle drives came around, people wanted a man with a gun for protection. I don't know that I thought about anything but killing and guns from the war to that day in Kansas. Maybe I thought coming back would change that. It didn't."

"It's not your fault."

"Nice words, Miss Reb, but a man is what a man does. I did stupid things and wrong things and they came back to almost kill you. When I heal, maybe it would be better if I rode on. Don't think Double J is going to cause you hurt and it looks like Lazy F isn't going to be your enemy any more. Not sure who Uriah may have told where I am. Don't want more trouble following me to your door. Way things were before Uriah came around, I got the feeling maybe I overstayed my welcome already."

"Stay."

"Why?"

"I want you to." Her hand reached out on the table to briefly touch his. "I got real mad when I thought you betrayed me with Oliver. I think he fooled you, and I think he's no good. But I think you wanted my aunt to be happy. I know I probably said things I shouldn't but when a girl gets mad, a girl says stuff. Aunt Jess knows enough to wait until I cool off before coming in range. You stood up to Jones for us. I don't know about men, Carrick. I don't know where any of this goes, Carrick—Double J, Oliver, any of it. I don't trust many folks. I trust you."

"Never done anything to hurt you, Reb, and I don't want to leave, but I'm not sure if stayin' helps you or works against you. I don't want anything bad to happen to you, Reb. It matters. I almost got you killed, girl, and I can't let that happen again."

144

"Cowpoke, I don't know whether you're much use moping around eating more food than the cows, but since I saved your life I own it, and that means you can't leave me all on my own with big ranches to fight, defenseless woman that I am." She hid the smile a minute, but no longer. He reached out his hand. She took it. "Partners." Their handshake said this was a business deal. Their eyes didn't. In the end, she cleared her throat and got up to break the stillness. She came back with a piece of paper.

"Texan had this on him, Carrick." She handed a piece of paper in a bold, florid writing style he had seen once before.

"Francis Oliver's writing," Carrick remarked. Carrick shook his head. He had been the one to tell Oliver about Texas. No. That was only a couple of days ago. No time for a letter to reach the fort. He looked again. It was Oliver's hand. Did Oliver write it when Carrick first showed? Had to be. If so, who told him about Carrick's arrival and who he really was? Maybe it was only bad luck Uriah was passing through the fort when the letter arrived. Hard to see a plot, but it was hard not to suspect one, either. Question now was: What to do about it? Was Oliver trying to ease Carrick out of the way? The man had an uncanny instinct for self-preservation. Did he see Carrick as a threat? Was it plain bad luck? Carrick was wondering, but there was no proof.

Noises alerted them to the arrival of Aunt Jess and Francis Oliver, accompanied by Lazy F riders. "Stay here," hissed Reb.

Carrick heard sounds of a brief conversation. Oliver's voice did, as Reb mentioned, carry a whining, wheedling tone. Carrick had not heard it before. The man was always working to make someone do something they didn't really want to do. As the talk continued, Carrick wondered if Oliver was there to see if Uriah had killed him. Maybe not. Everyone sounded happy as he heard a chorus of good-byes. Jess had a happy look on her face as she entered; one Carrick had not seen before. After an initial shocked exclamation at Carrick's condition, Jessie was silent as Reb and Carrick took turns telling the story—including Oliver's role. If it meant anything to Jess, it did not show in her demeanor.

"Mr. Carrick, if I recall your entrance to Lincoln Springs, it would give any man pause," she said. "I'm sure Francis was trying to protect himself. You and I can ask him the next time we see him, and I'm sure it will turn out that this was nothing more than Francis fearing for his future and some very bad luck."

Carrick was not so sure, but Jess was too happy to argue.

"Mr. Carrick? One more thing. While I was at Lazy F, I met a blacksmith named Carl Taylor. He had his own revelation for me. Would you care to guess it?"

"Carl must be about ninety-nine years old by now. How was he?"

"Sharp as a tack."

"What's this about?" asked Reb, returning with Jessie's tea.

"Some dispute, Reb, about who my parents were. Heard talk I was Josh's son by another woman. The way I heard, he had a child before his marriage. Some place down in Texas, where Josh lived long before he came north. Folks I called my parents weren't, so the story goes. If that was true, I'd have been the oldest, and would have been in line to inherit. The folks I thought of as mine never said anything. I thought it was range gossip. I couldn't ask them. They raised me. Thought of them as my parents. I know Samuel and Joshua had some fallings out in the last couple of years, but I didn't know what it was about. Uncle Josh never admitted it, but when I volunteered to join the army, he said some things about it making life easier for the family as well as for me if maybe the East was where I wanted to stay. They're all dead now. Dirty family laundry all it is now."

"Not really," said Jessie primly. "When Josh was dying, I took care of him. He talked about his son. He talked about you, too, but I assumed it was one of the boys who had died. I never told him they went before him. He was dying and didn't need that burden, too. There is a box, a small metal box, he said to give his boy when his boy came home. There was no one to give it to. I put it in the barn and left it. There were too many things to do to survive to care back then. It's yours if you want it."

"Maybe later, Jessie. Maybe after we figure out Francis Oliver, meanin' no offense, and if we end up all in one piece when this is over."

Jessie was defensive. "Francis agreed to accompany Reb and me to Lincoln Springs next week when Judge Wilson rides through to have the paper about the land signed and witnessed. I know he is a very contrary-appearing man, Mr. Carrick, but I think in this he is sincere. Even if he did write a letter, at the time there was not very much good feeling on this range."

Carrick hoped so. But he was starting to feel that sincerity and Francis Oliver did not walk the same trail.

# CHAPTER TEN

Carrick did very little but heal for the next few days. There had been an ornate funeral for Jackson Jones at the Double J, with an undertaker and a preacher up from Cheyenne for the day. Jones was buried on a hillside overlooking the valley. Jessie and Reb went along with about everyone else in Buffalo Horn Valley; Carrick did not. Double J was quiet in its mourning, too quiet for Carrick's liking.

Reb and Jessie were busy with ranch work, and planning for a rare trip to town to sign the papers. They might, they said, look at goods while they were there. Reb had the money she took off of Uriah tucked away. By rights it might have belonged to whoever the man left behind in Texas, but she was not respecting any proper customs for any man who came to kill Carrick. She didn't like Aunt Jess's upcoming marriage, and she would never think of Francis Oliver as family, but, if marrying the man made Aunt Jess happy, she would do her best to accept it while hoping her aunt would change her mind.

Carrick, who was moving a little slowly but otherwise had healed, was staying behind. Between the pain from his wounds and the nightmares that walked the floor of the Carrick family home, sleep often eluded him. It was so this night as well. At the edge of awareness, he heard a boot break a twig. The gun was in his hand. He struggled up to his feet. He had oiled the hinges of the Lewis front door. It swung silently. Carrick moved outside. There! A horse was by the barn. A man's form moved.

"Stop." The shape stopped. "Hands high and walk over here." The shape was still. Probably deciding his best chance. Carrick cocked the .45. "Hands high or I shoot."

The figure's hands were dark against the lighter darkness of the starlit sky. He muttered something and moved toward Carrick, who lit a match and moved it near the man's face.

"Colt?" The match died. "What are you doin' here?"

"Shh," whispered Ramsay. "Inside. Real quiet. I don't think I was followed but you can't trust anybody."

The inside of the house was dim, shadowy light from the unshuttered windows fading to deeper blackness broken only by the glow of the fireplace's embers. Ramsay looked out the window. After a minute, he stepped back.

"It's a man's life to be sure he's not followed," he whispered. "Colt, what are you up to?"

"Remember I told you I get paid to do things for people; things maybe they don't want to do themselves?"

"I remember. That's why you're kind of out on the edge there. You in trouble?"

"You are." Jessie made a noise in her sleep. They were both quiet. "I know somethin' you won't guess I know."

"Where there's a gold mine?"

Ramsay's teeth were white a second in the darkness. "Old man Rengert kept us lookin' for it that all one summer, didn't he? Remember how we got him back? I thought I was gonna die laughin'."

"I do that, Colt. But you didn't come here to talk about that."

"No, but I came to warn you and your friends, if they're your friends. I hear things. The girl here you're sweet on?"

"Reb? Who told you I'm . . ."

"Whole range knows it, Carrick. She don't point a gun at you, she must be sweet on you. Point is, she's heading to Lincoln Springs tomorrow. She and her aunt. Am I right?"

"How do you know?"

"Man offered me a job. Paid well. Bushwhack a couple of women riding to Lincoln Springs along the creek road. Them two."

"Why?"

"Man didn't say. Man offered five hundred dollars, Carrick. Me and Eileen could be in the land of milk and honey with five hundred dollars. Problem is, I can't do it. Heard through Bad Weather the way it is. You and the Lewis woman. Know you been shot. Can't do it to your woman. Don't know if I could do it to any woman. I had to tell the man I wouldn't take his job. First time I ever turned him down no matter what he asked me to do. Man didn't take it kindly. Said things that got me nervous. Said he would do the job himself if he couldn't find somebody else. Don't know if he did."

"First, Bad Weather ought to keep his mouth shut about things he doesn't know anything about. Reb's not my woman. I don't know. I am working here until I know where I'm going. The ladies have both been kind; that's all."

"Have it your way," commented Ramsay.

"But that don't matter. Who offered you the money?"

"I don't know I can tell you, Carrick. It would be worth my life. Make sure them women don't go anywhere tomorrow."

Carrick reached out and grabbed Ramsay by the front of his shirt. "Colt, you got to tell me. Even if they don't ride tomorrow, sooner or later they're going to be alone. You came this far. You know you want to tell me. If this is Double J, I'll find a way to protect you. Reb's Aunt Jess is marryin' Francis Oliver. Maybe he can get Lazy F to help you out."

"Carrick, you fool, it's Oliver who wants the women ambushed!"

Carrick first doubted Ramsay could be telling the truth. Then a wave of humiliation came over him. Reb had been right all along. He should have listened to her. Then a cold rage filled him, mixed with the realization that Oliver was a deadly enemy who would stop at nothing to get what he wanted.

"Why? Why, Colt?"

"He didn't say, full out. He had plans for the land. When they worked out I could be a boss working for some mine somewhere. There was some connection to the railroad. It didn't all make sense. I wanted to do it. Eileen would love to leave this life behind. But I can't ambush them women, Carrick."

"Colt, I don't understand. You been drinkin' too much? How does getting rid of them give him the land?"

"He has a paper. Paper's supposed to be found with them saying they signed their land over to him. He told me that it was legal so that no one—not even you—could lay claim to the land once he had that paper and they were out of the way. Carrick, you got to do something and you got to keep this a secret. Oliver is meaner than the worst snake. He's got ambition, and nothing is going to stop him. The man's driven like I've never seen him before. He'll do anything!"

Reb was clearly vexed with Carrick as she and Jessie saddled their horses and prepared to leave. He understood her feelings. They had had fragments of conversation all morning where he would stop and walk away. Every time he tried to figure out how to tell them women what Colt told him, it sounded like the word of a man who was a half step from a thief making wild claims about someone Jess Lewis wanted to marry. If he told them the entire plot and they ignored him and told Oliver, Ramsay could get hurt. If Colt was right, the women could get hurt. He thought about just telling Reb, but then she'd be on fire to do something that might get her hurt. He saddled Beast on the pretext that he and the horse needed exercise after his long rest. He dawdled a while so that whoever was waiting on the trail would have to wait. Impatient bushwhackers might ruin their own plans.

"Are you ready, Carrick?" Reb snapped. He thought of Colt's words. His woman? She was hers, and hers alone.

"Got your rifle? Got a spare handgun if you need it?"

"Got my head on, too," she snapped. "Think I never rode off my land before you got here, Carrick? Either get going or stay behind!"

He rode slowly. It hurt more than he thought. The rocking and pitching that were part of riding had been such a part of life he never felt it. Until now. Even Jessie seemed irritated by his pace, but unlike her niece she kept whatever irritation she had to herself.

Carrick knew of three places along the trail by the creek that were likely ambush places. Other places were either too open or near ranches or too close to Lincoln Springs. Two were near the ranch. The third was about two-thirds of the way. The first two were empty. Carrick was feeling the pain in his side and his gut. Then he smelled a faint trace of tobacco along with the scent of pine. He had worked out his plan along the way. The trail curved here. Since Reb led the way, he tagged a little farther behind Jessie than he had earlier until there was a sizeable gap. The women were accustomed to him falling back and didn't slow down for him. Anyone watching the women come around the curl in the trail would assume they were alone. He was guessing that they would talk first, lull the women into a false sense of security so that Reb's legendary hair-trigger temper would not be aroused. With Reb's reputation with guns, a hired bushwhacker might try to shoot first, but he was gambling it was Oliver waiting for the women. Oliver never did a straight-up thing in his life. He would try to fool the women one last time. At least Carrick hoped so.

Carrick lifted the .45 from his holster and spun the cylinder. Ready. Voices!

He slapped Beast on the rump. The horse galloped around the corner. Francis Oliver's face reflected a series of emotions— none pleasant. Shock and anger were the ones that registered the most. Four grim-faced men were behind him. Jessie's half-smile seemed frozen on her face as she watched Oliver's metamorphosis. Reb, born ready for a scrap, had her rifle from its scabbard the minute Carrick's entrance turned a happy greeting between Oliver and her Aunt Jess into a suspicious confrontation. Carrick stopped next to Jessie Lewis, a fact Oliver clearly resented from the look on his face. Jessie's face was about the shade of a thundercloud.

"Carrick."

"Oliver."

"Problem, son?"

"You tell me."

"I'm riding back to the ranch. Saw the ladies. Thought I would stop to say hello. Not a law against that, is there?"

"No law against shooting a man like you, either." He pulled his gun and pointed it at Oliver. "Man who writes letters. Man who lets other folks do his dirty work. Man who makes plans to waylay women."

Jessie's face now turned red. She whipped around, glaring fiercely at Carrick to put him in his place.

"Don't." Reb's rifle was aimed at one rider behind Oliver whose hand had been inching toward his gun. The hand stopped. Oliver's face grew redder.

"I demand to know what is going on!" Jessie exclaimed. "Carrick, have you lost your mind? Reb, put the gun down. I was at the Lazy F for several days and if anyone wished me harm they could have done it then!"

"Everyone knew you were there, Jess. If something happened,

153

Oliver would have been responsible. But what happens if a bunch of Oliver's riders say the boss was on the ranch when you were bushwhacked on your ride here today?"

Carrick turned away from Jessie and pushed his horse between her and Oliver.

"Want to tell her, Oliver? Want to tell her you figured a woman who could fight back against the whole range would be defenseless when you asked her to marry you? Want to tell her you're no better than Jackson Jones, only a lot sneakier?"

"Carrick, I heard you were shot. Your wound is ailing you," Oliver replied.

"Cover me," he told Reb. He nudged closer to Oliver, but kept his voice loud enough for the women to hear. "You ride well armed, Oliver."

"A man can't be too careful."

"Carrying anything interesting? Let me see." Carrick reached out a hand. Oliver backed away. Carrick cocked back the hammer of his gun.

"Last warning, cowboys," Reb called as her rifle fired over the heads of the restive Lazy F riders, who were held in check by two armed antagonists. "Carrick, I don't know your play but it better be good."

Carrick stared Oliver in the eyes; the man stared back with the grim determination of a desperate man who had been outplayed at his own game. Carrick reached toward Oliver's jacket.

"I am going to kill you, Carrick," Oliver hissed in a low voice. "You will regret this for whatever time you have left to live. All of you will!"

"You're gonna die tryin', Oliver, so I hope you try real soon." Carrick pulled Oliver's jacket open and extracted a paper from the inside pocket. He looked down and scanned it quickly. "Reb, kill this one first if he blinks the wrong way."

"Bein' shot maybe made you talk sense for once," she replied. "I thought you'd never come 'round to my way of thinkin'."

Carrick regretted the next step, but it had to be done. He handed the paper to Jessie Lewis. "Look at that, ma'am."

The document, which already had the signatures of Rebecca and Jessie Lewis upon it, stated they gave all rights to their land to Francis Oliver in consideration of the upcoming marriage between Oliver and Jessie Lewis. It was witnessed by a few Lazy F hands, or so it said. They had already either signed it or made their marks. It was dated that day. The forged document gave the impression that it was the document Reb and Jessie were en route to sign, but gave a very different outcome from anything the women had been planning.

"Francis, what is the meaning of this?" Jessie asked, as though she were the school teacher scolding an errant pupil. She waved the paper in the air. He said nothing. She leaned closer and waved the paper under his face. Silence lengthened. "Francis, I demand an explanation! This is not the paper we agreed upon. This is some kind of a fraud! How can it have my signature when I never saw this until now and it is not what we agreed upon, but the opposite? I want an explanation because I know what this looks like!"

The man was cornered. "Die an old maid then and lose your ranch, too!" Oliver roared. He turned his horse. "Your day will come, Carrick, and, when it does, you will deserve it!" Carrick backed away, ready for the man to pull a gun; hoping that he would. Instead, he galloped away. His men followed.

Carrick, Reb, and Jessie dismounted in a nearby grove of trees. When the wave of tears had stopped, Jessie Lewis demanded to know everything, with Reb echoing every word. Carrick told them the story, leaving out Ramsay's name.

"Didn't know how to explain it, Jess. Didn't think you'd listen."

"We were going to be married," she insisted. "I . . . I was certain there was something more than the land that he wanted! Oh, I am such a fool. Carrick, I don't understand. Why? Why, in God's name? He was going to be my husband; he could have used the range for grazing in any way he wanted."

"Ma'am, you were on your way to town to sign an agreement that he was going to sign as well. I read what Reb wrote, and that paper would have given Reb control over the land. Once that was signed, there would be no chance for him to control that land as long as Reb was alive. Must be something other than a place to graze his livestock that's driving him. He doesn't want to use it; he wants to own it. If he married you, as your husband he would control the land no matter what you wanted. But that paper with Reb's name on it knocked that deal apart. I guess this was what he thought of next. I don't know why. With Jones gone, there's no Double J pushing him. I can't figure his game, Jessie, but I'm sorry about it."

"There is no fool like an old one," she said, shaking her head. "I don't believe it. I thought . . . He made it seem so real." Another stream of tears followed.

"Ma'am, he fooled me and you. Only one of us never got fooled." He nodded at Reb. "If she hadn't been so all-fired stubborn, among other things, we might have found out too late what he was planning."

"I wish I was wrong, Aunt Jess," Reb said. "Now I want to shoot that weasel more than ever."

Carrick mounted up, scanned the road for other travelers, and then was back, urging them to move. "Ladies, I think we better move along. Oliver had five riders with him. There's three of us. I think we need to get back to the ranch and start preparing for trouble. I'm not sure how Oliver is going to take this, but I know we have to be ready for anything. I been bracin' for a war with Double J, but, as of right now, the biggest enemy we have is Lazy F."

Hoofbeats pounded into the Bar C yard even though it was hours before dawn. "Carrick!" The shaky notes of a woman in fear. "Carrick!"

Reb, whose turn it was on watch, opened the door for Eileen Ramsay. "He's here; we sleep in shifts these days. What's wrong?"

"He has to save Colton. Francis Oliver and a bunch of Lazy F riders calling themselves vigilantes took him. They went to Lincoln Springs to hang him!"

"Hang who?"

"Colton!" shouted Eileen, running over to the groggy Carrick who had been sleeping on the floor by the door and was awakened by the voices. In the two weeks since their run-in with Oliver, he had had little more than cat naps.

Lazy F had come to their place with about twenty riders, she said. They claimed they had proof Colton had rustled beef and stolen horses. With the circuit judge in town, they went to get him convicted and hung.

"Can't you do something? You and he were friends. Rory, you have to help me." Reb noticed the way the woman touched Carrick close, like they had been very close at one time. Carrick had never mentioned her. Then again, Carrick never said much about anything. She kept her thoughts to herself as Carrick mounted, leaving Eileen in Reb's care.

"I got to get my kids," she said. "Don't trust those men."

"I'll go with you," Reb said. "We'll be here when you bring Ramsay back, Carrick. Get goin'."

Morning had broken on the trail. Lincoln Springs looked empty, until Carrick saw the crowd by what had to be the town's hanging tree.

Firing his gun twice to scatter the crowd, Carrick rode into the mass of townsfolk. Hands behind his back, resignation stamped across his face, Ramsay sat on a horse with a massive rope noose draped about his neck. The other end ran to a huge limb twelve feet off the ground.

"Let the man be," Carrick called out. The crowd stood back from the armed man on horseback.

"Can't do that, Carrick," said Sheriff Dan Hill, trudging forward. "Jury found him guilty of stealing. Judge passed sentence. Thieves hang out here. This ain't vigilantes, Carrick. It's the law. The man got caught up in this range business, grant you that, but if he had clean hands he wouldn't hang. He ain't got 'em. Stand aside."

"What did he steal?" Carrick challenged. He noticed Oliver absent from the mob. Others do his work for him, he thought.

"There were cows with the Lazy F brand butchered by his fire," said Hill. "Five horses in his corral with Double J brands. Top stock, too. He was caught dead to rights. Judge sentenced him. You goin' up against the law, Carrick? If you are, we got room on that branch for one more. Law may not be what you want, but it's the law."

Emboldened by the sheriff, the crowd moved in. Carrick noted that several well-armed riders had gathered at the back of the crowd. If he was a betting man, he would bet they were from the Lazy F. He scanned the mob looking for a weak spot, a way out.

"Rory. Rory!" Hearing his friend's voice, Carrick moved his horse closer to Ramsay.

"Colt, I got a spare rifle the other side of me. Not sure we can make it, but we can try. Sidle over so I can cut that noose off of you."

"It's over, Rory."

"Colt, I've come out of worse."

"Carrick, listen to me! It's over. We've been living on what we

158

could steal for a couple of years. I lied to you the other day. Only thing I ever did with the railroad is steal from it. A man pays for a man's mistakes, Carrick. I'll pay for mine. You want to make it right; you make sure Oliver never gets his hands on more dirt than he can hold when he lays dyin'."

"Colt! You can't give up. Eileen? Your kids?"

"Maybe folks will be kinder knowing their man died like a man, Carrick." Ramsay's voice was starting to quiver. "You take care of 'em, Carrick. I know Eileen thought about waitin' for the war to end and you to come back, and maybe that would have been best but I love the woman, Rory. I know this is gonna break her heart, but tell her I love her. Tell my kids I died like a man. Do that, Carrick!"

Carrick nodded. He wanted to fight; he wanted to stop it, but he realized his friend had crossed a line years ago. Francis Oliver waited only until Colt had refused his blood money before striking against him. For that, Oliver would pay.

Ramsay was pleading with Carrick. "The longer I wait for this Carrick, the worse it gets. They can say anything they want, but none of 'em are going to see me tremble. Got that? Now can I get this done before they tell my kids that Colton Ramsay couldn't die like a man? Carrick? Please?"

Dan Hill had sidled up near Carrick. His childhood friend's eyes were pleading with him. There was only one brand of mercy left for Colton Ramsay. Carrick raised the gun and fired four quick shots.

The horse galloped away. Its burden jumped from its back, floundered briefly, twitched, and eventually was still. The crowd, which had started to flee at the shots, pushed closer until Carrick, atop a nervous Beast, waved his gun at them.

"Easy, Carrick," said Hill. "You fight a mob at a hangin' you end up gettin' hung. Ain't what your friend wanted."

Carrick wasn't heeding the voice of caution. Beast kept back the crowd. Hill walked over to Ramsay's dangling body. He nodded at Carrick. Standing in the stirrups, Carrick cut down his friend. He laid the body over his own saddle.

"Taking my friend home," he announced to no one in particular. "Anyone got a problem, I'll accommodate you when I'm done." He turned his back. Beast plodded away.

# CHAPTER ELEVEN

The small slope behind the old Bar C house was crowded. Folks Carrick didn't know and almost everyone he did know had come to bury his friend. Eileen and the kids were there. He had dug the grave. The territory had sent a preacher to bury Jackson Jones; no one came for Colton Ramsay.

Carrick stepped forward. He had no words. The words were blasted to pieces in unslaked rage and misery. But somebody had to say something. "Son," he said looking down at the box by the hole's edge. He had made the coffin. "You were my friend. This world's a worse place without you. You don't ride off too far from the river, hear, 'cuz the rest of us will be comin' across in a little while. And, God, you didn't make 'em any better than him. Maybe he was a little wild and maybe he did things that were wrong, but he never hurt anyone and he never broke his word to a friend. Let us remember how he died, and not forget until we make it right." There was a pause. Only Reb, next to him, knew he was barely keeping his tears within. "Ashes to ashes, dust to dust. Yea though I walk through the valley of the shadow of death, thou art with me; I am the resurrection and the life. We will meet over the river. God bless, Colton. Amen."

Bad Weather had appeared. He helped Carrick lower their friend's body into the hole. Carrick grabbed a shovel, hoping no one saw the wetness in his eyes as the clods of dirt crumbled against the wood of the coffin until the job was done. Some of

161

the folks who came to bring food for the Ramsay family walked back to the Bar C house. Carrick remained at the grave alone until it was filled and the wooden cross Reb made was put by Colton's head.

"Not your fault, Carrick," Reb said when she walked over after he had adjusted the cross. Carrick had told her, now that it no longer mattered, that it was Ramsay who warned him of Oliver's plan to kill them and take the land.

"Maybe it ain't in Aunt Jess's Good Book, Reb, but there's a law that says a life for a life. It may be later than sooner, but Francis Oliver is going to pay."

Jessie Lewis insisted that Colton Ramsay's family move in with her. "That man (what she called Francis Oliver these days) had him killed because he helped you, Carrick. This is the least I owe your friend's family."

Eileen had gratefully accepted the offer. Reb was not sure she liked a woman at the ranch who was so close to Carrick, but there was nothing she could do about it. Carrick rode out to where the remnants of Ramsay's crew remained. Some had scattered the day their leader was hung.

"Got an offer," he said when they were assembled. "Me and the Lewis women gonna run Bar C until they kill us or we put Double J and Lazy F in their places. There's no safe place on this range until this ends; you got to take sides with somebody. Me and the Lewis women don't care what you did. We'd both be powerful grateful for the help, but it's your business. It's work, it don't pay much, it's dangerous, and we all might be dead in a week."

"Hard to turn it down when you say it that way," said Pete Doherty, one of the older hands. "Saddle up, boys. Bring the women and kids. Double J or Lazy F are gonna wipe us out sooner or later. Colt was a good man. Gets hard to swallow when men turn on their partners. I'm going down fighting."

In the end, nineteen riders, eight with families, rode with Carrick. Jessie and Reb watched the motley parade of horses, carts, and a few cows trundle into the farm yard. Everybody unpacked into the bunkhouse.

"Quite an army you found there, Carrick. Bet Lazy F is shaking in its boots. They gonna run when it gets tough?" Rebecca Lewis commented critically, standing next to Carrick amid the confusion.

"Probably can't fight any better than a woman," replied Carrick, staring out across the valley but not quite controlling the smile that split his scruffy beard.

Reb, glad at last that he seemed to hear something she said, moved in front of him. "Remind me again who it was got shot, cowboy?" she challenged. Their eyes locked for a moment, then with a wicked grin she turned away to show the new hands where to settle in, not looking back. A stunned Jessie watched her niece saunter away with a sashay in her walk she was certain she had never seen before.

Carrick watched her go, feeling the stirring of a tomorrow that might be a long string of todays away amid the ache of a past that was gone. He was sure that wild Wyoming wind was blowing again, the kind that blew new hope into the worst of fools.

The bulk of Easy Thompson was unmistakable as he slowly rode up to the ranch. He was a big man. He was also, Carrick knew, a big threat because of his loyalty to Double J in general and Jackson Jones in particular. Even though the vitality and energy that made Double J an imminent threat to the Lewis ranch had been sapped with the death of Jackson Jones, the outfit was still the valley's largest. Unless the widow sold the spread, sooner or later, the drive for conquest Jones had started would begin again. It was, as Carrick had realized, the law of the range.

"Miz Lewis," Easy said, tipping his hat to Jessie.

Jess Lewis smiled for the first time in days. "Mr. Thompson, you have not been on our ranch in a year and more. I'm so glad you remembered the way. You should visit more often."

"Need to talk to this man here."

"Please don't shoot him today, Mr. Thompson. A lot of work has piled up around here and he will use any excuse to shirk his share."

Easy Thompson took his hat off, threw his head back, and laughed. "If you insist, I guess I can wait until tomorrow, Miz Lewis."

"Good! Now have your talk. Men talk; women work! When you are finished talking, permit me to show you around."

Thompson looked over the Lewis ranch as Jessie wandered off toward the barn. "You settlin' in here like you were a-gonna stay."

"Happened that way. Ramsay was a friend. Family's here."

"Don't live out no more in that shack that crazy old man built by the pass?"

"Nope. Thought it wasn't proper to stay here with the women, the way gossip gets, but life changes what's necessary. The way things are on this range, there's no way I'm leavin' 'em alone. Not safe." The real reason he lived in the shack was no one's business. After whatever he did when he was shot, nightmares didn't seem like they mattered anymore. Thompson didn't need to know that, either.

"Heard about Oliver. Ran into Dan Hill the other day and he believes what you say, but Oliver denies every word and he's got witnesses say he never left the ranch that day. Shame what he did to a fine woman like Mrs. Lewis. Sorry, in a way, about your friend. He wasn't much good, but he was better than some of what killed him. Surprised it ended that way. He knew what he could get away with—understand, Carrick? Double J wasn't going to ride him down for a steer or two a year. More work than it would be worth. Surprised he ever got greedy with Lazy F."

"He didn't."

Thompson waited for elaboration. None came. "He went like a man, they tell me. Awful good of Miz Lewis to take in his family. She's a fine lady."

Carrick, who knew Ramsay's crimes were used as a pretext by Oliver because Ramsay had sided with Carrick, felt uncomfortable with the knowledge that he had a hand in his friend's death. "Easy, you didn't come here to talk about Colt. Maybe you came to tell me why someone from Double J was dumping salt in that water hole a while back? As I recall, the boss was pretty upset about it and you were nowhere to be found. I know a lot happened since then, but I never heard an explanation."

"I never ordered that!" Carrick wondered if an earthquake could approximate the sound of Easy's voice when he was angry.

"Who did?" asked Carrick quietly, trying not to rile Easy; they didn't need any more enemies than the ones they already had.

Easy Thompson looked embarrassed. "I don't know."

Carrick was not sure he heard right. "You didn't do it?"

"Carrick, use your head for something more than a place to set that hat. Neither Jackson Jones or me would have ever done anything that sneaky. Jackson Jones was a straight-up man! If he wanted you off the land, you and the ladies would have been off the land. Only one we can figure did it was Lazy F, but nobody saw Larry Gordon anywhere near Lazy F. No extra money turned up in his bedroll. Maybe Double J has spies; maybe one of the hands missed something. Now can we talk about something important?"

"Ruining a water hole is pretty important to us, Easy."

"Carrick, when I hear something, I'll tell you. We got more important business. Came to talk to you about that shack and the goings-on up at Black Wind Pass."

"What about it? I slept in it a few nights. Figger other folks use it. Looked used. Not Double J land. Not your concern."

"Tell me about it."

"Tell you what?"

"What did you find that made it look used?"

"Easy, you got a reason to ask this stuff?"

"Always have a reason. Talk without a reason is for fools, Carrick."

It was a standoff of wills. Carrick weighed his options. Double J wasn't pushing very hard lately. Easy Thompson wasn't asking anything important. So why did it seem right to be so contrary?

"Blankets, eatin' stuff. Drinkin' stuff."

"You leave it there?"

"Easy, one day I rode away from that shack expectin' to come back and I haven't gone back there since. Of course it's there. Fancy stuff, some of it. Look for yourself. If you see something you want, just take it."

"I looked. Nothin' there."

"Somebody took it, Easy. Not me. Your stuff?"

A scornful glance was all the response Carrick got. Easy Thompson stood like a mountain. The man was lost in thought. His eyes walked the ridge line at the horizon, then focused back on Carrick. "Obliged."

"Don't like mysteries, Easy."

"Lot I don't like in this valley lately, Carrick. That's a fact. Don't know I'd pay unannounced visits to many places if I was you. Weren't for the fact Dan Hill is drunk and lazy, Lazy F would have had him out here to arrest most of everyone livin' here including the livestock. Man's got a grudge. Feel sorry for

Miz Lewis not knowing what he was really after. Got to be hard on her, Carrick."

"Life's hard. What's my standing with Double J?"

"The less we see you, Carrick, the better we like you. If I knew you killed the boss, you'd be dead, Carrick. Don't matter how fast you are; don't matter nothin'. I'd get you. Some say you did it. Quite a few. It still fits like a bad boot. If I ever figger the boot fits, I'll be back and it won't be to talk."

"Mr. Thompson!"

Easy Thompson moved faster than Carrick thought possible to take off his hat in a sweeping bow as Jessie Lewis brought him coffee. A genuine smile broke across the man's face.

"If you are only going to visit once a year, you have to at least let me show you around," she said.

The smile that sprang to Easy's face transformed the man. He cut his eyes at Carrick, as though ill at ease being seen as someone other than the Double J foreman, but Jess Lewis had her hand through his arm and was pointing out where they had made changes to the ranch. She did not mention most of them were Carrick's work.

"Now, Mr. Thompson, you must tell me something."

"Anything, Mrs. Lewis."

"Jess. The whole world calls me Jess, Mr. Thompson. Do you have a name other than 'Easy'?"

She watched his face redden like a ten-year-old.

"They were Bible folks, my family, but we was too poor to have one. Named me Ephaniah Zaphaniah 'cuz they thought they was Bible names. Mouthful for a boy to say. It just became easier to be Easy, you might say." He smiled at her as though he had said a clever thing.

"Well, that mystery is solved," she said. "Now will you indulge me, Mr. Thompson?"

"Is that a pie I smell, Mrs. Lewis?"

"Jess. Yes; it might not be ready for a while, so we will have to walk a bit longer. I'm sure the valley knows all about me. What about you? What did you do before you came here?"

His face clouded. Easy Thompson knew how far down he had been when Jackson Jones plucked him from the alley in Cheyenne and gave him a place and a purpose in life.

"Rode around some." It was the best he could do. Jess Lewis understood cowboys. She wondered at times if any of them did not have a part of their lives they were ashamed of. She stopped and they looked out at the range together.

"I suppose we could see if that pie has cooled enough to eat. I could let you have Mr. Carrick's piece if you'd like."

Easy Thompson could not restrain himself; Jess Lewis was not only pretty, she was observant. "Guess I could tolerate that," he replied.

Carrick watched the two walk in companionable conversation around the ranch's yard and into the house. He could hear Easy Thompson's rumbling laugh in harmony with Jessie's low alto tones. And he wondered what bee was buzzing under Easy Thompson's worn brown hat that had to do with the shack at Black Wind Pass.

The next morning, Carrick saw the smoke. There was only one thing that close to the pass that could burn—the shack. If enough of it had burned to send a huge column of dark smoke smudging the sky it would most certainly be gone, but curiosity is a powerful itch. Carrick figured it was worth a look, at least.

He reached the remains of the shack to find the fire pretty well burned out. There was a lot of charred wood, some still smoking. There was no trace of anyone anywhere. Anyone who burned it could have left the valley through the pass. Carrick had not met any riders, but the fire was probably set around dawn. Maybe even before. He dismounted to look around. He though he smelled some kind of lamp oil, but mostly the place stunk from the smell of the old wood and whatever junk had been lying around. Some of the old wood in the wood pile was partly charred; some was too rotted to burn. There hadn't been much stuff in the shack to begin with and most of what there had been was now gone. It was another fool's errand.

He looked up as hoofbeats resounded from a rider coming hard across the valley. His heart sank. It was Easy Thompson, riding hard. Easy had clearly seen Carrick from the way he was looking up at the shack. There was no way to avoid him now. Carrick found a rock a ways from the ruined shack to wait. He stood up when Easy arrived only to find the big man pointing a gun at him.

"Easy, what are you doing?"

"Thought you were square, Carrick. Maybe. Them ladies seem to cotton to you, but you fooled them like that Oliver fooled them."

Carrick cringed. He could smell the liquor from several feet away. Anger and alcohol. Never good when they mixed. "Easy, what are you talking about? I lived here half the time when I was a kid. I saw the smoke from the house and came looking."

"That doesn't square, Carrick. I asked you yesterday about this place, and today it burns. You were the only person off of Double J who knew I was curious about the goings-on up here. I know where the hands were yesterday and today and it wasn't one of them."

"Easy, there are probably all kinds of people who come up here. Somebody probably got drunk and careless and started a fire by accident. Old dry wood, it wouldn't take much." Especially, thought Carrick, if that oil he smelled was splashed a few places to help a fire along. That was not a thought to share with a man who was already angry, smelled like he had had a few drinks from a bottle of something cheap and powerful, and,

169

worse yet, was aiming a gun at him.

"What did you have to hide, Carrick? What were you up to? What did this shack have to do with the boss? Tell me or I will shoot you here and now."

"Easy, I did not shoot Jackson Jones, and I did not burn down this old shack. Ask the women where I was last night. I was at the old Bar C."

"Jessie Lewis is too honest a woman to understand she's been deceived again, and you probably got that little one fooled," Easy replied. "Talk or die."

"Easy!" Carrick felt rising panic. Easy was like a train accelerating down the track and Carrick had no idea how to stop him short of taking a bullet. "Easy, I didn't do anything to anyone. Why don't we ride to Bar C and talk this out?"

Easy Thompson had lived his life by the simple code of faithfulness and loyalty. He knew other men were smarter, and other men were better at many things. As he watched Carrick insist upon his innocence, he could see the face of Jackson Jones, lying still in death, and the closeness of Carrick and Lucinda Jones when he had told her of her husband's murder. "We don't ride nowhere, Carrick," Easy said. "You pay now."

Easy clicked back the hammer of the gun. "You deceived me. You deceived Jackson Jones. Not even gonna waste rope hangin' you."

Carrick saw the death sentence clear in Easy's eyes. He feinted running to his left and then dove for Easy Thompson's legs. Easy had half expected the man would run, but when Carrick came straight at him, he was slow in reacting. Carrick felt the heat of the gun's barrel over his shoulder as the explosion above his right ear left him deaf to anything but the sound of his own pounding pulse. He reached for Easy Thompson's gun, but Easy swung it and slammed Carrick's hand away. He swung it back and caught Carrick on the left cheek. The blood dripped down. Carrick got two hands around Easy's gun hand, but Easy had one hand free to push Carrick off of him. Easy shoved hard and Carrick felt himself falling. He rolled on the rocks. The muzzle of Easy Thompson's gun followed him. Then it fired.

Rebecca Lewis had been certain there was gunfire, but she had been in the barn and could not be sure of its origin. She was on edge again. The fire was a bad sign, even if Carrick said it might be an accident. She looked toward the pass.

"Aunt Jess, look!" Two horses were coming down the trail that led to Black Wind Pass. Both had riders slumped in their saddles. The men were silhouettes against the sky, but the gray horse was clearly Carrick's; the other, the chestnut stallion that was one of the few horses on the range big enough for Easy Thompson to sit comfortably.

"Aunt Jess, somebody's coming and they're hurt!" Reb yelled as she ran toward the horses, which were coming at a walk.

Carrick's face was bloody, and there was blood all over his shirt. He was reeling in the saddle as she came near. "Carrick, what happened?"

"Easy's hurt," he gasped. "Shot in the leg. We'll live."

"What happened?"

"You got to bandage Easy, first. Move, girl. I only got a cut; he's hurt."

Reb reached up to yank the reins of Easy's horse from Carrick's hand. Reb walked the horse fast, careful not to bounce Easy out of the saddle.

Jessie Lewis sputtered as they approached. The two women struggled to lift Easy out of the saddle and then half-walk, half-haul him into the house. There was a huge purple bruise by his jaw that looked as though he had been hit with the butt of a gun. The gunshot wound in his leg was high up on the outside of his left thigh, almost as though he had shot himself. It was relatively shallow and had missed doing major damage. The bullet had passed through. All that remained was a hole, and a long time of painful hobbling before he could walk without a limp. The women worked on Easy. It was moments before Reb realized Carrick had not followed them.

He was walking toward the door, staggering slightly. His head and shirt were soaked. There did not appear to be fresh blood on his face, but Reb could see a raw mark where a bullet had missed his right eye. A massive bruise discolored the left side of his face.

"How's Easy?"

"Shot in the leg. Aunt Jess is bandaging it. He'll hurt but he'll live." She had to repeat it twice for him. "Why do you care so almighty much how he is after you shot him, Carrick?"

"Didn't want to. He didn't give me a choice. His gun went off by my ear. Sound is kinda hollow. He's gonna be all right?"

She nodded.

Carrick plunked down on the porch of the house and stared at the hills. It had been close. Too close. For both of them.

"He's all set, Reb," came Jessie's voice as she emerged from the house. "Carrick! What on earth happened?"

He explained. Talking hurt and it echoed in his ears.

"Fool men!" Jessie Lewis said when he was done. "Always ready to shoot each other. I should give both of you a piece of my mind."

Reb, with whom Aunt Jess had shared more than a few pieces of her mind over the years, smiled at the picture in her mind of two bandaged, bleeding cowboys on the receiving end of a scolding from Aunt Jess. "And what are you smiling about, young lady? Help me get the wagon hitched so I can take Mr. Thompson home after he wakes up. It is a miracle any work ever gets done here with all of the shenanigans going on."

The liquor-fueled fever of righteous anger that had been

driving Easy Thompson up at the shack had cooled by the time he woke up with Jessie Lewis glowering down at him. It grew even colder as she delivered the promised scolding to both Carrick and Easy, with Reb maintaining a discreet distance and turning away to hide her smirks.

"Easy," said Carrick when Jessie had ended her summation regarding the juvenile nature of men who shot each other rather than talk calmly, "whatever you think I did, I did not do it. I could swear to you on a Bible, on my mother's grave, or anything you want. I did not kill your boss. I do not know why someone shot him. It wasn't me. I didn't come here to this valley to do anything but see my home. If it wasn't me, and it wasn't Oliver, maybe it was one of these syndicate things Jackson Jones was talking about. Way I hear it, he killed one of their fellas last year. Maybe somebody wanted to teach ranchers a lesson. I don't know, Easy. I don't. I promise you I'm going to find out."

From the look of doubt on his face, Easy was clearly still suspicious of Carrick but he was also squirming under Jessie's glare. "Carrick, you say one thing, but it don't always look that way. Double J is my life, whether the boss is alive or dead. I . . . I know Jessie here and her niece say you don't potshoot people, but you killed enough folks by now that I know they don't know you all the way through. Best I can tell you is that I won't come after you until I get me the kind of proof that will stand up in that circuit judge's court. Maybe it don't exist. Maybe you didn't do it and don't know anything. But until I know for certain sure who killed the boss, I'm going to suspect everybody."

There was a silence in the room. Easy's eyes met Jessie's stare. "No, not every last person, Jessie. I hope for your sake and his he didn't do it, but, if he didn't Jessie, I don't rightly know who would other than Francis Oliver and he's too much a weasel to even think on it. Carrick doesn't look or act like an innocent man to me."

Jessie took the wagon and drove it to Double J. Easy Thompson was not willing to let a woman drive him home, but after a long lecture about preventing further bleeding, he surrendered. Carrick offered to ride behind to be sure Double J didn't retaliate, but one glare from Jessie and a reminder from Easy that Double J didn't act without his orders ended that.

"You been quiet, Carrick," Reb said after the wagon left as they stood in the ranch's yard. "Your head still hurt or are you thinking?"

"Easy was after something. Got more questions than answers, Reb. Maybe Lincoln Springs has the answers. So far, we been lucky . . ."

"Call this luck?" she said, waving her arms at his bloody clothing and all of the families and men behind her from Colton Ramsay's hideout.

"We been lucky," he stressed. "Lazy F went for Ramsay. If he hadn't come here that time, it would have been all over for us. Double J barked more than it bit. Hate to say it, but whoever killed Jones bought this ranch some time. What happens when they decide to come after us? It was one thing when Jackson Jones was grabbing for more. He was sure you would fail, and wanted to grab the land first, but he wasn't going to push too hard to make happen what he was sure would happen anyhow. Now that it looks like you might be around a while, what happens if someone decides to speed up things a mite? And if they could use the law to hang Colt Ramsay, what happens if the law comes after you out here? Easy Thompson is a popular man. I had better square this with Dan Hill before someone else makes it look like what it wasn't."

"Dan's lazy," she said. "He'll never come out here to see what went on."

"We have to clear it with the sheriff. Dan'll bless vigilantes if two ranches want him to," he replied. "I know town's a risk, but it's a risk we have to take."

She nodded. It made sense. It was still a risk. She knew better than Carrick how much the town relied on Double J for business, and how Dan Hill was Double J's man. Setting up an ambush—even in the motley collection of buildings that comprised Lincoln Springs—would be simple. She could not shake the thought that this could be the last time she saw him.

"Carrick," she said, not knowing how much emotion was in that one word. He stopped and looked back over his right shoulder. "Did a good job of sewing on you. Don't really like sewin' much. Don't ruin all my work by stopping another bullet."

"Don't plan to. Appreciate the concern. Could buy you more thread if you want it."

"You know what I mean, cowboy. Come back in one piece. I figure all this excitement's good for Aunt Jess. Only reason you stay on."

He walked back closer. "And what about you?"

"What about me?"

He was now so close the brim of his hat was almost shading her face. "You got any thoughts on the subject of me, or you still spend your dreaming time sighting me down the barrel of your rifle?"

What happened next was a surprise to even her. She put two arms around his neck and leaned up—the heels made it easy—and kissed him hard on the mouth. He rocked back on his heels for a second, but not much longer. Two arms wrapped around her tightly, expelling breath from her mouth into his own. He held tighter and kissed her back.

How long they were like that, she did not know. There was a windy glorious freedom and feeling of strength flowing through

175

her. There was power and joy and happiness and redemption in that one kiss.

Then it hit her that they were in the full view of everyone seeing every last thing she did. She realized that gasping and kissing did not work well in the same minute, and pulled her head away, noticing that no one was staring, which meant everyone was doing so. She moved her head back, and he did the same. She took her arms away slowly. He released her but kept his hands on her waist. She stepped back, out of his arms, breathing faster. She flicked her hair and it felt wild and free. His eyes were glittering.

She wanted to laugh and cry and put a fist in the air and dance on the nearest table and run off to the hills. Oh, it was good to be alive! For the first time in forever, it was good to breathe and feel and see. She could feel the grin on her face and she knew it was wicked and the grin refused to quit. And it didn't matter if Double J and Lazy F and every Indian west of the Mississippi descended upon the old Bar C right about then. She stepped back into his arms.

Jess Lewis was more than a little concerned as she drove the wagon over the rough track to Double J. One reason Double J grew so powerful was that Easy Thompson's personality blunted many of the rough edges of Jackson Jones. She could not imagine what would make the man snap and want to shoot Carrick, although Carrick seemed to have the ability to find trouble on a sunny day.

She took a quick look back. Easy was piled against some sacks of feed. Not very comfortable, but he would get there. His horse was tied to the wagon behind. She was wishing as she drove the team that the valley could be what it had been when the war was on. For all the hard times, people were not at each other's throats. Everything was different now. Reb had been a

176

playful girl, but now she was fierce, ready to fight anyone who posed a threat to what she held most dear—that old ranch. Jess feared for her niece. Not many men appreciated a strong-minded woman. Carrick? She snorted. They would breed a race of warriors. The image of that made her laugh. She looked back again at Easy. He was stirring again. It was not much farther.

Jess had never been to Double J; she had visited the old Johnson place, but never the new ranch. She was somewhat relieved when Henry Petersen, the ranch manager, was in the yard to greet her. She had been worried how to explain to a fool cowboy how Easy got shot. Petersen seemed to understand. Although the man made Jess's skin crawl, he had never been anything but polite on the few times they had met in town. Reb had complained once that she thought he was staring at her inappropriately, but since Petersen worked for Double J, Reb was hardly an impartial source.

Petersen ordered some hands to carry Easy from the wagon. Before they did, she checked on him.

"Easy, now no more of this, you understand?"

Easy Thompson smiled amid his discomfort. "Ma'am, Miz Jessie, you give the best scoldin's ever."

"Well, I don't want to give another one, so no more getting shot, Mr. Thompson!"

"Miz Lewis, everybody else calls me Easy. It's ain't hard to say. It's easy."

"Very well, Easy," she replied. "And you can call me Jess. I suppose, since we won't be having a range war, we can start living like civilized neighbors."

"I'd like that, ma'am, um, Jessie."

Aware they were attracting a growing audience, Jess Lewis wished Easy Thompson fast healing and went to climb back onto her wagon. Petersen, who had disappeared into the ranch house while Easy was unloaded, returned. He very politely asked

Jessie in for tea, which she declined. She noticed that Lucinda Jones did not make an appearance. She assumed the widow was staring out from a window somewhere. She never was very friendly. Reb disliked her.

Petersen discussed the details of the shooting again. Jess, who was by now tired, wanted the questions over. "Mr. Petersen," she snapped, "I have told you what I know. Easy Thompson was there. Carrick was there. If you want to know what they said and did, you should be asking them. I need to get back before dark."

After refusing a Double J escort—she wondered if Reb would use them for target practice and decided not to find out—she climbed onto the seat, clucked the team into movement, and rode away from Double J with the vague impression that something was not right there, a feeling she decided was caused by nothing more than too many cowboys with guns. She needed some quiet. This was one of the few times in months she had been out on the plains alone, and she decided that, this one time, she could take a few minutes off from running a ranch that was nothing short of swimming upstream every day. Maybe she would take the long way home and look up at the sky at sunset. It had been a long time since she did anything that simple. She was overdue.

Lincoln Springs was quiet when Carrick rode in the next morning. His head still hurt, but a man lived with hurts. The way of the world. A few people were here and there, moving slowly. Dan Hill, whose attitude toward Carrick veered with the winds of the range and his opinion of whether Carrick was trying to survive or running a deep game Hill could not fathom, was less than happy to see him.

"Thought you'd want to know I shot Easy Thompson

yesterday," Carrick began when the perfunctory greetings were completed.

Hill sputtered his beer across his shirtfront.

"He ain't dead," Carrick added. "And it was his own gun that did the shootin', if that makes it better."

It didn't. "Carrick, this range wasn't perfect before you rode in but it ain't been nothin' but trouble since you got here. Why'd you do a fool thing like that? Everybody likes Easy Thompson."

Carrick explained that Easy suspected him of killing Jackson Jones. He told the lawman about the cabin and the fire. "I did the least I could, Sheriff, to stop him. He was going to shoot me if I didn't do something. Man's got a right to defend himself. Easy's not gonna die; maybe limp a while. Jess Lewis took him home."

Hill shrugged. Nothing he could do, anyhow. Everybody knew Easy had been on the prowl for revenge and there were more than a few folks who saw Carrick's arrival and Jones's death as too close to be coincidental.

"OK, Son," Hill said at last. "But don't expect me to play hero if your friends at Double J and your friends at Lazy F pay you a visit one night. Wouldn't take much to rile a mob into thinking they were vigilantes because of that stunt you pulled at Ramsay's hanging and his gang living at the ladies' ranch. Folks wonder if you and your old friend had something in mind. Way the townsfolk see it, you're the reason for the gunplay and the fighting. I hope that Double J and Lazy F and the ladies figure everything out and all you fools put the guns away when you ride in here. Now let me have my beer. An old man deserves one quiet minute in the morning to have a glass of beer."

Carrick left the saloon. The quiet on the street was even deeper than when he rode in. Not a soul to be seen. Carrick's pulse raced. He'd seen streets this empty before, and always for the same reason. He was walking out into some kind of a trap that no one in Lincoln Springs thought he should be warned about.

In the shadows by the dry goods store, watching every step Carrick took, stood a man who could only be Gordon Crowley, still with a bandage on his head. Crowley realized there was no further point in waiting now that he had been seen. He moved forward to stand in the light. There was a shotgun in his hands.

Dan Hill had emerged from the saloon. He looked at Crowley. Shook his head. "Good Book says you reap what you sow, Carrick. Don't tell me I didn't warn you to keep ridin'." The doors swung as he walked back through them, giving the doorway to onlookers as the word spread.

Behind Carrick, boots scraped on wood as boys and men pushed to find places for a good view. Crowley held the weapon with his right hand on the trigger, the barrels in his left. Twenty yards. Too far. Carrick knew he might hit Crowley. He might hit a kid watching. No! Abilene was the past. He focused on the man wanting him dead. Patience, he thought. Patience. The Crowleys had been bullies and brawlers. Standing alone in a street required a whole different brand of sand in a man. Carrick started walking. Slowly.

"You killed my brothers, Carrick." Some men had to talk. Carrick hated talk. Since Abilene, he also hated what was going to happen next.

"They pushed it, Gordon. Didn't have to be that way then. Don't have to be this way now. There's been enough of this. Put the gun down." Thirty feet. Crowley shifted position, Carrick stopped.

"Heard you killed Jackson Jones, too. Man hired us when no one else would. Man didn't deserve to be shot down like that."

"Didn't kill him." Carrick had no time for chatter. He was fifteen feet from Crowley. It would do. When a six-gun faced a shotgun, the six-gun had to fire first. Crowley was not a gunman. He would need to take the time to aim. Carrick hoped so.

"You been ridin' with rustlers and thieves," Crowley called out. "Country's overrun with them now; even them ladies' ranch is a hole for outlaws. You're never gonna do anyone's dirty work again. I'm gonna save the town a hangin'."

Sweat dripped. Nothing moved except a horsefly. Any second. Carrick saw the gun was cocked. The hammers were visible. He would have no time at all. He had to shoot first. Crowley's facial muscles showed tension. Maybe fear.

Crowley was raising the shotgun to his shoulder when Carrick's first bullet hit the man's hip. He staggered. The second bullet clanged off the barrels of the gun. The third was dead center.

Carrick's legs smarted from the rocks kicked up as the shotgun slugs plowed into the hard-packed dirt of the street, where they would be dug up for souvenirs by the kids. He walked rapidly through the cloud of dust to Gordon Crowley. Crowley was dying fast. Carrick felt that hollow feeling again.

Dan Hill had emerged from the saloon. Carrick turned his wrath on him. "You happy now, Sheriff? You knew he was in town! I'm sure someone told the sheriff! You could have disarmed that man. He would have listened to you. He didn't have to do this. I couldn't let him kill me. You know I don't run."

"Crowleys lived by some hard rules, Carrick. Maybe I could have stopped it today, but it was gonna happen. Warned you that the man was going to be primed for you. Don't think it's over, even now, Carrick. You and Lazy F and Double J solve your problems outside of town. Or next time you show up, I'll clap you in jail—all of you, any of you—and find a reason later. Not lettin' you start a range war to bring back your old spread and I'm tired of buryin' folks every last day of the week."

"Never wanted it, Sheriff, but I'm not gonna let two women

be pushed off their land. Maybe the law here isn't about right and wrong; maybe it got sold to the highest bidder; but I didn't kill nobody that didn't ask for it."

Hill's face was flushed. He stepped down toward Carrick with his hand on the butt of his gun. "You better go, Carrick. You got no claim to talk to me that way. Law doesn't always come down on the side you want it, but it's not here to help you when you want it and not when you ignore it. Saddle up and go."

Carrick unhitched Beast and rode out of town. The crowd around Crowley had grown now that the showdown between Carrick and the sheriff had ended. No one looked him in the eye. He would be condemned for the killing as he would have been equally condemned for running.

Carrick knew he'd been unfair to Hill. He knew that killing Crowley was necessary and was probably better happening in town than anywhere else. If the man didn't brace him face to face, he would have been sniping in the hills. Jackson Jones was proof that when a man wanted you, he could get you. The murder still disturbed his thoughts. Lazy F's way wasn't that direct; he bet his bottom nickel Oliver was basically a coward. If Lazy F was suspected of killing Jones, Easy Thompson would not have been going after Carrick. He would have been focused on Lazy F. But who else would want Jones dead? Carrick had been hoping the rancher was going to find a way to work things out with Reb and Jessie. They didn't want the man dead. Jones had raved about cleaning out Ramsay's crew in the broken lands, but Ramsay didn't have the kind of killer instinct to strike first and strike hard. Something was troubling Easy Thompson about the cabin. Easy had assumed that Carrick had burned it to keep Easy from finding something out. Maybe it was time for another look.

# CHAPTER TWELVE

There was still a shimmer of heat radiating off of the blackened pile that once had been Crazy Charlie's shack. Even with gloves on Carrick all but singed his hands searching. As he swatted aside the remains of the walls, he looked for something in the pile of ruined wood.

Nothing.

Then he saw where the chimney had knocked the floorboards to pieces. Hoping nothing more would fall, he crawled on the wood after clearing away debris, covering himself in soot. He reached through the boards—which were charred on the top but still more or less solid—for something. Anything. Mostly he found rocks. Some dirt. The pass was uneven there; that's why the floor was built. A piece of floor gave way under him. Carrick decided against rolling down the hill amid the shack's ruins.

He took a close look around the shack. Carrick looked further, down the hill from the smoking ruin. Sunlight glinted on metal. A fancy cuff link, the kind rich men wore for their fancy shirts with thick, heavy, white starched cuffs, was lying in the tall grass by the edge of the small landslide of dirt that slid downhill when the shack burned and crumbled. It had fancy initials that Carrick could not read. He couldn't see *JJ* in them. Nor *FO*. As for Crazy Charlie, he barely had shirts, let alone jewelry. Somebody who took off his jewelry had been up here— somebody who was fancy enough to have Eastern affectations in the way he dressed. Carrick stuck the link in his pocket and continued looking. He found a long pin, the kind ladies wore to keep their hats perched at the odd angles. It was heavy, and looked like solid gold. His fingers could feel some kind of lines carved into the metal, but he could not read any letters. He pocketed that as well.

The shack had never had a lock. The door barely worked. Anyone who wanted something hidden there would probably not have put it where any passersby could find it. If someone was using the shack for a meeting place, and they left things there that had not been destroyed, there was only one place left to look—the woodpile.

About five rows of wood from the top, tucked in the back were bottles of wine. Wine was pretty scarce on the Wyoming range. It was the fancy drink for fancy ladies and cultured men. Fancy ladies? Lucinda Jones was a fancy woman married to a man who was a slave to his dreams of an empire on the range. She was also at least ten years younger than her deceased husband. He recalled Easy Thompson's flare of suspicion when he found Carrick with Lucinda. Lucinda would not be the first woman who found someone else's companionship a substitute if her husband ignored her. Who would drink wine with her? Francis Oliver? Carrick thought he was a whiskey man, but perhaps he would have tried to wound Jones in the most personal ways possible. The shack was not that far from either ranch, so it was possible.

Carrick wanted answers. He needed to find out who drank wine with French labels. And maybe—if Carrick's reputation was as sinister as Dan Hill painted—he could use that to his advantage to force that whiny clerk Godfrey to tell him if anyone in Buffalo Horn Valley had bought cuff links.

Carrick did not want a showdown with Dan Hill. The sheriff was backed into a corner, and thought Carrick was responsible.

He hitched his horse at the end of Lincoln Springs's main street and took side alleys to the mercantile.

Godfrey insisted that the cuff link came from a St. Louis store, or maybe a fancy place in Denver, but that they were nothing he had ever sold. "Only people who wear starched cuffs use those," he explained to Carrick. "This is Wyoming. Not even Jackson Jones starched his cuffs." When asked if he sold wine, he volunteered that only two crates had ever arrived to Lincoln Springs in the past five years—one for Lazy F and one for Double J. Carrick was no closer to an answer. Godfrey did say that Francis Oliver had mentioned buying fancy items lately but had never purchased anything.

Carrick recalled Lazy F. Oliver would never wear anything fancy; he liked to dress like one of the men. There was nothing fancy he ever saw at the ranch.

"When did he talk about buying this stuff? The other day when he was marrying Jessie Lewis?"

"Long before that," Godfrey said. "He came in and said he had good news; he had been to a meeting that changed his life. At first I thought he meant the tent revival had come through, because my wife likes to go, but he laughed and said that treasures in Heaven were nothing compared to what was right underfoot. I didn't understand it, but I do not question my customers."

Godfrey either could not or would not add to that, leaving Carrick mystified.

He walked the street, looking at the signs. Nothing that stood out. Saloons, the barber shop, a few stores that sold dry goods, guns, saddles, and the like. A tiny one selling fancy dresses. He walked past one before he realized it—the sign read, "Union Pacific."

The railroad was nowhere near Lincoln Springs. Carrick had picked up all kinds of talk around the range, but nothing that said the railroad was coming through any time soon. It was something every rancher wanted, and every town schemed for, but Lincoln Springs seemed too remote.

He walked into the office. It consisted of a desk, a table, and a few chairs. A bored-looking young clerk sat at the desk. He gave Carrick a cursory glance that was not in Carrick's favor.

"Do you have an appointment?"

"I'm curious," said Carrick. "Why would the railroad have an office here when there's no line?"

"The Union Pacific is the greatest transportation artery in the world . . ." began the man.

"I didn't ask for a speech," said Carrick, stepping closer to loom over the man in his chair. "I want an answer."

The clerk looked up at the man he was facing. Carrick had unconsciously drifted his hand near his gun. He looked like what he was—a man more used to the saddle than the indoors and a man who was accustomed to settling disputes with violence. The clerk decided quickly that whatever the man wanted, he could have it.

"The railroad buys supplies, mister. There are a lot of ranches around here that sell us supplies."

It made some sense, but not much. Carrick looked at a vacant desk covered with papers and maps. The top one caught his eye. It was a map of the valley, with a lot of shading in the central and western parts–some of it covered lands occupied by the Lewis women and some of it was the land where Colt Ramsay's crew had lived.

"What's that?" he asked.

"It's a map," the clerk replied.

Carrick's fragile temper snapped. He grabbed the man's shoulder. "A map of what?" he snarled.

"Coal. Men came through a while back to take samples. There's coal all through that valley. The map is pretty much where the most of it is. The railroad is *negotiating*," the clerk stressed the word as though it somehow was important "with a major ranch owner to open up a mine there that would provide coal for the Union Pacific. Because property records here in Wyoming are so informal, the owner is in the process of clearing title to the land, proof that any court in the United States will accept, without which, of course, the Union Pacific cannot enter into a binding agreement."

"Who is the owner?"

"I'm sorry, sir, but business deals are confidential . . ."

"That's my range, mister, and nobody is digging it up for coal while I can run one cow or one horse on the land above it. Now who is telling you he can let you turn that range into a mine?" The clerk stammered. Carrick's hand was now tightly gripping the butt of his gun, a fact not lost on the clerk. "Who?"

"The man's name is Francis Oliver," said the clerk. "He will sell us all of the land he owns, but we won't take it all for the mine. We will work with the ranchers in the valley, because we know they supply beef for our camps and trains. You should welcome progress and not fight against it. Mr. Oliver has been very accommodating. The Union Pacific was approached by this man months ago when he said he was sure there was coal on his land. If there is a problem in . . ." he squinted at the map ". . . the Buffalo Horn Valley, it has nothing to do with the railroad. We need coal and we will buy from those who can provide it. We have an agreement with Mr. Oliver that is good until the end of the month. If there is something you wish to discuss, I suggest you talk to him. That was the advice I gave the other man."

"What other man?"

"A much nicer and more polite gentleman," the clerk replied. "He was about your height, clean-shaven, and dressed nicely. He was asking about the kinds of deposits in the area. I think he was thinking about mining for iron, but I told him that the railroad has a very strong market for coal and that it would be very much to his advantage to supply us with it. He thanked me very much for my time. I did not see him again. That was, oh, perhaps a month ago. It was before Mr. Oliver's agreement was prepared, but after our surveyors conducted their expedition to the valley."

Carrick roughly thanked the man for the information and left. He wondered about the identity of the "other man." Was there someone in town who was speculating in land? One of these syndicates Jones had mentioned? It was possible. He tried to think of the men he had met in the valley. No one came to mind as a match.

Coal! Oliver didn't care about the range; he wanted to get rich in coal. Carrick guessed Oliver wanted title to the range; then he could either own a mine or sell the land to one of those syndicates. That made sense. If he did that, he would not care what the range said about him after he was gone. Carrick thought back. Oliver had known for months about the coal; he probably had lied to the railroad men who took samples that it was his range. That's why he was trying so hard to grab the old Bar C range. He could try all he wanted, but, as long as Carrick was alive, and Reb was Reb, he'd never get it.

Ranch life resumed what could have been normal except Carrick knew storms were brewing. The new hands didn't mind work; Jess liked having a crew. Carrick tried telling Jess about Oliver's plans for the land but she started crying when he mentioned Oliver's name, then said a bunch of words ladies don't usually say. He didn't bring it up again. When it was over they could figure out what to do with the coal that could make the ladies rich. First, they had to protect it, something Carrick had grimly promised himself he would do, no matter what it cost.

Jessie noticed a change in Carrick since the death of his friend. He spent more time with the widow and her children. He had carved toy horses and cows for them. They played roundup with the toys. At night, Carrick often went to the bunkhouse where all the families were living to tuck the children in. One day she commented on it to Reb.

"As if he doesn't have enough things to do!" the younger woman shot back. Jess did not raise the subject again.

When Carrick was sleepy one morning after staying up through the night when one of the Ramsay children was ill, Reb had lost her temper. "Them kids are her business, not yours. Her kids always need something. Why are you the one that has to be there for 'em?" All she got by way of a reply was a mumble.

One morning when Carrick had ridden to the south pasture to check with Randy on the cattle, Eileen Ramsay and Reb all but collided in the ranch house kitchen. Reb felt sorry for the woman, but, from what she could see, Eileen was trying to put a rope around a horse that already had another brand. She grumbled a greeting and hurried to finish her coffee so that she could get her own work done.

"Rebecca?" Reb stopped. The woman must need something. Her kids always needed something. "When are you and Rory getting married?"

Whether it was the coffee spilled all over the floor or the look on Reb's face, Eileen was launched into a spasm of laughter to which even Reb was not immune. When they were through, they sat down at the table—one Carrick had recently made so more adults could sit together at a meal.

"I guess I asked the wrong question," Eileen began. "I'm sorry. I look at you two and I remember Colt and I when we were first married."

189

"Carrick hasn't asked me about that," Reb said. "Don't know what he's thinking. I got work to do."

"He probably never will," Eileen replied, putting a hand on Reb's arm to keep the high-strung young woman from darting off again. "He was never a talker. Before I married Colt, when I was a girl, I would have some wild times with Colton and Rory. Even when we were having fun, he was quiet. He was either listening or watching. He could spot adults before they got anywhere near. Now, he acts like a cat almost—looking whether there is anything there to see or not."

Reb didn't know what to say. Social talk with other range women happened once a year and usually revolved around them asking her when she was going to get married or talking about sewing and things she didn't know anything about.

"You two are made for each other," Eileen continued. "I . . . I know that it may sound odd to you after the way things worked out, but Colton was a good husband. I know it was not the life everyone would choose, but he was what he was from the day I met him until . . ."

Reb hated tears. "Don't cry, Eileen. You and your kids are safe here and . . . and you folks are welcome here. I know you know Carrick right well, but he ain't the only one here that fights for what he wants. Aunt Jess and I, we've had people after us a long time and they haven't gotten us yet."

"I only wanted to tell you, Rebecca, that men are funny animals. If you love a man and want to marry him, don't wait forever. I don't know that Colton and I lost a day. Maybe we knew from the start we wouldn't have forever. One day, it ends." Eileen Ramsay stood up and patted Reb softly on the shoulder. "You can lose a lifetime waiting, girl. Don't."

Francis Oliver was drunk. He was so close to everything a man could ever want, but he had been blocked again. He'd known

190

the day he arrived in the valley that it could be an empire. He'd come with nothing, and was making that into something when Jackson Jones appeared, better-heeled and able to move faster. Lucinda had been bought. She should have been his.

He had been shrewd and skillful in seizing every opportunity that came along. He was a better businessman than Jones. The women who ran the old Bar C were teetering, and he was sure he was going to get their land. Then Carrick came back and ruined everything. Even having Jones out of the way didn't make things easier. There wasn't enough common border between Lazy F and Double J that he could grab what was now available because no woman could properly run a ranch. Ramsay had seen the price of crossing him. Pretty soon, Carrick and the women would learn that lesson, too. It would need to be soon. Time was not on his side. He avoided direct confrontations because he knew the risks were higher. This time he might have to make an exception, or be relegated to an obscure ranch forever.

His confrontation with Lucinda Jones at the funeral had been typical of his luck. After paying his respects, he turned the conversation to the future. That fancy ranch manager Jones had hired—Petersen—was glued to her side. When Petersen got called away, Oliver had broached the subject of marriage now that her husband was gone. Combining ranches would make them the king and queen of the valley, once the old Bar C was out of the way. She all but slapped him. "I am not that desperate," she had snapped.

"How desperate are you?" he shot back. She had blanched at that, eyes coals of hate staring back. There was more than anger. A nerve had been hit. He had ridden home from the funeral wondering what Lucinda Jones was hiding. Lucinda was only a woman, though. This Carrick was the problem. Unless his luck changed soon, he'd have to risk taking the old Bar C on. Then, anything could happen.

Oliver was sitting in his usual chair by the fire, bottle on the table to his right. He didn't bother with a glass. This night he had drunk more than usual. Instead of retiring to bed, he leaned back in the chair and closed his eyes. As he slipped into a sleep, he slid lower and lower in the chair.

He snapped awake as the chair pitched forward and wood splinters dug into his face. He rolled onto the floor. More splinters flew as he saw a chunk of the chair fly up. He heard the distant sound of voices yelling.

"Boss?" Harvey Edwards, his foreman, rushed through the door. He saw Oliver on the floor, blood from cuts on his face and holes in the chair he sat in every night by the fire. "Boss is shot! Get help!"

Edwards ran to Oliver, who was sobering up rapidly. "What happened?" said Oliver.

"Somebody took a shot at you, Boss," Edwards replied. "Sniper from up the hill. We heard the buffalo gun. Didn't think about the first shot much. Second one didn't sound right. Too close. You hit?"

Oliver explained it was splinters and sent Edwards and the crew to chase whoever had taken the shots. Edwards returned after a while, crestfallen.

"No luck, Boss. Whoever it was knows his way around. Horse was saddled over the hill; sniper must have walked down on foot and then rode away."

"Ride into town. I want Dan Hill and the law arresting Carrick. Had to be him. Hill needs to arrest him, and if he won't ride out there and do his job I'll find a sheriff who will. Tell him that!"

Dan Hill rode slowly and reluctantly to the gate of the Lewis ranch. Reb Lewis's temper and affinity for guns were legendary.

Carrick had proven himself a killer. Only the prodding of the town's council had pushed him to make the trip at all. He was sure it was a fool's errand. Whether Carrick was guilty or innocent, he was hardly going to admit trying to kill Oliver.

Jessie Lewis ushered Hill inside with as much respect as she thought the law was entitled to, no matter who wore the badge. He stumbled through a recitation of his mission, while staring at Jesse. He did not want to antagonize Carrick or Reb, both of whom had been waiting when Hill rode up—armed as always. It was silent for a while after he finished talking.

"Didn't shoot at him," Carrick said. "Wouldn't miss if I did."

"Me, neither," said Reb. "What makes you think Oliver didn't make up this story?"

Hill explained that there were witnesses, and the town was worried that there were too many shootings on the range. If the army and the territory had to step in, it would be bad for everyone, he told them.

"Sheriff," said Jessie, "none of us want anything from Francis Oliver except to be left alone. We have one buffalo gun at our ranch. It's too big for me, with too much of a kick. Reb doesn't use it. It probably has so much dust on it that you can tell from looking at it, assuming I can find it, that it hasn't been fired. Would it help you if we showed you that?"

"It would, Miz Lewis," Hill replied. "I got to answer to the town."

"Well, tell them Carrick was with me," exclaimed Reb.

"Rebecca Lewis!" interjected Jess.

"We were sitting in the front yard of this house with rifles waiting for Francis Oliver to ride in so we could shoot his fool head off," she said, turning red and stammering. "That's where we were! Taking turns sleeping by the fire and guarding. Anyone doesn't believe that, they can come here and tell me to my face!"

Carrick nodded regretfully. He had not wanted anyone to know he was keeping watch. "I'm not taking chances, Sheriff. Nobody left here that night. Oliver leaves us alone, I'll do the same."

Hill still asked to be shown the gun. The range was starting to believe that between the two of them, Reb and Carrick might be the most deadly shooters in all of Wyoming. Taking their word to the town on a subject that involved guns was like a promise from a snake not to bite. Jessie showed him the weapon, which not only had dust, but cobwebs. Hill sputtered apologies and fled, moving more quickly leaving than he did arriving.

"What do you think this is all about, Carrick?" asked Reb.

"Oliver trying to get to us through the law, Reb," said Carrick. "No better way for him to pretend that someone is after him than to have a hand shoot his chair and then use that to get me arrested. Man's got a million angles; none of them work. Sooner or later, though, the man is going to have to do his own dirty work, Reb. That's the day that worries me, because it can't be much farther away."

Now that the custom of keeping watch at night was no longer a secret, Carrick adopted the Double J habit of stationing someone armed by the ranch house every day, as well as standing guard at night. He had no idea where, when, or how trouble would strike; only that it would. He cleared the ranch yard of anything that could be used by an attacker as a place to hide if they were forced to defend the house. If Oliver was up against a deadline, he was going to have to either act or throw away his dreams.

It was a clear cloudless night, with the summer heat fading as the sky darkened into a blue-black backdrop for the stars. Carrick was standing by the gate to the ranch yard. He could smell the coffee before he heard the footsteps.

"Gonna stand guard every night if I get coffee."

Reb smiled. "I couldn't sleep. I don't think Aunt Jess sleeps much these days, either. It's odd, Carrick. We got the biggest crew I think I've seen in years. Eileen drives them harder than I do. Double J isn't always pushing the way they were. That snake Francis Oliver knows he can't do something sly to get his hands on our land. We're stronger than ever but I feel more nervous than ever."

"You know with livestock what you got," he told her. "Disease, weather, they get hurt. People? You don't know with them. It goes back to Jones. His power, his ambition ruled the whole valley. Now there's no one in charge; no one controls all the rest. By the nature of things, this place will grow stronger. Double J is going to stay strong. Lazy F ended up the odd one out. He did everything he could on the sly to get rich. He reached for what wasn't his and got his hand slapped. Sooner or later, and my bet is on sooner, he's got to come out in the open. When he does, Reb, the man pays."

"Keep your voice down and watch what you say about shooting people around Aunt Jess," Reb chided. "Or do you want another scolding?"

"Think she'll scold me for pointing a gun at Oliver the same as she would with Easy Thompson?"

She laughed. "Easy is such a big old bear. I think he read his manners in a book somewhere, about the only one he ever read, but he is so nice to her. A woman likes a well-mannered man, especially if a woman thinks she might want to get married to said well-mannered man."

Carrick tried to fathom Reb's expression in the darkness. "Somebody tryin' to tell me something?"

"Somebody ever gonna ask me something? Girl keeps waitin'. Girl gets impatient. Impatient girls have itchy trigger fingers, Carrick. Read that in a book, once, I think. A book of manners for frontier girls."

Carrick drew in the dirt with the toe of his boot for what seemed to Reb like forever. "Reb Lewis, I don't have the slightest idea if either of us is gonna be alive tomorrow. I don't know anything but living with a gun in my hand. I've ridden from Kansas and Texas here, and I see men settling down. I don't know if I know how to plant and plow and sell and buy. I still wake up and see that Abilene street. I dream about Uriah's brother. Forever is a long time, Reb, and it scares the life out of me. You need a man who is everything you deserve, not the nearest cowboy who doesn't think he can live without you."

"Oh, Carrick! What if a girl knows better than some cowboy does? Ever think about that? Ever just plain think, period? If I waited for you to tell me what I wanted I'd be waitin' forever. Girl knows what a girl needs."

"In that case, come here!" He set the coffee on a fence post and opened his arms. She came into them. In time, they sat on the fence and held each other's hands underneath a black sky dotted with stars, a map of heaven bigger than any words. They sat closer. She put her head on his shoulder. And underneath a sky filled with the silent wonders of a Wyoming night, she drifted and dreamed.

She awoke with a start. Carrick had lifted her to her feet and was moving toward the sound of hooves. He chambered a round.

"Gonna shoot if you don't stop and tell me who you are."

Randy's voice emerged from the dark. "It's me. I rode to warn you. We may be having company soon."

A small fire, for warmth, was flickering by the house. Carrick led Randy to it, holding Reb's hand as they walked. Carrick saw Randy notice and returned the questioning glance with a tight smile. His friend knew better than to say anything.

They sat down by the fire. Randy spoke at last. "Remember Will Greene?"

Reb flushed. "He wanted to marry me when I was fourteen and sang to me and I threw mud on him. Poor man. I think he ended up singing to Aunt Jess mostly because I hid whenever I saw his horse. Didn't he get married to that Anne Williams girl?"

"He did. He's the blacksmith for Lazy F. I don't think he is comfortable with some of their recent actions, but a man has to eat. He came to see me last night. There's some kind of plan in the works. All the men are being gathered; a lot of talk in whispers. A couple riders said they need new shoes before their horses take that rocky road over the hill. You know where that lets out. There have been some meetings between Lazy F and Double J, he thinks. I do not know if those were meetings that resulted in the ranches being allies or if they failed to reach an agreement. Easy Thompson hates Francis Oliver, but no one really knows Henry Petersen, the ranch manager, or even who is making the Double J's decisions. The Lazy F hands think the range is going to be divided between two outfits and they think they are fighting for their survival. He thinks they plan to put the old Bar C out of business once and for all."

"Easy to say," Carrick replied. Reb caught defiance in the tone; a touch of arrogance. Nice of him not to worry. She was scared half to death.

"Carrick. We can't stand up to both of those outfits—you, me Aunt Jess, Bad Weather, and a few . . . whatever they are!"

He did not respond. She poked him. "Carrick! You gonna answer me?"

"Oliver is planning a raid."

"What?"

"Reb, the only way to get us off the range is to kill us, and kill us all. Oliver needs to act soon. They will wait for a time when they think we are all here, and then wipe us out. This isn't about control of the range or the stock or even Colt's men. This

197

is about you, me, and your Aunt Jess. If Oliver kills us all, no one will stand in his way. Bad Weather might fight because he's stubborn, but no Indian can hold title to land, so, once they kill us, they have no one to stop them. Oliver needs the land, and he is running out of time. He's going after us because we are all that stands in his way. Colt's folks are not going to fight for the range like we will. If we go down, they will drift. Maybe, if we know when Lazy F is coming, we can have a surprise of our own. Maybe we should give them an invitation so we know when they plan to attack. Bad Weather, anyone know you rode over tonight?"

"I don't think so; I waited until after dark."

"Did your friend say when they were coming? Tonight?"

"Didn't sound it. I got the impression it's maybe a day away. Not much more," replied Randy.

"Go back, then. Act normally. Tomorrow, we will send someone to spell you a day or two down there while you go for supplies, some such excuse. Lots of cover down there; easy for them to spy on you. They may be already. If they figure you're in town, they might make their move sooner."

"You want them to attack?" asked Reb.

"Lazy F knows the country as well as anyone else. I know which way they'll come. You know that back trail that leads out by the barn?"

"It's steep and narrow going over the hills. There are lots of rocks along the way. No one rides that."

"A man can ride that trail if he goes slowly enough. A man like Oliver might not care if a few horses fall by the wayside trying this in the middle of the night as long as most of 'em get through. Think about where that trail comes out. No one can see riders until they are on top of the house. Perfect surprise. They could put twenty, thirty riders here before anyone knew they had arrived."

"Then what do we do?"

Carrick grinned. It was wolfish. Savage. "Put Francis Oliver in a place where he can't ever hurt anyone again."

The sun would be poking over the hills to the east soon.

Everything was ready. Randy had ridden in the day before, after making sure the riders who relieved him were told, loudly, he was heading for town. Every window of the house had someone waiting with a rifle. Even Aunt Jess, who tolerated hunting to eat but hated shooting anything, insisted she wanted a gun.

"It wasn't you he fooled," she had told Reb earlier with no small amount of asperity. "I want the man in my sights for one second. I have never been so humiliated and degraded in my life, Reb."

"We'll pay him back, Aunt Jess."

Reb was dubious, however, about the upcoming fight. She expressed her doubts to Carrick. "If Randy and Aunt Jess are the best we got, Carrick, we're in trouble. Both of 'em are good people but they aren't soldiers or killers. Eileen Ramsay and her bunch are willing, but I don't know if they'll stand. If Lazy F puts all its riders against us, Carrick, we can't hold them off. What good is all this if Aunt Jess is killed?"

"We don't let that happen," he told her. "If Oliver comes at us, we fight back with every last thing we've got. Bullets can kill anyone when there's a scrap, but Randy's supposed to watch your aunt doesn't do anything stupid like try to kill them all. Oliver has to kill you and me. If we aren't in the house, he's not going to be trying to take it. You've got to focus. Your horse saddled?"

"Yes, Carrick," she repeated like a child telling an adult something for the thousandth time. "Two rifles, two guns over the saddle horn, enough bullets in the saddlebags to last as long as the Alamo held. Same as you told me and told me and told me." He smiled at her; she paused. "You aren't planning on you and I running away and leaving Aunt Jess to fight this out, are you?"

"You think I would?"

"Nooo, but . . ."

"A little faith, woman. A little faith. If I tried that, you'd shoot me. If war teaches one thing, it's how to surprise the folks that want to surprise you. What Francis Oliver thinks he's coming up against and what is actually ready to meet him are going to be two very different things."

Carrick's shadowed face was grim. His tone was as cold as death. Reb shivered. "I'm cold. I'm scared."

"Scared is good; keeps you thinkin'. Keeps you alive. Everybody's scared before a fight. Can't do much about that. Might do something about the cold part, though." He held out his arms.

She was half-dozing on his shoulder, underneath his jacket, when he shook her roughly awake.

"Hey!" she started to yell. His hand was over her mouth. He pointed with the rifle he held in his other hand.

This was it. She looked out the barn door. There was a shadowy shape moving beyond the tall grass. Another. And another. Fear was in her stomach. Her lungs. It broke out in drops on her forehead.

"Easy. Easy." The words staunched the advance of fear, but didn't vanish it. "Nothin' happening we didn't expect. Glad they came the way we suspected. Gettin' tired of stayin' up all night waiting for 'em."

She could not share his calmness. She was always ready to fight back when provoked, but this was beyond what she knew, this cold planning to kill people. "How many are there?" she asked, hoping for a number that would ease her mind.

"Twenty, maybe more. It's not going to matter. Wait until Bad Weather opens the ball, then we do what I told you."

She peeked out the door again. The pre-dawn light was spreading. Figures of horses and men were becoming distinct. Incongruously, the birds had started singing in the distance, as if this was another peaceful Wyoming morning. She was up around this time every day to start chores. For a moment she wondered if she would be getting up tomorrow.

He slapped her rump. Anger flooded her. "Mount," Carrick growled. Miserable man! Then she looked at the riders in the half-light. They would pay, too. She didn't see him grinning as he watched the anger take root and blossom. Anger was good. It would get her through the next few minutes. That, and a little luck.

Bad Weather's rifle opened. A moan responded. Milling riders were thrown into confusion for a moment, then responded by firing at the house. A volley answered back. The volume of sound made the sides seem evenly matched. Lazy F hadn't brought everyone. Good! Carrick wondered if that was because some riders wouldn't have stood for murder, or whether Oliver was that confident. Either way, it was what he was hoping for. Firing now became general; everyone shooting at what they thought they saw.

"Now, Reb!"

Carrick and Reb pounded out of the barn and down the pathway towards the main trail that would lead to either Lincoln Springs or Black Wind Pass. Reb fired blindly as she rode, not caring what she hit but hoping no one took good aim at them.

"Come on, Reb," Carrick called loudly as they passed through the Lazy F riders, standing up in the stirrups and waving. It was almost too dark, but he hoped they were visible. He stopped and leveled the rifle, firing into the horsemen. Then he nudged Beast to a gallop. If that didn't get their attention, nothing would!

Francis Oliver saw the two riders gallop away. Carrick! The other one had to be the girl. They were the thorns in his plans—the girl and the man who had ruined everything. He pulled his best riders aside and left the rest to continue the attack on the farmhouse. They couldn't get away. Jessie Lewis and the dregs of Ramsay's gang wouldn't matter. It was like a snake. When he killed Reb and Carrick, the head would be dead and the body would die.

Lazy F's men galloped down the flattened trail. It was flat land here; no chance of an ambush.

"Boss!"

One rider was pointing. Dust kicked up from two sets of hooves was visible in the light; then they saw the two riders heading across the flat prairie for Black Wind Pass. Oliver spurred his mount harder. They had to catch them before they cleared the pass. Even Dan Hill might have to do something if Reb Lewis came bearing this tale. There was always fear the army might look into this if it got big enough. If anyone poked into the valley to investigate, the railroad might get skittish and look elsewhere for its coal, and all of this would be for nothing.

"Ride!" he growled at his men. They cut through twists and turns in the woods to gain on Carrick and Reb, losing sight of their quarry now and then in the process. Once they heard them firing back. They must be getting close.

Soon, they were on the last winding uphill piece of the trail to Black Wind Pass. They had to have come this way, or the riders would have run into them. Oliver spurred his horse in desperation. His men followed.

Orange from the rising sun filled the pass ahead with a glow. The riders were not visible. Oliver moved out further from the rest. As he and his men neared the pass, they saw the blackened remnants of the ruined cabin. The sun was in their eyes, making it hard to discern the riders they were chasing, but they knew there was no other trail; no other path. They were up there somewhere.

Then Oliver saw the silhouette. One black shape against the deepening reddish orange of the sunrise. One defiant man in the middle of the pass. He was standing in a relaxed posture, with his right hand leaning casually against a rifle. That loose, unconcerned stance reminded Oliver of a big cat watching prey, not caring if it was seen because it knew it would kill whomever came close.

Something in Oliver shivered as he reined in his horse. He was not a man who believed in anything, but, for a moment, he thought he was seeing death. No one could have gotten there that far ahead of them. They had been on their heels forcing them to fire wildly only a few moments ago. No matter. Carrick was there and if he wanted one final showdown, Oliver would give him one. He growled and cursed and turned in his saddle, pulling his horse to a stop. His men were soon behind him.

"Calhoun! Smith!" Oliver called. He pointed. "Get rid of him."

The two Lazy F riders did not hesitate. They drew their guns and rode into the pass, where the trail narrowed to allow only a few horsemen at a time to enter. Oliver watched through the dust kicked up by their horses. The lone cowboy was lost in the cloud. Guns fired. Oliver saw red flashes wink within the dust. He held up his hand to block the sun from his eyes but the glare was too strong.

Silence.

The fine cloud of dust dissipated slowly as the faint morning breeze blew through the pass.

No one was in sight. Beyond the pass stood Calhoun's gray stallion, riderless. There were two lumps on the ground that looked like bodies. Oliver cupped his hands to his mouth and called the riders' names. No one answered. For one final moment of rational thought, Oliver knew fear and knew the only way to live was to slink away. Then his desperation returned and he waved his gun theatrically over his head and pointed it toward the pass.

"Boys! Get ready to charge!" The remaining eight riders drew rifles.

One let loose a scream and pitched from his horse. Another crumped silently in his saddle. Another cried out. From the shack, rifle fire was moving down the line of mounted targets, picking them off one by one, like targets on a fence rail. Oliver and his men had no choice. They could either rush the pass and face Carrick or remain sitting ducks for the hidden sharpshooter.

Oliver pointed to the pass. "Ride him down! We'll come back for her when we're done!" Slowly, stirrup to stirrup, he and the three remaining unwounded Lazy F men rode. Oliver's eyes probed for the target he sought. The rifle fire behind them continued, but was now more of a nuisance than a threat.

There! A silhouette moved as Carrick jumped from one rock to the next. Oliver's riders anticipated his command. Rifles opened fire. Bullets ricocheted off the rocks to their left where Carrick had taken cover. Oliver knew from his days in the war that men on horseback were an easy target.

"Dismount." Oliver waited. Carrick thought he was tricky. Oliver had a few tricks of his own. They slapped the horses ahead of them. As the horses galloped through the pass unmolested, the gunmen advanced under cover of the dust. They used the screen to reach the rocky edge of the pass. They spread out to flank the rocks their antagonist had used as cover. The breeze was stiffening. The dust was dissipating. They moved fast.

They froze.

Above them was the clear sound of a cocked hammer. "Drop 'em or die."

Oliver roared out a curse, firing up the slope of the pass until a bullet stifled his rage and sent him toppling over. The rider next to him went down as well. The shooter ducked back to avoid the fusillade that erupted from the remaining two riders.

The tableau held. The sun rose. A crow called. Two men pressed against the rock had lost any reason to fight, but would not give up. This was no longer about Lazy F. This was a fight to the finish. They had beaten longer odds. With one look, they nodded. They split up, one each way. They clung to the rocky sides of the pass. Waiting. Sweat trickled down their faces. Dust-caked lips were dry. Silence. There it was! A boot moving rocks. They leaped up the final few feet to the top of the rocky sides of the pass. Each saw nothing but the other. Trap!

They started scrambling back down, but the hidden sharp-shooter who had moved away from the ruined shack to take up a new position in the rocks opened fire on them. When they stopped to return it, Carrick ended it quickly, emerging from his own hiding place with his gun blazing. Then he held up a hand toward Reb. "Stop!" he yelled.

There were distant sounds. Somebody was moaning. Then it stopped. The clinking sound of metal casings hitting rock was the only sound to break the silence. Then the chamber of a revolver spun, clicking faster as it whirled until Carrick stopped it and locked it back in place. Footsteps warily moved toward the men. Dead. Carrick let loose the breath he did not know he was holding. It was over.

Oliver alone had not died instantly. He was leaning against the rocks at the side walls of Black Wind Pass. His chest was red and wet, but his eyes were still alive with fury. He had his revolver in his hand, waiting for one clear shot at his enemy before he died. Laboriously, he worked to cock back the hammer of the weapon, his hand trembling as he put every bit of effort left in his life into taking Carrick or Reb with him.

From nowhere, a boot kicked the gun out of a hand too weak to hold it. The dying rancher looked up. The sky was a faint pink dotted with blues and white. A woman knelt down next to him.

"You killed Carrick's friend. You humiliated my Aunt Jess. You tried to take my land away from me!"

"I . . . I . . ."

"I wanted to finish you off, Oliver. I wanted to finish you myself! You aren't worth it. I think I'll let you die slow instead."

Francis Oliver saw Rebecca Lewis stand and walk away. Her figure merged with the shadows that were converging on his sight until it seemed the girl had walked away down a tunnel that was closing slowly, closing faster, and then closed altogether.

Reb stood next to Carrick, looking down upon Oliver's barely dead form. "He died too fast," she said with anger and regret.

"It only matters he's dead, Reb. He got what he deserved. Help me heft him."

"Can't we leave him for the vultures? I'm not going to bury him."

"We need to end this, Reb. There's been enough killing. His men aren't going to fight for Lazy F once they realize Oliver is gone. They need proof. Time for Francis Oliver to do something good for once in his life."

They threw him over a horse and rode down the pass. Distant desultory gunfire said the old Bar C house was still under siege. At a safe distance, Carrick surveyed the scene. The Lazy F men had found such cover as they could. There must not have been enough to rush the house because Oliver split the men. Now he had to hope nobody wanted to be a hero.

Carrick tied a white cloth to his rifle. He waved it as he rode up to the scene of Lazy F surrounding the old Bar C house.

"Lazy F, this here is Carrick! Listen here! Got Francis Oliver here, boys. Dead." He pushed Oliver off the saddle. The rancher lay sprawled face-up in the dust. Carrick walked Beast around in a tight circle as he spoke. "Oliver wanted the ladies' range; he got the dust he can swallow. He had a scheme that was going to make himself rich and nobody else. The man was out for himself, Lazy F. Not you! Way I figure this, it ends here. Your boss told you lies, you swallowed them, and you rode with him. All of that is over. Not minded to vengeance, but if you aren't off the Lewis ladies' land in the next minute, every last mother's son of you gets the same."

For a moment, nothing happened. Then Harvey Edwards, Lazy F foreman, stood with his hands up, walking toward Carrick.

"Boss said you and Double J were going to raid us. He said you sniped Jones to get your old home range back, and you and that Ramsay crew were coming for us next. It was us or you, Carrick. That's what the boss told us. Isn't that right, boys?" A murmur of agreement swept through the ranks of Lazy F riders, who were emerging from cover and walking over to look at their dead boss.

"He lied. Been doin' nothin' but tellin' people I only want to hold this land for these women and I'm gettin' tired of no one believin' me. Oliver was looking for his own gain, boys, and he didn't give a hang about any of you. He was looking at sellin' off the range to mine coal, and then every one of you would have been out of a job. Harvey, you get these men out of here, take this with you," he gestured at Oliver's corpse, "and then maybe we can see about fixin' all the troubles that he started. We got to find a way that all this land can hold the people in this valley without everyone wantin' the whole range for themselves. Never thought I'd see a day when this valley needed ink and paper to draw lines people could live by, but I guess the way things changed out here, that's what it has come to."

Edwards and the other Lazy F survivors picked up their dead. Two men rode to the pass to collect those who died with Oliver. Once they were done, with prone figures over the backs of too many horses, the remaining dispirited Lazy F riders trooped away.

"Carrick!" Jess Lewis was calling. "Carrick!" There was urgency and panic in her voice. He ran inside.

Lying by the window he picked to defend, Bad Weather was lying on the floor, too much blood next to him to signify much hope for his life.

"I called to him while they were shooting; I didn't get an answer, but I thought he was trying to stay hidden. When you came back I found him like this," she said.

Randy was still breathing shallow gasps. Carrick called his name over and over until his eyes flickered. Recognition flared.

"Remember. Lone Warrior. The last journey. Tell me, Carrick. Tell me, Clawing Wolf?"

"I remember."

Reb's boots stomped her way in. She saw Carrick openly crying. He had Randy's head in his lap, and was bending down as he spoke.

"And in the end," Carrick began, "when all the warriors were gone but one, and the enemy was at the gates of the place of the People, the Lone Warrior listened to the wind. The wind told him of heroes. The wind told him of his purpose. The wind told him that even if there was no other warrior to fight for the people, this warrior had himself. And he believed in himself, and he went forward, and the enemy was defeated." Carrick looked at the face; at the closed eyes. He could barely form the words. "And the people rose and saw the Lone Warrior bleeding from his wounds and ascending to the sky. He was not dead.

And they took strength that the Greatest Spirit would send him when next the People were in need. And the Lone Warrior was honored forever, for he kept faith with the People."

Randy had stopped breathing during the story. Carrick looked at Reb. "As kids, we agreed when it was our turn to die, the survivor would tell that to the one who was passing." He sat, holding the body of his friend, eyes focused on the place the friends of the dead go when those they love have left them behind. "Figured . . . I figured, Reb, when this was over we'd have some time to be friends all over again. Never gonna happen is it?"

Reb had no words. She put her arms around them both, the living and the dead, and like that they stayed, undisturbed but for the sound of Carrick's tears landing on the old wood of the floor.


The standoff had produced relatively few casualties aside from Randy. Two Lazy F riders were killed; one of Ramsay's old gang was badly wounded but would live. Several Lazy F riders had wounds, but most were minor. Many in the house were wounded by flying wood, but the cuts and scratches would soon heal.

"If they had rushed us it might have been a close call," Jessie Lewis told Reb later as they inspected the house for damage. "It is one thing to fire a gun through a window; another thing to fight someone up close. I kept waiting, expecting it—especially when you were gone so long. They never did."

"Maybe they knew somehow that whatever Oliver was up to, it wasn't worth dyin' for," said Reb. "Not much is."

Jess volunteered to relay the news to Dan Hill at Lincoln Springs so that the story got to him correctly. She returned with the news that Hill seemed to have once again changed his tune about Carrick. Even Hill seemed to understand that the ranch had a right to defend itself. If Oliver had built up any stock of goodwill, it had evaporated before he died. She also mentioned that there was a man in the Lincoln Springs hotel who had checked in, accompanied by two very well-armed men who appeared to be bodyguards. The man, who said he was from Chicago, claimed he was there to do business with a local rancher, but had not moved from the hotel since his arrival. Hill said most of the town was waiting to see what the man was up to.

"I guess now that the sheriff thinks we are not going to be killed off or chased off, and we seem to be either lucky or good at surviving, we might be someone he has to deal with," she said. "I guess he thinks the man from Chicago is one of those syndicate people we have heard about. I made it clear that no one on this ranch is selling anything, as if everyone in Wyoming doesn't already know that. He said he's sick and tired of all of it, by the way, and wondered if this is the end."

"I wish I knew," said Reb wistfully. "I wish I knew."

Carrick saddled Bad Weather's horse and draped his friend across it. "I'll be back," he told Reb. She offered to ride with him. "Nope. This I got to do alone. Randy wanted what he wanted. Back in a couple days."

While Carrick was gone, Reb had riders stationed at Black Wind Pass and up the hill from the old Bar C to watch for signs of anyone coming. She was taking no chances. If Double J thought they had been wounded, it might be them riding up next.

A day after Carrick left, one of the lookouts reported seeing smoke a range of hills over. "Randy once told me that his Cheyenne ancestors were buried over that way," Jess told Reb. "He must have told Carrick that, too."

The next day, Carrick rode back, gaunt and ghostly. He had

clearly not slept in the time he was away. He showed no interest in food, or even coffee. He took Randy's belongings to Eileen Brown, telling her the horse and saddle and guns were hers. Reb had almost forgotten that they had all once been friends together—Carrick, Randy, Eileen, Colt Ramsay, and even that Jones woman.

Reb gave Carrick a day or two in hopes that he would return to normal; then she sought him out.

"Carrick, you got to come back to us. I know he was your friend. I'm sorry he's dead. We've living. I'm living. I need you! You want to talk about what you feel?"

"Reb, I hurt right now in more ways than I thought a person could feel and be alive. Maybe it would have been better for everyone if I had kept riding on, never come back to the valley."

Her boot shook the ground as she stomped her foot. "No! Jess and I were gettin' pushed out by two bullies. This whole range was gonna go up in a war that was gonna take them friends sooner or later along with anyone in the way of that weasel Oliver or that bully Jones. I know you lost your friends, Carrick, but don't it matter at all that I'm safe?"

The hurt in her voice reached him. " 'Course it does, Reb. Of course it does." He opened his arms and she held him tightly.

"It'll get better, Carrick," she said. "It'll get better now that it's over."

"Not quite," said Carrick. "It's not over. The shadow on this range—the one that's gonna hang over every one of us that ever raised a hand against Jackson Jones—ends the day we find out who killed Jackson Jones," Carrick said. "Not sayin' the man was perfect. He was a threat to you and anyone who got in his way. Nobody deserves to die like that. Somethin' else. Until we know who killed him, there's gonna be talk I did it. We got to figure that one because until whoever killed him pays for what they did, we're all going to live looking over our shoulders, when we're gonna end up like Colt or like Randy—or even like Jones."

# CHAPTER THIRTEEN

Carrick went to feel the night. No moon. Windy. This next step was something he didn't have to do. He knew that. It was a risk that could get him killed for no gain other than some intangible thing he and Jackson Jones both understood—doing what was right no matter what the world thought. In the end, living and dying didn't matter. Death was only a moment to spend alone. Not that much different from living on some days. It wasn't death that drove him. It was fear of failure. And fear that the guilty would go free and the innocent would suffer. There had to be no one left who could pose a threat, and, when all the fancy stuff was through, it still took a man with the nerve to risk it all to make sure that everything was right. Enough of it all. Time to think about nothing else but the final act that he had written, but had yet to play out.

Mortality walks before dawn. Be a shame never to smell the breeze again when it's Fall and the rocks are damp with a smell that only comes by once a year. Be worse to not do right by a man who never much cared about doing right by anyone except himself. The faint breeze moved the night around him. He smelled distant mown hay and a far-off campfire. There was a horse far, far away talking to the stars. Or another horse. Enough thinking. There was work to do. By this time tomorrow, it would be over. Reb would be safe with no clouds over her future. He'd either be with her, or he'd have spent that moment called dying and be on the other shore. Whatever it was, it didn't matter anymore. All that mattered was thinking fast and shooting straight, and the rest of it would take care of itself. And in the night, beyond fear and anxiety, he could slowly feel the ice, as if it were a sheath, covering the nerves, covering the thoughts, and leaving the mind racing forward to the only thing that mattered anymore.

Retribution Day was going to dawn. About time.

Rebecca Lewis was angrily attempting one last time to persuade Carrick of his folly. She had spent half the night watching him walk around outside the ranch house. She wanted to talk to him, but in the end the only one she talked to was God. Carrick had cast off some of his shell, but since Randy's death he was distant and withdrawn. She was not entirely sure whether the plan he told her was primarily designed to catch Jones's killer or risk Carrick's life. She told him that bluntly. He didn't seem to care.

"The only thing Double J wants to do with you is kill you!" she insisted one final time.

"Think they can?"

"I'm afraid they can."

"There is only one way to end this, Reb. We got to find out. I owe the man."

"And you don't owe me? Go ahead! Get dead. See if I care."

"Got a better idea? Got a way to end this once and for all without any risk to anyone? There are not any such things, Reb."

"You get dead in there and I'm never forgiving you." She had not liked his plan from the start, and now that it was time to enact it, she was certain it would end in disaster. She knew nothing would stop him. A man had to live with this thing men called honor. Carrick was no different.

"I got faith, Reb." He left her under the trees with eyes that were no longer dry and rode on alone.

Carrick slowly rode up to the Double J gate. He wondered how many guns were trained on him; how many trigger fingers were itching. The gate was not guarded. He rode in unchallenged. Cowboys watched. No one spoke to Carrick. They might have allowed him to come and go, but they did not have to like it. About the only noise was the black stallion Jones never got to ride. The animal was in a corral alone. No one knew what to do with him. He belonged to Jones; everyone was afraid to get on his back.

Henry Petersen emerged from the big house, adjusting his stiff, starched cuffs again and fidgeting with the black tie around the heavy, thick collar that poked up above the black suit jacket he wore. He walked quickly and nervously to greet Carrick. He escorted Carrick inside the old house that had been used by Jackson Jones as an office. Carrick had asked to meet there. The table by the window was where Carrick remembered it, and was piled high with papers. A grim smile passed across his face. A man's life so often depended on a stray piece of a memory. The windows near the table offered a spectacular view of an oak grove ten yards off and the mountains beyond. Carrick looked out through the glass—more of it in one place than any house he had ever been in—as Petersen excused himself to find Lucinda. Carrick wondered where Easy Thompson was. It had been long enough since the incident at the shack that Easy should be healed, but not long enough that Easy would have forgotten it. He was hoping not to run into the foreman, at least not until his business was concluded.

Carrick kept looking out the windows, talking to himself and then waiting as though he expected the trees to talk back.

Lucinda Jones swept in, a black armband around the sleeve of her royal-blue dress. The swishing of the voluminous folds of the material preceded her arrival, with Petersen following her.

"Luce," Carrick said, tipping his hat. He gave the world outside the window one last look, tugged on the brim of his hat once, and turned back to the business he came there to do.

Lucinda Jones exuded the warmth of a ball of ice. She stood at the far end of the table from Carrick and looked over his head as she talked. "I have agreed to this meeting that you requested, Mr. Carrick, because I agree it is time to resolve the issues concerning ownership and grazing rights. I believe that by inheritance you are the person who has legal title to the land occupied by the Lewis women and known on the range as the old Bar C."

"Guess so. Don't really care much. Ladies' land. Think I've said that about a thousand times. Some fine day, maybe somebody'll listen."

Exasperation crossed Lucinda's face. Petersen tried to speak but she cut him off. "The papers that Henry has in front of him will formally set out the range limits of Double J and what we will call the Bar C, because the Lewis women never created any registered brand of their own. They are not invited to sign this document because even if they were given use of the property by your late uncle, they are legally nothing more than squatters." Carrick marveled at Lucinda's command of business. Then again, he guessed, a woman couldn't dream of ruling the range without learning something along the way. He also had a sense that this was personal. He wondered what Luce and Reb had done to each other over the years.

"Carrick, are you listening?"

"Yes, ma'am."

Her voice had an angry, precise edge to it as she continued. "I believe that the document is a fair proposal. Although my dear late husband had dreamed of owning all the range, I believe that, in the present circumstances, it is best to recognize that acquiring all the land will take a higher price than he may have foreseen. The document is there to be read. If you need assistance, Henry here . . . Mr. Petersen . . . will read it to you."

"Nope. I can read everything that's going on, Luce."

She gave him a very sharp and inquisitive look. "In addition to a formal agreement upon range limits, there is also an agreement between yourself, as the heir of the Bar C, and me, as the heir of the Double J, that there will be peace between the two ranches and that any and all disputes over boundaries and the activities of cowboys who are too trigger-happy will be resolved through the sheriff and the circuit judge in Lincoln Springs."

"Maybe instead of all that we could simply talk to each other, Luce," said Carrick.

"Of course," she replied, barely losing her train of thought. "And, lastly, there is a paper I will sign and you will sign that declares an amnesty for any and all activities taken during these past few weeks that, in the years to come, might be seen as a violation of the laws of the territory of Wyoming. I am willing to forget the past. I understand that, on both sides, passions over the range have run very high and that actions may have been taken that should not have been taken. I believe that the range will be best served by moving forward and not looking back to drag up old disputes."

She caught him staring away again. "Are you listening, Carrick?"

"Not really, Luce. But I am understanding the lay of this land for the first time."

"You have your ranch; you have your precious gun-toting woman. What kind of riddle are you spouting? And why are you looking up at my hat that way?"

Carrick dug into his pocket. Still there! He hadn't checked on the ride over to the Double J. He threw the cufflink on the table towards Petersen. It clattered. "You dropped that."

"Why so I did!" the ranch manager exclaimed. "I looked all

over for it. How ever did you find it in the ranch yard?"

"I didn't."

Petersen looked puzzled. Lucinda Jones was growing red and frowning. "Where did you find it?"

"Where you lost it. At old Crazy Charlie's cabin up by Black Wind Pass. You know, the place you went to meet Luce, here."

There was a brief reaction of horror on both of their faces. Petersen's urbane mask returned first. "I do not understand you. I have never been to that cabin, which I think you mean is the one that burned. As ranch manager, I do not ride the range. I manage this ranch from here."

"Is that what you call it?"

"I beg your pardon."

"Since when is adultery with your boss's wife managing the ranch?"

"How dare you!"

"Cuz I'm right." He turned to Lucinda. "Your husband asked Easy how to get to the cabin. Easy thought he wanted to meet me. He wanted to find out what was really happening right under his nose, didn't he? That would have meant the end for either or both of you. Which of you killed him?"

Petersen took a step towards Carrick. "If anyone in this room killed Jackson Jones, it was you."

Carrick stood his ground and looked hard at the ranch manager, then Lucinda. "You know, Luce, I wondered about it a few days back when I recalled that Reb was still grousing about some sharpshooting contest at the fair a couple years that she should have won, but you won instead. She said that a while ago and it took a while to settle. Your father hunted buffalo. You're no stranger to the kind of gun that killed him. You did it, didn't you? I bet you got a huge bruise on your shoulder where the gun kicked, don't you? Bet it's even bigger from trying to kill Francis Oliver in his own ranch house. You missed him, maybe because with a shoulder already hurting you couldn't hold the gun right, but you killed your own husband. You might not want us men to see that bruise, but I can get Jess and Reb Lewis over here and you can show it to them."

Purple-faced and angry, Lucinda Jones jerked open a drawer of Jackson Jones's desk and grabbed the .45 that lay inside. She trained it on Carrick. "You were always clever, Carrick. Lucky, too. I was sure Easy would kill you. Francis Oliver and all of his devils could not kill you! I had someone watch you so Gordon Crowley could find you alone. He botched it. A woman always has to do everything herself, Carrick. Do you really think you could walk in here and leave, free to do whatever you want? You leave on my terms, or you leave dead."

"Lucy, what is he talking about?" Petersen asked. "You said this man killed Jackson. He didn't? Put that gun down. It might go off!"

Carrick kept pushing. "After the fire I went up there to see if I could find any reason why a worthless old cabin would be torched. Found a gold hat pin with the cuff link. Didn't mean anything at the time. Godfrey in town said all that was stuff he didn't sell, so it must have been bought out of town. Not many folks travel, Luce. Not many. Got me thinking. Somebody put a bottle of imported fancy French wine in the wood pile."

"Fool," she hissed at Petersen.

"Lazy F and Double J bought the only cases of wine in the past year. Then I recalled the hat. You wore one when I met you in town. You didn't wear one the other day when your husband was killed. Hat couldn't stay on without a hat pin. Bet not too many ladies in Buffalo Horn Valley have gold hat pins. Put that together with the cuff link to hold those starched cuffs of your ranch manager, and the story is plain. So, I got the two of you there, which means I know what you were doing. But it don't make sense, Luce. You were queen of the range. Why kill the king?"

"Queen!" She snorted with derision. "We left this ranch once—once in all the time we were married. We spent two days in Denver, most of that at the stockyards breathing cattle dust. I wanted San Francisco. I wanted Saint Louis. I wanted to tour the East, and see cities and bring the best of their comforts here so I could have a proper life. What is the use of having all this money if you can't have luxuries and enjoy life? Do you know the only thing he ever talked to me about?"

"An heir."

"That's right. I was allowed to share this ranch house on the condition I produce an heir, as if I was another head of livestock. I could have fine dresses, but there was no place to wear them because society out here is nothing but horses, cattle, cowboys, and women who follow cowboys! Can you imagine what it was like being wife to that man? Once he all but bought me from my family, all he wanted was to show off that he had the prettiest woman in the prettiest dresses, as if anyone in Lincoln Springs has any taste! And he wanted an heir. He was starting to sour because we didn't have children yet. He was starting to look at me as though I was one of his prize stock that didn't reproduce upon command and because of that ended up as steaks for the crew! He was going to divorce me unless I had a child. He told me that if I didn't do my job as expected he would find someone who would, as if I was a lazy cowhand! Henry's different. With Jackson gone, we can manage the ranch from Denver, or maybe even Saint Louis. I can enjoy my life. Jackson Jones put me in a cage. I had to break out the only way I knew how."

"You walked into that cage wanting fine things at any price, if I hear right, Luce," Carrick said.

"The price was too high!" she replied.

"You sent that rider to salt the water hole, didn't you?" Carrick asked.

"Do you know how easy it is when you are the only woman on a ranch to get a man to do what you want?" Lucinda asked. "It was simple! You were lucky that day—always lucky, Carrick!"

"You . . . You killed your husband?" Petersen's voice sounded like that of a twelve-year-old boy. He had been trying to utter words as Carrick and Lucinda talked. "I thought . . . we could get . . . The syndicate man was one thing, Lucinda. I was willing to talk to him for you, for us, but this is something different. No one would have known about it until we had left the range. I . . . I . . . The sheriff. We have to tell the sheriff. I could be arrested." Petersen turned to Carrick. "I never meant . . ."

"Really Henry? Squeamish at this late date? Don't turn sanctimonious on me. Did you think we could hide what we were doing forever?" Lucinda's tone dripped with scorn. "I knew the old war horse was getting suspicious. It wasn't love, of course. The man did not know how to love anyone but his dreams. I was a possession. No one was going to touch one of the great man's possessions." Bitterness, anger, and hate mingled in her voice.

She turned to Carrick. "When you showed up, it was time. I wanted to wait until some time when I was sure you could be blamed, but then he wanted to go to that cabin. I don't know if he suspected or was curious—he was intrigued by you, Carrick, because you stood up to him. I had to be sure he never got there. I rode up ahead of him, and it was simple. The first shot was because I had to, but let me tell you Carrick, the next two were to prove to him that I'm not merely a thing to be used and tossed aside. I showed him that a woman can do a lot of things on this range, and I taught him the last lesson of his arrogant life!"

Carrick heard hysteria creeping into her voice.

"All these men never once suspected a woman. Easy is sure you did it. Even though he has some unrequited feelings for Jessie Lewis, that does not extend to you. When you shot him, I was so hoping he would die because if he did, the crew would have gladly gone out to exterminate you. But he recovered. You have all the luck, Carrick! Or rather, you did." She laughed. "I will tell you what happens next. Henry and I will tell him we trapped you into confessing. By the end of the day, you will be swinging from a tree here at the Double J. I will cry a lot and for me—for me, Carrick—they will do anything. Did you think you could walk in here and expect to walk back out again? You and your family acted as though you were somehow better than everyone when you lived in the same dirt as the rest of us. I am going to be the one to get out of that dirt. You always thought your luck would last forever, even as a kid, but it has run out at last."

"Lucinda, this . . . this is wrong," said Petersen. "You killed Jackson? I cannot in good conscience condone that. You must turn yourself in . . ." He took one step toward the door. "I must summon Easy."

The gun in Lucinda Jones's hand spoke once. Peterson staggered back, hand to his chest where the red was already flowing. The surprise on his face was frozen as he staggered. The second shot knocked him down as the words he tried to say became whispers, then gurgles, then moans, then nothing.

The gun now covered Carrick, held in a steady hand. "It was interesting to have Henry around, but he was too weak for my taste," she said. "You would think a man who scruples to adultery would not get squeamish at getting rid of the husband, but men are unreliable. I'm sure where I am going, I can find someone else. I will let Easy run the place while I avoid all these bad memories and live in Denver, or California. By now,

Carrick, Easy Thompson and the others will be coming to investigate the shots. I will tell them you shot Henry and tried to kill me, but I got the drop on you. They won't really care if the story is good or bad. They want to hang someone to avenge Jackson, and you will do fine. Shooting Easy was hardly the way to get him on your side, Carrick. I will get what I want. Do you know what your problem always was, Carrick?"

"I didn't kill my friends?"

Her lips pressed together to the point where they were bloodless. "You never cared," she sneered. "When we were kids, everybody else wanted something. They wanted gold; they wanted land. You wanted to ride in the wind. You're no different now. You could have had a ranch, and that no-account girl you seem so fond of. Little Reb! Even Jackson raved because she caught some stupid horse! It wasn't enough for you that she was going to keep her pathetic ranch. You had to keep interfering. You had to stir up trouble as you blundered around without any idea what you were doing! How much like you!"

Easy Thompson burst through the door. A square of light opened then shut behind him, sealing off any escape.

"Thank God you're here, Easy," Lucinda exclaimed. "Carrick killed Henry. He admitted killing Jackson. I found Jackson's spare gun to defend myself. He was going to kill me. You have to help me."

Easy moved past Lucinda to look at the ranch manager's body. He rose, face dark with anger. "Boys!" he called out.

"She's lying, Easy," Carrick said, wondering whether to go for his gun now or try to talk his way out. He kept taking fast glances out the window. "You know I didn't kill the boss. Boss and I understood where we were headed. Showdown was a ways off yet. Bet he told you the same. Some day. Not yet. He tell you?"

"Easy, ignore him!" The foreman's hand was on the butt of

his gun, frozen as Lucinda and Carrick tried to pull him in different directions. "I'm Double J now, and this cowboy wants to pull down Double J."

"Easy, she's lying. You knew something was going on at that cabin," Carrick said. "Bet somebody saw a rider in a woman's hat heading that way, and you didn't hear about it until later. Or somebody saw Petersen up where he didn't belong. Maybe somebody saw him at the railroad office. Bet I'm the only one not Double J you asked. If I wanted to, Easy, I could have killed you that day. Didn't want to then and don't want to today. No crime being loyal. Only one person in this room wasn't loyal. I found one of her hatpins and one of his cufflinks up there, Easy. Bottles of wine up there, Easy, only came from here because nobody else on the range drinks the stuff except Francis Oliver, and she sure wasn't with him. Bet one of the hands saw her take the oil up there to burn the shack. She can shoot better'n a lot of men, Easy. Reb had told me that but I had forgotten. Bet there's an old buffalo gun lying around that she used."

Carrick breathed in fast and hard as he finished. Sweat was dripping down his back. Loyalty was a hard habit to break, and Easy was a loyal man. His face had the look of a man struggling to swallow bad-tasting medicine and ready to spit it back in somebody's face. Carrick had seen the same look when Easy wanted to kill him up by the shack.

He took a shot in the dark. "Easy, it was all about money, not the range. She was gonna sell everything to that man from Chicago staying in Lincoln Springs, that syndicate man. Somehow, she heard about Oliver looking to sell land to mine coal. Petersen here went to spy out those rumors. Railroad man can identify him, I'll bet. She could have made a fortune by selling all the land that has coal. He was gonna buy the land, send all of you packing, and run the place from the East. Maybe they would run a ranch; maybe it would have been a mine.

Fortunately, we're never gonna know. She would never live here; she wants to spend Jackson Jones's hard-earned money in places like San Francisco. Right, Luce?"

Lucinda's face was purple with anger. He knew he was right, but she had enough self-control not to blurt out anything in front of Easy. Carrick had failed to bait her into a confession while Easy Thompson was there to hear it. He had set this up; now he had to finish it. He had a flash of Colt Ramsay's face. He gave a thought to Reb. Wherever she was. Well, it was his play. If words weren't going to save his life, then he could go down like a man. He waited for her to make the first move, or Double J would certainly kill him. He looked at Easy Thompson. The shoulders tensed. Easy was going to go for his gun.

Lucinda had been watching both men. She had put her gun down on a chair when Easy Thompson arrived. Now, she frantically picked it up. "You are not going to stop me," she yelled, her voice echoing loudly through the room. "Carrick, you killed my husband and you have to pay for it!"

Boom! Something exploded as Lucinda continued to shriek. The house's wall shook. Mortar billowed from the wall by the windows and plaster cascaded from the ceiling. Easy stepped back as the dust flew. Carrick reached for his gun. Lucinda, who had ducked on reflex when the gun exploded not far from the open window, now took a step back to the table and aimed, squinting as she looked at Carrick with his back to the sunlight streaming in the room.

Two guns fired, almost together. Glass smashed as shards flew everywhere. Lucinda's exclamation of anger was stifled as she staggered to her left, into Easy, who roughly pushed her away. Carrick's shot at the reeling target went wide. He never fired his second. More glass shattered. Lucinda lurched sideways. Red blossomed through the pale-blue material by her left hip, matching the stain on her right side. "Kill him . . .

225

Easy . . ." she croaked open-mouthed. "Kill . . ."

She staggered into another bullet that passed through her chest and buried itself in the wood of Jones's vast desk. No more coherent sounds emerged as Lucinda wobbled rubber-kneed and bleeding, before falling to the floor with a final anguished groan.

Easy looked at the dots of Lucinda's blood on his clothes, then at Carrick. No expression. He had never drawn his gun. The massive foreman stared at Lucinda's body. He looked out the window and nodded as though to himself. He moved his feet out of the way as Lucinda's blood trailed towards him across the wide planks of the floorboards. His face showed disgust as he watched her dying spasms.

The door burst open. Men with drawn guns spilled in. "Not now!" Easy Thompson roared, holding up one hand. "It's all over. You can clean up the mess. Then you can take these two—" he gestured at Lucinda and Petersen "and dig a deep hole and toss 'em in."

The Double J men holstered their guns. Buzzing. They did what they were told, unasked questions in their eyes.

"Boss told me what he suspected, Carrick," Thompson said to Carrick, ignoring the commotion around them. "He thought it was you meetin' Lucinda up there. It was Petersen?"

Carrick nodded. "She confessed before you got here. She mentioned the syndicate man to Petersen. He knew Oliver had coal in his lands and that there was coal on the old Bar C lands. They could sell it all and leave the range rich. I figured it was one of them; Reb was sure it was her. I wasn't entirely sure I had any of it right until I saw the way she reacted."

"Never did tell you." Easy's mustache wriggled as his face worked with emotion. "Don't like bein' wrong, Carrick. Remember Larry Gordon?"

"Rider I killed? The salt?"

226

"Him. One of the boys told me Larry seemed to think he was somebody important lately. Saw him talking quiet with Petersen the mornin' of that day. Fella was out north most of the last few weeks. Didn't know until the other day."

"So you had your suspicions, Easy?"

"Had questions, Carrick. Didn't quite connect until now. I figured this was some dirty deal between you and her. Boss knew a syndicate man was around, wondered a bit if you were workin' with them. He sent Petersen to spy on with Oliver, but he never suspected her. He would have in time. Boss was startin' to realize she wasn't what he thought she was. Not sure that he really wanted to know, long as she gave him a child." The sigh Easy Thompson let loose came from the tired soul of a worn-down man.

"I wanted it to be you, Carrick, no matter what Jessie said. You put fear into Jackson Jones, Carrick. No man should have done that. Jackson Jones gave me my life back when he made me foreman. I owed him everything. He told me once you were a shadow in his path. Never saw the man afraid of anything until you came along. Guess I only saw what I wanted. Didn't start thinkin' about anyone else until after you shot me that day I braced you at the shack. You could have killed me and the law would have had no problem. No. I got you wrong, Carrick. Got a lot wrong. Got to tell Miz Jessie she was right. Got to see her soon and tell her." Easy put out a massive hand. Carrick shook it.

"Might have been nice to know what you were thinkin' in there, Easy," Carrick remarked. "Didn't want to kill you unless you were in on things with her. Don't think Jess would have approved."

Easy's chuckle at his own joke rumbled as he and Carrick walked out to the suspicious eyes of Double J riders who watched from a distance. Then he looked away from Carrick towards the small oak grove by the old house. He stopped and shook his head before turning back to face Carrick. "Guess you plan as good as you shoot, Carrick. She set you up to die by puttin' a gun in that room; you set her up better. Hand it to you." He took off his hat.

Rebecca Lewis—emerging from her lair behind a tree ten feet from the old house's gaping window—came striding over to meet them, her rifle in her right hand and a massive buffalo gun in her left. The flame of anger was still in her eye. Underneath her old brown hat, her black hair streamed around and behind her like a battle flag. She waved both arms as she greeted Carrick, wincing in pain as she moved her right arm to point it accusingly at Carrick. "No, she ain't gonna be like a rattler in a corner. No, she ain't gonna move some place a girl can't see. No, she ain't so evil she'll try to kill every last living thing to survive. No!" She was shouting louder and louder the closer she got to Carrick. Easy was grinning. Carrick discomfited was too good a show to miss.

"Reb, whoa up one minute!" Carrick replied. "You know as well as I do there was not one bit of proof what happened. If she didn't feel like she had the upper hand enough to spill her guts, we never would have known. The risk was the only way. Seems to me you told me you could have my back when I told you the plan."

"Told you more than that! Told you she wouldn't go gentle, Carrick. Told you she wouldn't sit still for you so you could do things nice and neat your way." She hefted the buffalo gun in her left hand. "Told you she might move to places I couldn't see her and not sit nicey-nice and confess prim and proper as if she was a lady. Told you it was a risk! Told you you could get your head shot off, as if I was supposed to care!" She shook the buffalo gun in his face. "This can blast a hole in anything. Good thing for you I distracted her before she blasted a hole in you. Maybe now that I think of it she should have so a girl could get some rest from a crazy man that never does nothin' the proper way!"

"I would have gotten her," Carrick said. "I had her lined up."

"She got one hole in her from you? You even wing her?"

"No."

Reb snorted her conclusion concerning Carrick's aim. Easy Thompson worked very hard at not laughing.

Reb stalked away from Carrick, walked up to the windows, looked in at Lucinda's body through the shattered glass, gave a satisfied grunt, and turned back to Carrick, stone-faced and still intense. "Told you I was better than her, Carrick, even if she got that shooting ribbon at the fair."

"You did," answered Carrick. "And you are."

# CHAPTER FOURTEEN

The wheel had come full circle. Once again, Carrick was walking into Everett Morrisson's saloon in Lincoln Springs. This time, everything had changed. Instead of a man who was unsure what he was doing and where he was going, Carrick was very certain of his purpose. He looked around him. There were familiar faces sprinkled among the crowded tables and along the bar. Not friends, but not enemies. No more Crowleys. No more like them.

In the corner, three men sat facing everyone else. The Chicago man Carrick had bumped into in the street a while back was flanked by two men who gave a hard stare to every person that walked past the table. All three watched Carrick warily as he deliberately walked up to their table. Their hands were by the lapels of their jackets; the whites of their eyes were showing as they looked up at him. He leaned his hands down, palms flat, on the table, spilling some of their whiskey across the wood.

"You leave town today."

"Somebody appoint you the king around here?" asked the man in the suit. "Free country, friend." The men on each side were fidgeting. Carrick wondered if their guns were in their jackets or around their waists.

"Not for you. Lucinda Jones is not going to meet you to sell you her range. Neither is Henry Petersen. They're dead. What anyone in Buffalo Horn Valley does with our range is our business. You go back East and you stay there. Never come back, or you can join them in the ground."

"You been drinkin' too much too early, friend, to be talkin' that way," the man replied. "I see one man talking wild and three men here who don't care to listen. Now run along and scare somebody else."

The table crashed to the floor as Carrick kicked it over. The men rocked back in the chairs to avoid it.

"You're a dead man, cowboy," he hissed at Carrick while reaching for a gun in his jacket.

"Don't think so."

The men facing Carrick became aware of the silence in the saloon. A small, dark-haired woman had a rifle trained on the three men. She looked very ready to fire. Downright anxious, in fact. All three men showed their hands, palms out.

"I told you to git," Carrick said. "That means you git. You don't need anything on your trip, like the checks you brought to pay for the range no one is going to buy." He pulled pieces of paper from his pants pocket, ripped them into tiny shreds, and scattered them on the floor. "Found 'em in your hotel rooms along with some interestin' reading. Real interesting. The kind of reading that would tell the army or the territory the things you syndicate men will do to get a toehold on our range. I think once that gets read, you're going to find your welcome is about worn out here in Wyoming. Now put the guns on the floor, get up, get out, and tell your Chicago bosses and the rest of your high-powered money men that the Buffalo Horn Valley is not for sale to people like you."

The men fumed in place.

"If you ain't gone in about the time it takes to count three, I'm gonna step back and let nature take its course, friends," Carrick said.

Dan Hill walked in. "Sheriff," the man in the suit called out.

"This is illegal. You cannot allow this treatment."

Hill looked at Carrick. "It ain't the way the law is supposed to work, Carrick, but your way does kind of grow on a fella." Hill walked to the back corner and stood before the three men. "If you three were here—which you ain't because I don't see you and don't hear you—and did something to make folks mad that got you killed, which you still might, I wouldn't know a thing about it. Way the law out here works, if you three were partners with the folks who killed Jackson Jones, why that implicates you in a murder. This valley has been havin' a terrible problem with vigilantes who hang men from the nearest tree or shoot them in a saloon no matter what the law might say. Terrible problem. Guess it's a good thing you decided to leave before anything happened. Good thing you decided to leave this minute."

Sheriff Dan Hill turned away and, after tipping his hat to Reb, walked out, head much higher than the three men who, moments after he left, dropped their weapons to the floor of the saloon and scurried out the door to find their horses saddled and ready. The saloon was quiet as Carrick followed them out to the street. A smattering of townsfolk had come to watch. For a moment, he locked eyes with Willard Godfrey, before the man grimaced and turned his back on Carrick, slamming the door to his store behind him. Always someone unhappy, Carrick thought. Always someone.

The syndicate men mounted. One looked down from his horse at Carrick.

"You can't stop us," he threatened.

"Just did," said Carrick. "Git."

One rifle clicked. Jed Owens was in front of the stable, aimed and ready to go off. The men snarled at each other and, with baleful glances at Carrick, turned away. Carrick and the settlers of the Buffalo Horn Valley listened to the fading hoofbeats of the syndicate men.

"Now, it's over," Carrick said to no one in particular.

The September sun shone on the Buffalo Horn Valley. Jessie Lewis was walking purposefully toward a place her niece and Carrick called Cougar Rock, although anyone who could see a cougar in that weathered hunk of rock had a great imagination. She carried a small metal box, pitted with dents and layered with dirt and dust. For once, she was not carrying a gun. There was no real need. The territory and the army had both gotten wind of the disputes in Buffalo Horn Valley, but by the time they sent anyone to investigate, it didn't matter. It was over the moment Lucinda Jones died. The army and territory each sent folks for a few days who ate a lot of food and bought a lot of drinks in Lincoln Springs, and then left saying friendly things no one cared about hearing as long as it meant the visitors weren't coming back. The valley might have had its differences, but there was nothing like a pack of outsiders poking their noses in the valley's affairs to convince ranchers to stand together.

It would be roundup time soon. Then it would be time for the early winter that followed on the heels of summer—one of Wyoming's trademarks. Winter would be good, for once. The range could use a rest. The past weeks had seen nothing she had ever seen before. Everyone's stock was pretty well mixed up, with a lot of riders leaving the valley—riders who had appeared to play a part in a range war and were no longer wanted or needed. New riders showed up who had lots of ambition but not much sense. No one knew who was in charge of what. No one but Reb and Carrick.

Jess had never understood how much her niece knew about running a ranch. Reb had grown up in the space of a few weeks. The girl was giving directions on different days to cowhands running two ranches and if she had made a mistake yet no one had unearthed it. Reb hadn't pointed a gun at anyone in days. Nothing went according to anyone's plan, but the work got done, the hands got fed, and the only person shot in the last three weeks had been a foolish young rider who tried to kill a snake and shot off a toe.

Carrick had, in time, shaken off the effects of the episode of violence that had rocked the valley. Jess had difficulty convincing the man to speak in more than the fewest words necessary, but there was no question that his work as a carpenter and a cowhand had helped the ranch. He would be gone hours at a time, eat, then ride out again. Of course, the biggest impact he had was on her niece. They were rarely apart except when ranch work demanded it, and rarely indoors at all. If she wanted them, other than at meals, she had to go looking.

She came upon them enjoying a rare moment of peace. Reb was nestled in the crook of Carrick's arm as they looked across the valley. She looked happy; content. The bruise on her shoulder from the buffalo gun—nothing compared to the one they found on Lucinda Jones's body—no longer pained her, at least not very much. The pine above them danced delicately in the breeze; around them the grass flexed to the rhythm of the wind as shadows from the passing clouds sent dark patches meandering across the range. Jessie had not quite become used to seeing Reb as someone's woman. The girl would always be a girl to her. But life changed. Some changes were for the better. Easy Thompson had managed to find his way to Bar C twice in the last two weeks for reasons that no one discussed. No fancy words. No fancy promises. She would never be fooled again. But it was nice, she did admit that.

"Told you I had this," Jessie said, handing Carrick the box. "Took me days to find it and more days to dig it out!"

"What's in it?" asked Reb.

"Suppose we can find out," she replied.

Carrick tried to pry open the box, but it would not give. He shot the small, crusted lock to pieces. The box, sealed shut by years of heat, still took a knife to open.

There were two bundles. One was a very short will. "I, Joshua Andrews Carrick, leave everything to my natural son, Rory Carrick, because my other children are either dying or dead. Rory was my son by an Irish girl I knew in Texas who died after he was born. I brought him with me to Wyoming, but when I married I wanted my children by my wife to inherit my lands. If he reads this, I hope he will forgive the deception. He needs to know he had two fathers who loved him." It was dated the day before Joshua Carrick had died, witnessed by one of the hands with his mark. Jessie did not know he had been that clear at the end.

The other bundle was big. By the time they unfolded it, and sorted through all of its tattered sheaves, it was two documents—a map of the valley and a deed to the old Bar C. It covered a large chunk of what had become Double J and most of what was Lazy F. Between the map and the will, it was clear that Carrick was, in the eyes of the law, the legal owner of a large section of the valley.

Carrick thought about the map, and what it meant. He could be the king Jones never lived to be. One night a few days ago, he and Easy had used the natural features of the land to divide up the valley. Carrick figured there needed to be room for everyone, and a place for everyone. No plan would last forever. There were too many changes buffeting the range to do more than give everyone a breathing space. In the back of his head, he understood the logic Jones espoused: If there was a competition for survival, the best and biggest would win, not necessarily the people who deserved it. He could see the time not far off when that law would rule the range. As the first settlers pushed out the Indians, some day the men from Chicago would be back and push out the small settlers. However, in the Buffalo Horn Valley, that day had not yet dawned.

Eileen Ramsay and her children received a patch of ground that included the largest coal deposits. She was likely going to let the railroad mine the coal. That would feed her and her kids for life and spare her the need to try to run a ranch on her own. Jess and Rebecca Lewis knew too well what that was like.

Double J was deeded to Easy to run as his own, since it had been his as much as it was anyone else's. It remained a large spread because Carrick couldn't quite shake the feeling that he owed it to Jones. He was careful not to mention that feeling too often around Reb; she had very firm convictions to the contrary.

The Lewis women received the old Bar C range in between the other two ranches, including the land that was Ramsay's. The final deeds had not yet been drawn up, because there seemed to be some question about whether Jessie Lewis was going to live much longer on what was now Circle L, or whether she would be moving to Double J as Jessie Thompson. If that happened, the land would belong to Reb. Jess was going to make up her mind any old day, or so she said every day when Reb asked her. Every last thing would be signed by everyone and filed with the territory so there was none of this range war nonsense in the future—at least as long as any of them were alive. Carrick groused again about papers and ink, but he knew the old days of handshake deals and an open range everyone could share were gone forever, if they were ever as real as his memory made them.

Carrick had been very comfortable not owning a thing. Lucinda Jones had been right. He didn't really want to have it; he only wanted to live on it. Now, he had to make that decision all over again.

"What are you going to do about it, Carrick?" asked Reb

once again, elbowing him sharply to get a response this time, after she was done looking at the deed. Her voice tried to mask any emotion she felt. One day she might have owned everything she ever wanted, but she could see now that it had never been hers to have. She'd fought hard, so long, that she could not have kept silent.

Carrick understood. He returned her answer with a smile. "You know if we got married it would all be yours," he said.

"That's not an answer, unless it's the best you can manage by way of asking me to be your wife, which is something you still ain't managed to say right and proper so a girl could say yes or a girl could say no."

"Kind of thought we were moving in the direction of yes for quite a while now, Miss Rebecca Lewis who gets all proper."

"Proper girl needs to be asked proper. I'd like you to do it before I'm so old it don't matter. But don't start confusing again. What are you going to do about the land now that you got that paper in your hands?"

"Nobody ever listens to me. Reb, I told you and Jess the day I got here that it was yours, not mine. I happened to get born on it; you put your lives into it. Figure I was meant to own the land the day I was meant to own the wind, girl."

"Carrick, be serious!" Before she could say another word, he acted.

The match in his hand flared as he scraped it across a rock. He touched it to the dry, cracked papers. In moments, the paper was pieces of black flying about in the wind. Jess Lewis gasped but stood watching, frozen in place, as Carrick threw his inheritance literally to the wind. They watched gusts blow the pieces away and apart. "Maybe a smart man doesn't own land; maybe he marries someone who does. Then he doesn't have to work because it's all her responsibility."

"Still waitin' for a proper man to say it the proper way."

237

"I'll think on it." His grin matched the one she gave up trying to hide. "Plenty of time for saying proper things between now and when that travelin' preacher shows up next month. Jess told me; maybe she has plans, too." Reb started blustering; her aunt had never told her! Jess was red as a sunset.

Carrick stood and dusted off his pants. "Well, Reb, it's been right nice talking about proper things with you, but I got a chore to do been on my mind a while. Want to come to Double J? Figure you got a stake in this business."

"What business?"

He told her. She smiled.

This time, no one was guarding Double J. They stopped by the white cross that marked Jackson Jones's final share of the Wyoming range.

Reb had picked some columbines, and left them by the foot of the cross, set on a hillside that overlooked everything Jones owned and everything he wanted to own. "Mr. Jones, you were a hard man who lived by some hard rules and you died a hard death. I forgive you, but I can't say I'm sorry." She touched the cross and backed away.

"Man had a dream this valley would amount to something, Reb. Shame he never wanted anyone in that dream but himself," Carrick said. Turning to the cross, he added, "Wish we could have all ridden the same road, Jackson Jones. Hope that across the river there you finally got what you wanted. Maybe they got enough."

Reb touched his arm lightly. They left to head down to the ranch yard.

Easy Thompson wasn't overly friendly, except to Reb, but he agreed that what Carrick proposed was a sound idea. He did make sure to send best wishes to Jessie, something Reb promised to do with more than a small grin on her face.

"Can't go back, Easy," said Carrick, extending a hand. "Got more respect for you than most. There's a valley to grow, Easy. What do you say?"

Easy Thompson all but crushed Carrick's hand. "Boss never got what he deserved, Carrick. World works in its own way, I guess. Not gonna forget, Carrick. Not gonna live looking hindwards, either. Double J and I got a future." He looked at Reb. "You know what I'm talkin' about."

Reb wanted to speak, because Easy Thompson was a man in agony waiting for Aunt Jess to say she would marry the man, but the last time she got into Aunt Jess's business with someone wanting to marry her it didn't come out too well. She said nothing.

Carrick swallowed. "Place up north, Easy. Bad Weather and I used to hunt there. Haven't seen it since I was a kid. Real quiet. Real pretty. Maybe sometime. Me and you. Get to know each other when we ain't trying to kill each other."

Easy Thompson measured Carrick, pursed his lips, and nodded. "Some time real soon then," said Easy.

That settled, Reb and Carrick set to their task. No one helped them, but no one got in the way, either. They rode to the spot where Jackson Jones was killed.

"Stand back," Carrick commanded. They had alternately dragged and been dragged by the black stallion Reb had trapped all those days ago. The stallion was having none of anything Carrick wanted to do. Carrick was driven back by hooves each time he went to loosen the rope around the animal's neck. He pulled the knife from his boot and sliced the rope as close to the stallion as he dared, then jumped back as the animal leaped forward.

The white rope was a bright necklace against the black neck of the stallion as he shook himself and, for one moment, stood still. He looked out at the range, at the free wide open lands where the strong survived and the wild wind never stopped. He took one look at Carrick and Reb, then started to lope, as though not entirely sure of what to do with his new freedom. Then he caught a scent, or heard a sound, because the loping gait turned into a gallop. Hooves pounded the ground. When he came to the barrier of the muddy banks of the creek, he simply leaped the ribbon of water, sailing over it as though born to run and born to fly.

Carrick and Reb watched as the king of the wild Wyoming range returned to his empire. They sat their horses as the Wyoming wind sang its own song. They watched the free stallion until he was a distant black dot in the lengthening shadows. Dismounting, they walked to an oak that was scarred by storms, and sat beneath its gnarled limbs. They watched the shadows climb Red Butte until the sun's rays barely touched the top layer of red-brown rocks, then left the formation in the shadows. They watched as hawks and clouds streaked across the red-orange sunset. They sat as the breeze stiffened, and even as the sun faded into purple smoke in the west beyond the distant hills and the first fireflies began dancing above the waving grasses.

They sat awhile longer, in a silent shared place that was deeper than any words could shape. They knew that the world would call soon enough, bleeding troubles and dumping its wreckage at their feet in the unholy chaos of reality. It could wait. For now, as the past stepped grudgingly aside for the future, it was enough to share the relief that they had survived, and the hope that they could endure.

# ABOUT THE AUTHOR

**Rusty Davis** is a freelance writer. His first novel, *Wyoming Showdown*, was published by Five Star Publishing.